# S H A D O W E D

A NOVEL

# SHADOWED

THE FINAL JUDGMENT

# JERRY JENKINS

TYNDALE HOUSE PUBLISHERS, INC.
WHEATON, ILLINOIS

Visit Tyndale's exciting Web site at www.tyndale.com

TYNDALE is a registered trademark of Tyndale House Publishers, Inc.

Tyndale's quill logo is a trademark of Tyndale House Publishers, Inc.

*Shadowed*

Designed by Dean H. Renninger

Edited by Ken Petersen

Published in association with the literary agency of Vigliano and Associates, 584 Broadway, Suite 809, New York, NY 10012.

**Library of Congress Cataloging-in-Publication Data**

Jenkins, Jerry B.
  Shadowed : the final judgment / Jerry Jenkins.
    p. cm. — (Underground zealot ; bk. 3)
  ISBN-13: 978-0-8423-8414-8
  ISBN-10: 0-8423-8414-6
  ISBN-13: 978-0-8423-8415-5 (softcover)
  ISBN-10: 0-8423-8415-4 (softcover)
  I. Title.
  PS3560.E485S48 2006
  813'.54—dc22                                                    2005013444

Printed in the United States of America

11  10  09  08  07  06  05
 7   6   5   4   3   2   1

*To*
DR. JOE STOWELL
*mentor, example, and friend*

---

*Thanks to*
DIANNA JENKINS
DAVID VIGLIANO
RON BEERS
KEN PETERSEN
JEREMY TAYLOR
TIM MACDONALD
*and*
DEBBIE KAUPP

---

*With gratitude to*
JOHN PERRODIN
*for research assistance*

---

*And to the always outrageous*
MCNAIR WILSON

## AT THE CONCLUSION OF WORLD WAR III

in the fall of 2009, it was determined by the new international government in Bern, Switzerland, that beginning January 1 of the following year, the designation A.D. (*anno Domini,* "in the year of our Lord," or after the birth of Christ) would be replaced by P.3. (post–World War III). Thus January 1, A.D. 2010, would become January 1, 1 P.3. *Shadowed* takes place thirty-seven years later in 38 P.3.

---

**AFTER THE THIRD WORLD WAR,** a so-called holy war that resulted in the destruction of entire nations, antireligion, antiwar factions toppled nearly every head of state, and an international government rose from the ashes and mud. Religion was outlawed around the world in an attempt to eradicate war.

The United States was redrawn into seven regions and renamed the United Seven States of America (USSA), the president deposed, and the vice president installed as regional governor, reporting to the International Government of Peace in Bern, Switzerland.

When he completed his graduate studies in religion, **Dr. Paul Stepola**'s wife, **Jae,** urged him to pursue work with the National Peace Organization. Her father, retired army general **Ranold B. Decenti**, had helped build the NPO from the ashes of the FBI and the CIA.

Paul slowly works his way up in the organization. When the NPO initiates a new task force, the Zealot Underground, to expose and eliminate religious influence in the USSA, Chicago NPO bureau chief **Bob Koontz** taps Paul as a key member.

Paul becomes enmeshed in the NPO's covert operations. He is the decorated sole survivor of a raid on a house church in San Francisco where he shoots and kills the leader, a widow. In a Texas investigation of oil-well sabotage he witnesses the stoning to death of an underground Christian. In a subsequent oil-field fire, Paul loses his sight.

While recovering, Paul meets **Stuart "Straight" Rathe**, a volunteer at the hospital and, unbeknownst to Paul, a secret believer. Paul asks his superiors for the contraband New Testament on disc so he can brush up on the beliefs of his targets, should he ever be able to see and work again. His exposure to Scripture and to Straight lead to his conversion and the dramatic restoration of his sight.

Paul cannot tell Jae, fearing she will tell her father and expose Paul to the death penalty. Straight introduces Paul to the leaders of the Christian underground, one of whom—code name Abraham—challenges Paul to become a double agent, staying in the NPO while secretly aiding the resistance.

Paul is able to appear committed to the NPO by arresting phony people of faith, but his true allegiance is put to the test in a major operation in Los Angeles. Paul is suspected and nearly found out as he secretly works with underground factions to protect them from genocide by the NPO. In the end, they pray for God to judge their enemies with a drought that affects everyone in L.A. except true believers.

Following three horrific terrorist attacks in Europe spearheaded by a man claiming to be a Christian believer, Paul is sent overseas to thwart him. There Paul secretly engages with underground believers and determines that the terrorist is not, in fact, a person of faith.

Though Paul is suspected of treason, followed, and monitored, his role in eliminating the terrorist buys him time and temporarily squelches the threat that he will be found out. Meanwhile his wife has begun listening to his New Testament discs, alternately worrying that he has become a believer and finding herself overwhelmed with the claims of Scripture on her own life.

The international government sets a deadline for all citizens to sign a pledge of loyalty that reads:

> *By order of the Supreme Council of the International Government of Peace, headquartered in Bern, Switzerland, and dated this Monday, January 21, 38 P.3., it is resolved that within sixty days, or by March 22, 38 P.3., every citizen of the world community who has reached the age of eighteen years shall be required to stipulate by signing this document and having it on public record, thus:*
>
> *"Under penalty of life imprisonment, or death in extreme cases, I hereby pledge that I personally support the global ban on the practice of religion. I am not affiliated with any group, organization, or individual who acts in opposition to the ruling of the international government on this matter, and I stipulate that if I become aware of any citizen violating this ordinance, I am under obligation to report the same, failure to do so resulting in the same punishment."*

With input from the underground leadership of Christian believers in Europe, the USSA, and throughout the world, Paul crafts a response to be disseminated as far and wide as believers dare, including to the major news organizations in their respective countries.

It reads:

> *To: The Honorable Baldwin Dengler, Chancellor of the International Government of Peace, Bern, Switzerland*
>
> *From: The worldwide church of believers in the one true God of Abraham, Isaac, and Jacob, and God's Son, Jesus the Christ*

*Re: Your decree, announced this Monday, January 21, 38 P.3.,*
*which we call the year of our Lord, A.D. 2047*

*Chancellor Dengler:*

*We aver that the current world system, which has banned for*
*nearly four decades the practice of religion by people of faith, is*
*an abomination in the sight of Almighty God.*

*We believe that you and your government, as well as most*
*of your loyal citizens, are unaware of the size and potential*
*influence of a people that has, by your actions, been pushed*
*underground and forced to practice their faith illegally.*

*We ask that you rescind immediately the decree announced*
*today and put a moratorium on laws prohibiting the practice of*
*religion until you can determine how people of faith can peace-*
*ably live in this society without fear of reprisal.*

*We are beseeching our God to act in judgment, should this*
*request not be carried out within forty hours of when the*
*decree is announced, or midnight, Bern Time, Tuesday, Janu-*
*ary 22. We believe that He will act to deliver us from you, our*
*oppressor, as He did in Los Angeles, California, last year.*

*We respectfully warn that you will regret ignoring this*
*request, as we are calling upon God to specifically act as*
*He did thousands of years ago against Pharaoh in Egypt,*
*when Pharaoh refused to let the children of Israel flee his*
*domain.*

*We refer you to the Old Testament account of the ten*
*plagues God unleashed against Egypt. There are those among*
*us who are asking God to eschew the first nine plagues and to*
*refrain from hardening your heart, and it is our heartfelt wish*
*that you avoid the dire consequences of the tenth plague at the*
*forty-hour mark. Short of this, we fear that God may not limit*

*this plague to the seat of the government but rather that it will affect the entire world.*

*To our brothers and sisters around the globe, we remind you that you need not feel bound by the Old Testament caveat of protecting your own households by sprinkling blood on your doorposts to identify yourself. We believe the blood of Christ has already been shed on your behalf and that God knows His own.*

*In conclusion: Rescind the loyalty decree, lift the laws against the practice of religion, or proceed at your own peril.*

*For your reference, following is the text of the carrying out of the tenth plague on Egypt, which we fear God may administer upon those who turn a deaf ear to our plea:*

*So Moses announced to Pharaoh, "This is what the LORD says: About midnight I will pass through Egypt. All the firstborn sons will die in every family in Egypt, from the oldest son of Pharaoh, who sits on the throne, to the oldest son of his lowliest slave. Even the firstborn of the animals will die. Then a loud wail will be heard throughout the land of Egypt; there has never been such wailing before, and there never will be again."*

*. . . And at midnight the LORD killed all the firstborn sons in the land of Egypt, from the firstborn son of Pharaoh, who sat on the throne, to the firstborn son of the captive in the dungeon. Even the firstborn of their livestock were killed. Pharaoh and his officials and all the people of Egypt woke up during the night, and loud wailing was heard throughout the land of Egypt. There was not a single house where someone had not died.*

**International Chancellor Baldwin Dengler** responds that there will be no negotiating, claiming that believers are a very small number who don't really have God's ear. He reminds the world that such beliefs caused the very world war that resulted in the outlawing of religion.

Jae travels to Europe to visit Paul and discovers on his computer that he authored the Christian Manifesto. If she exposes him as a traitor, he will be put to death. Despite her upbringing and lifetime of atheism, she feels compelled to pray for him.

When Paul finally returns safely, she tells him she knows his secret. "Paul," she says, "I don't know where I am in all this, but you must know by now that I am not going to turn on you. Whether or not we ever agree about God, I don't want to lose you."

**"I CAN'T GO ON LONG** with the NPO regardless, Jae. Even if I don't reveal myself today, when I have not signed the loyalty document within sixty days, the truth will come out. You need to decide what kind of a life that means for you and the kids."

• • •

On the plane [back to the States, January 22], Jae told Paul straight-out, "I do not believe this slaughter is going to take place. If it doesn't, it will tell me a lot about your fellow believers and the effectiveness of their prayers. If it does, besides being the most shocked person in the world, I can't promise how it will make me feel about God. I suppose I will have to believe He is real, but I would have a hard time understanding Him or liking Him much."

Paul worried about Jae, of course, and he couldn't quit looking at his watch. Midnight in Bern would be 6 p.m. in Washington. With the time change they expected to touch down in D.C. midmorning. Stretched way past his level of endurance, Paul didn't know what else to say or do. He let his head fall and he slept the entire flight, not rousing until touchdown.

• • •

Jae was spent too, but she could not sleep. She wanted to find the verse that had been bugging her. She put the Hebrews disc back into the player and listened straight through until it jumped out at her:

*You see, it is impossible to please God without faith. Anyone who wants to come to him must believe that there is a God and that he rewards those who sincerely seek him.*

She prayed, *I want to believe that there is a God, and I am sincerely looking for You.*

• • •

Jae's mother picked them up at the airport. The kids were in school and, she said, already enjoying it and making friends. "Your father is at work, of course. But he can't wait to see you both. Berlitz and Aryana [Jae's brother and his wife] are coming for dinner at six-thirty."

Jae felt as if she had come out of a haze of craziness into some semblance of sanity.

When the kids [Brie and Connor] got home from school that afternoon they attacked Paul and wrestled with him on the floor, telling him about everything they had been doing, friends they had made, and their teachers.

"Do we have to go back to Chicago now that you're home?" Brie said.

"I thought you *wanted* to," he said.

"We do, but not yet."

Ranold pulled in at about five, hurrying into the house in his nicest suit but already pulling off the tie. He squeezed Jae's shoulder and vigorously shook Paul's hand. "I want to hear everything, son," he said. "Everything. Let me get out of these clothes. Your mother tell you Berl and the new wife will be here for dinner?"

Paul nodded as the kids screamed, "Yay!"

Ranold bounded upstairs with more energy than Jae had noticed in ages, and he soon returned in a flannel shirt, wash pants, and white socks. "Pardon the informality," he said, "but I didn't need one more minute in that monkey suit. Paul, come on into the den and join me in a stiff one. You can debrief me, and we can catch the news before the other kids get here."

• • •

[In the den] Paul kept glancing at his watch, and Ranold finally noticed. "Almost time for the news." He switched on the TV. The last couple of minutes of a five-thirty sitcom were playing.

Paul drummed his fingers on the arm of the chair.

"Couldn't be more proud of you," Ranold said. "Hey, you haven't touched your Coke."

"Not thirsty, I guess." In truth, he wanted to be with Jae right now. He could hear her talking with her mother and the kids playing in the other room.

At six straight up, it was as if the power went out in the house. Everything went black—every light, the television, everything. Brie screamed.

Ranold said, "What the—?" and Paul heard him rise and move to the window, pulling back the curtain. "Streetlights too," he said. "Power outage."

And just like that, the lights came back on. The kids laughed. Margaret said something in a high-pitched, relieved voice. The TV picture sprang back to life, showing the anchorman slumped over the desk and his partner, a woman, standing, screaming for help.

"Would you look at that?" Ranold said, leaning forward. "Guy looks like he passed out. Heart attack or somethin'."

The phone rang, and Paul heard Margaret answer. "Aryana," she said, sounding alarmed, "what's wrong?"

• • •

Jae looked up at her mother as the kids came bounding into the kitchen. "The lights were off!" Connor shouted, just as Margaret slumped to the floor, the phone clattering away.

"Daddy!" Jae called, and the men came in from the den as she picked up the phone. "Aryana?"

The woman was hysterical. "He just collapsed!" Aryana said. "When the power went out, or whatever happened, even our headlights went out. I told Berl to stop, but I could tell he wasn't steering. I grabbed the wheel and could feel him just sitting there limp. I was able to get my foot on the brake when we hit the curb. Then the lights came back on. But, Jae, he's dead!"

"What?"

"He's dead! No pulse, nothing!"

"Dad!" Jae said. "You need to talk to Aryana."

Jae took over trying to rouse her mother, who lay still on the floor, while Ranold took the phone.

"That can't be, Aryana!" he said. "He's a young man! Call the paramedics!"

Paul's molar vibrated with a tone, and Ranold turned away as if also taking a call. "I've got to take this, Aryana," he said. "Get help and call us back."

• • •

Paul answered his call. It was [Italian underground leader] Enzo Fabrizio from Rome. "It's happened, Paul. Are you watching the news?"

JERRY JENKINS • xvii

Ranold, pale, answered his private phone. "Oh, Bia! No!" he said. "My son too!" He slammed his fist on the kitchen counter. "I've got to get to Berlitz and help Aryana," he said. "Paul, will you come?"

"Let him stay with Mom, Dad," Jae said.

"Ranold," Paul said, "it's happened."

"What's happened?"

"The curse. The plague. The warning from the underground."

"What? What!" Ranold looked wildly at everyone in the kitchen, his eyes finally landing on Connor. "But, but your son, *your* firstborn son is fine!"

The kids burst into tears. Ranold stormed out.

Jae helped her mother into a chair and fanned her. "You kids help me with Grandma. Now! Get me a glass of water. Paul, you'd better check the news."

Paul made his way back into the den, where news bulletins of millions of deaths poured in from around the globe. And knowing his and Jae's and the kids' lives would never be the same, Paul heard the report from Bern, where it was announced that International Government Chancellor Baldwin Dengler was mourning the loss of his own eldest son.

# 1

**PAUL STOOD BEFORE THE TELEVISION,** fighting to keep from hyperventilating. He had been in life-and-death situations, had faced his share of kill-or-be-killed scenarios. He had long trusted his instincts and had proven that his prodigious intellect could sort through myriad possibilities even under pressure and keep him calm enough to make wise decisions.

But never had he been awash with so many consequences, all bad. Could anyone anywhere doubt that this global catastrophe—the sudden, inexplicable death of every firstborn male child, regardless of age, in every family that refused to acknowledge God—was anything other than what had been warned?

On one hand, Paul envisioned a mass turning to faith on the parts of terrified people around the world. On the other, the carnage was unimaginable. What percentage of the global population lay dead where they had stood, sat, lain, run, walked? And what would this mean to the economy, to service industries, to law enforcement, to the military? For that matter, what would it mean to normal existence? How would people simply get around?

There had to be bodies everywhere, and if it was true they were supernaturally slain by God, not one would likely exhibit any examinable pathology. There would be no bleeding, no trauma, no evidence of why hundreds of millions of men and boys and even infants merely ceased to live. Perhaps rather than a massive turning to God, the opposite would be true.

Jae herself had said that a global curse like this would have to persuade her of the intervention of God into the affairs of man, but that she would also have a hard time understanding or liking Him much. And this from a woman clearly on the cusp of belief. Surely millions would use the chaos and mourning to justify their hatred toward such a seemingly vengeful and spiteful God.

It would be quite a step, Paul told himself, from atheism to begrudging acceptance that there was a supreme being. But most, he was sure, would have preferred to have been convinced there was a God who was about only love and peace and harmony, not also about justice and righteousness and judgment.

As he flipped through the channels, Paul was reminded of the amateurish TV news work he had perused in the archives during his doctoral studies years before. History had provided occasions when events overwhelmed even the most professional newsperson. The assassination of U.S. president John F. Kennedy, nearly eighty-five years prior, had caused reporters to pale and a celebrated anchor to succumb to emotion.

A U.S. space disaster in the previous century had left news journalists scrambling, airing rumors and unconfirmed reports, reading from newswires rather than teleprompters and then having to correct misinformation, often in obvious anger.

Terrorist attacks from before Paul was born showed broadcast journalists clumsily trying to sort fact from rumor and appearing to try to maintain an air of professionalism while plainly ashen with fear. Historical broadcasts during World War III showed the same, as the death tolls from the tsunami and other nuclear-caused massacres overwhelmed on-air personalities.

It was the same now. Just minutes old, the horrific news from around the world unmistakably rocked broadcasters appearing desperate to remain objective. But as the enormity of the situation hit them—several newsrooms with talent and behind-the-camera staff lying dead—those remaining seemed to realize the ramifications.

If this was what the underground zealots had predicted, had prayed for, and now claimed, everyone would be affected in some way. Rare was the person who didn't have a relative—father, brother, grandfather, uncle, son, cousin—who was a first-born male. And what about friends and acquaintances? Paul saw the truth begin to register on the faces of the reporters and anchorpeople. They had to be frantic to get off the air and onto the phone to confirm their worst fears.

And with every second, the death toll rose. Of course, it was not limited to firstborn males. The slaughter extended to innocents, to passengers in planes piloted by firstborns, or driven in cars, trucks, buses. Pedestrians had been wiped out by driverless cars; surgeons had collapsed onto patients; fathers had dropped infants; electricians had fallen into live wires; firefighters had dropped on the job, their fire hoses shooting away from blazes.

The extent of the cataclysm would not be known for days, perhaps weeks. Paul couldn't imagine the demand for funeral services. Surely there could be no keeping up with the corpses already piling up around the world. Mass graves would become necessary, colossal funeral pyres, refrigeration for those who could afford to wait for burial space.

Atop all this, of course, would be the devastating toll of human grief. How does a family, a clan, a people, a nation, a world mourn a loss so all-encompassing? Nothing would ever be the same, Paul knew. Not for the USSA. Not for the world. And certainly not for him.

It was a fearful thing to fall into the hands of an angry God.

# 2

**IN THE KITCHEN,** Jae was unnerved at the silence of the children. Normally rambunctious and talkative, they were, naturally, stunned. Their grandmother had fainted and was just now rousing. Their grandfather had railed at their dad and seemed angry that Connor, Paul and Jae's firstborn son, was alive.

Jae couldn't tell how much either Brie or Connor had absorbed. She prayed that at eight and six they were too young to understand. But still they moved stiffly, faces pale, merely following their mother's orders. "Everything's going to be all right, kids," she said. "Just keep helping Mommy."

"Where'd Grandpa go?" Brie said.

"To pick up Uncle Berlitz and Aunt Aryana."

"Why?"

"They're coming for dinner, remember?"

"What's wrong with their car?"

"We'll have to ask when they get here."

Jae didn't know why she was lying, delaying the inevitable. It was unlikely they'd see even Aryana this evening, and no way would they see their dead uncle. In fact, it was becoming plain to Jae, they had better not be here when her father returned.

"Is it true?" Margaret Decenti managed as her eyes fluttered and she sat up. "Is Berlitz dead?"

Jae saw the children turn. "Daddy's gone to help," she said. "We'll know more when—"

"Dead?" Connor said.

"Mommy!" Brie said, wailing.

"You two do me a favor," she said. "Run upstairs and start packing your stuff."

"Why? Where are we going?"

"We have to hurry," Jae said. "Can you help Mommy, and I'll explain later?"

"I want to know now," Connor said.

"No!" Margaret said, trying to stand. "Your mother's right! You must leave and soon. You must not be here when your grandfather returns!"

Now both children cried, and Jae called for Paul.

•  •  •

Paul hurried into the kitchen. His mother-in-law looked terrible, Jae shaken, and the kids out of control.

Mrs. Decenti, usually docile and tentative, reached for Paul and pulled him close while barking at Jae. "Take the kids," she said. "I'm fine. Now, Paul, listen. My husband may be many unsavory things, but he most certainly is not stupid. He figured this out before he left the house. You heard him. I was barely conscious, but I heard him. We'd been talking about this since the warning came from the underground. He pooh-poohed it, but he always added that in a way he wished it *would* happen. He said it would make it easy to know who the enemy was. They would be the dogs whose firstborn male children remained."

Paul was at a loss. She was right, of course. But where would they go? How long would it take Ranold, even in his grief, to sic NPO forces on his own family? Paul and Jae would be easily recognizable sitting ducks, especially with two small children. There was a chance that the sheer pandemonium might give them time. Surely the NPO had more important things to do than to worry about a turncoat agent, even if he was Ranold B. Decenti's son-in-law.

But who could measure the depth of Ranold's rage, his determination, his vengeance? Might he harm his own daughter? his own grandchildren? Ranold would feel obliged to protect his grandchildren from their own father, a traitor.

Jae was dragging the children toward the stairs, though they fought to stay in the kitchen.

"Lots to do, Brie, Connor," Paul called after them. "Show me how responsible you can be." What a nightmare for them. No kid of any age deserved this kind of calamity. Yelling, fainting, talk of death, parents on the edge of panic.

Paul pulled the curtain aside and peered out the kitchen window into the blackness of the driveway until his eyes grew accustomed to the faint light from a bulb at the peak of the garage. The driveway was empty. In his haste, Ranold had raced off in Paul's rental. The only car left was Ranold's NPO-issue sedan in the garage. With a radio connected to NPO headquarters, perhaps Paul could stay ahead of his pursuers. Once he knew their plans, he could initiate his own, and if he heard they knew what car he had taken, that would signal the time to switch, hide, lie low.

But where would they go? They were a long way from the Detroit salt mines or Chicago. And dare they drag frightened children along on an escapade like that?

It was as if Paul's mother-in-law could read his mind. "Let me keep the children," she said.

He shook his head. "We've been away from them too long as it is. Besides, Jae would never allow it. And who knows what Ranold might do?"

"He'd have to kill me before he could lay a finger on either of them."

"I know, Margaret, but—" He helped her stand.

"You have to do what you have to do, Paul. But you had better do it soon."

The phone rang and Margaret picked up. "What's happening, dear?" she said, rolling her eyes at Paul. "Aryana's okay, under the circumstances? Me? Well, what do you expect? I'm numb. . . . He's right here. Sure."

She handed the phone to Paul and leaned close so she could hear too. Ranold didn't even take the time to greet him. "Listen, son, I need help. I need counsel. You don't have to fear me, because it's all clear to me now. You're right. I've been wrong, and I need to know what to do about it. I might even need you to pray with me; could you do that?"

His answer would confirm for the first time for Ranold where Paul stood. What point was there in hedging now? Connor's well-being was all the evidence Ranold needed. "Well, sure," Paul said, "I—"

"This is so hard, Paul, so difficult on your mother-in-law and me. Promise you'll be there for me when I get home. Aryana is going to stay with Berlitz until we can determine some disposition of the body. Will you be there, Paul?"

"Hurry home, Dad."

As soon as he had hung up, Margaret said, "You didn't buy a word of that, I hope."

"Not a word."

"You've got to get out of here—and fast. How can I help?"

• • •

Upstairs Jae was packing like a madwoman. Would she be able to talk her mother into coming with them? Not in front of the children. She had promised she would explain everything if they would just help her get packed. They were sniffling, clearly terrified. She wished she could sit and cry.

When she heard footsteps on the stairs, she panicked. Had her father returned already? Her mother and Paul entered, and Paul immediately took charge of the kids while studying his personal digital assistant. As soon as the kids were preoccupied and out of earshot, Jae pleaded with her mother to pack a bag and join them.

Margaret Decenti began shaking her head from the first word. "I can take care of myself," she said. "Your father will demand to know where you've gone, and I'll say I thought it was his idea and that he knew. He'll explode, but I've been through that before. He'll yell and scream, but he won't hurt me. Now hurry."

# 3

**IN ALL THE CRISES** Paul had found himself in over the years, he had never really worried about the kids. Oh, he wondered if Jae would be all right taking care of them if anything happened to him, and while he hated to dwell on it, he knew a young, attractive woman like her wouldn't stay single long. And besides, the kids needed a father figure.

But this was different. They were with him now, under his charge—and he had become an international fugitive, punishable by death. Besides the crushing burden of responsibility for their safety, he had never had to act decisively in a professional sense in their presence. How would he be able to concentrate? Would it be fair to Jae to lay on her the responsibility of keeping them quiet so he could think?

He lugged down a couple of the suitcases, found Ranold's car keys on a hook in the kitchen, and made his way to the garage.

When he returned, Jae and the kids had brought down the rest of the luggage, and she was assuring them she would keep her promise. They would know soon enough what was going on.

Paul knew he was exacerbating the tension by grabbing stuff from the kids and slinging it into the trunk, but he didn't see an alternative. Time was not their friend.

As Jae herded the kids into the backseat and buckled them in, Paul whispered, "Your mother will be okay?"

"Do me a favor," she said. "Help me decide. Say good-bye to her and tell me what you think. Everything in me says to not leave her here alone."

"Jae, we've got to go."

"Please, Paul. It'll take less than a minute."

He rushed back in and found his mother-in-law sitting and rocking before the television. She was moaning, "Berlitz, Berlitz."

"We're going, Margaret," he said. "Are you sure you don't want to come along?"

She shook her head, but she looked wasted. How could she not? Her grown son, her only son, was one of the dead. Millions of mothers were grieving, but that made her pain no less personal. Would she be able to stand up to Ranold in her condition? He would erupt when he found Paul and Jae and the kids gone. In no time he would make them targets of a massive manhunt, numbers one through four on his Most Wanted list.

"Paul, sit with me a moment, would you?"

"Margaret, I'm sorry, but we have to—"

"Just a moment."

He checked his watch and peeked at his PDA again.

"I saw the letter from your father, you know," she said. "The one he sent you to open on your twelfth birthday. Jae showed it to Ranold and he showed it to me. He thought it would infuriate me, make everything clear to me. I haven't been able to get it out of my mind. It had the most profound effect on me. Your father was devout. He truly believed. And oh, how he loved you."

"He did."

"I'm not stupid either, Paul. I live in the shadow of a powerful man, and I've learned to keep my place. But that doesn't mean I don't know what's going on. That Connor is alive proves you are a believer."

"Actually it doesn't, Mom, in spite of what Ranold thinks. By 'firstborn male,' we think the Scripture refers to a child that is both male and born first, not simply the first male born in a family."

"But you, Paul, you qualify."

"I do."

"And so you are a believer."

"I am." How freeing it felt to say so.

"And Jae?"

Paul cocked his head. "She's close, if not there yet."

"It won't be long. She's a lot like me, and I don't need any more convincing. Person would have to be a fool not to see what's going on here. I don't know what it's all leading to, but I want to be on the right side of it when it happens. I've already lost my son. I don't want to lose my soul."

Paul was stuck. He couldn't walk out on his mother-in-law at a time like this. And yet he couldn't stay and suffer the consequences of the rage of his father-in-law either.

"You don't have to lose your soul, Margaret."

"I know. I'll figure it out. You go."

He shook his head. "I don't feel right leaving you—"

"Nonsense. I'm a grown woman who has lived decades with a difficult man. For once we'll have something to share. He loved Berlitz too, you know, in his own clumsy way."

"You think you can comfort each other?"

"He won't likely think of my grief," she said. "Keeping him from exacting revenge will keep me busy."

Paul couldn't remember feeling so torn. He had to act fast and decisively, but he was being pulled in too many directions. Part of him wanted to just stay and have it out with Ranold, to challenge him, dare him to take his grandchildren's father out of the picture.

He heard the door between the kitchen and the garage and prayed it wasn't Ranold. He wasn't ready.

Jae appeared. "Listen," she said, "both of you. Maybe this isn't my decision. Maybe I'm out of place here. But I have made up my mind, and I cannot be dissuaded. I'm staying with Mom until Daddy returns."

"Oh, honey," Margaret said, "you can't. You must—"

"I said I could not and will not be dissuaded. Paul, I know you have some plan, so take the kids and put it into action. Send for me or I will come to you, whatever you concoct."

"That won't be easy, Jae. Your dad will have this place under surveillance, and—"

"Just go, Paul. This is your life. You'll make it work. We're out of time. The only reason Daddy isn't back yet has to be the traffic. Go."

• • •

Alone with her mother at last, Jae found herself a wreck emotionally. She wanted to be alone to deal with God about her own faith and about the loss of her brother. And she desperately needed to be with Paul, because now it was clear she could lose him in an instant. The NPO would be under orders to shoot and kill traitors on sight. On top of that, she had just reunited with her children and had been with them only a few hours.

But right now her mother was top priority. Margaret could

work herself into such a state that she might faint again, or worse. And what if she hit her head? Could she be suicidal? Jae didn't think so, but the loss of a child, even a grown one, had to put any mother on the brink. Then there was the trauma of waiting for her volatile husband to find the target of his vengeance gone in *his* car. . . .

• • •

Connor had done what Paul wished he himself could do. Retreat. The boy had simply shut down. He buried his face in his sister's shoulder and appeared to be sleeping. No crying. No moaning. No talking. He was just still.

Brie was stony too, but she hauntingly reminded Paul of his mother-in-law as she sat rocking in the backseat. As he fired up the car, he swiveled to face her. "You trust Daddy, don't you?"

She nodded.

"Once we get where we're going, I'll make sure you understand what's going on. Okay?"

She nodded again. "Where're we going?"

"No place you've ever been before, but I think you'll like it."

"Are there kids there?"

Paul hadn't even thought of that. "Yes. Yes, I believe there are."

He used the remote to open the garage door and shut it again as he pulled slowly onto the street. The sky was pitch-black and the night frigid, but the neighborhood of stylish brownstones was alive. Three cars were disabled, two in a ditch and the other lodged against a power pole. People milled about outside, moving between houses, talking, arms around each other, some apparently near collapse from grief and fear.

As Paul picked his way through the neighborhood and onto the main streets, he saw more damaged cars, some off the road, some on. Every intersection was a muddle of fender benders, people crying, civilians trying to direct traffic, the occasional emergency vehicle creeping through the snarl. People poured in and out of stores and auto-recharging stations, carrying supplies, blankets, first-aid kits.

"What happened, Daddy?" Brie called out.

"Lots of accidents, huh?" he said.

"Yeah, but why?"

"Remember, you're going to find out later. Daddy has to be on the phone for a while, so you be patient, okay?"

Paul was trying to connect with Straight, his faith mentor and underground contact in Chicago, but he was getting no answer. Straight was either trying to reach Paul or was inundated with calls from other zealot underground cells throughout the world.

Between Paul's attempts, a call got through to him, the caller ID showing a Chicago number. "Paul?" It was the voice of his secretary from NPO bureau headquarters.

"Felicia? Where are you calling from?"

"A pay phone." Her voice was shaky. "Did you know Bob Koontz was a firstborn?"

# 4

**JAE SWITCHED OFF THE TELEVISION** and sat knee to knee with her mother, holding her hands. Both women wept, commiserating over the loss of brother and son.

Jae had never felt the presence of God so clearly, and it terrified her. She had loved getting to know Him through the New Testament discs, realizing that along the way she had come to understand what had happened to Paul and what must happen to her. She believed, she knew, and yet she didn't understand how or why things had come to such a state that God had to act in this manner.

Strangely, though, while she had predicted that she wouldn't understand Him or like Him much if the curse was enacted, she found only the former true. The latter somehow was not part of the equation. It wasn't that she was happy about what had occurred. Who could be? But that it was so specific, so definite, so crystal clear, made her fear God with such profound respect and awe that any doubt escaped her.

It was almost like cheating now, she decided, to place her faith in a God who had revealed Himself in such a dynamic, obvious way. When she had been pondering all this, trying to piece together the puzzle Paul had become while gaining glimpses of God through the recordings of His Word, everything she had been taught and come to believe had been challenged. When she allowed for the possibility that this might be true, her little-known muscle of faith was stretched and tested and strained beyond capacity. When she had found herself *wanting* to believe, Jae fought against a lifetime of programmed-in resistance and knew it would take some real heart-to-hearts with Paul and maybe with Straight and who knew who else—God Himself?—before she could surrender her disbelief.

Well, that had certainly been taken care of in one fell swoop. The international tragedy had blown her back on her heels, and she sensed that the full intensity of it would not scratch the surface of her consciousness for days. But it had had the opposite effect on her soul than she had envisioned.

At first she had thought those praying for such an act from the Almighty were capricious and mean-spirited. And she assumed that if God was who she was slowly coming to believe He was, He would not allow Himself to be talked into such a horrific deed.

Somehow He had agreed it was necessary. No one who could do this would be weak enough in character to be able to be talked into it against His will. What He had wrought in Los Angeles the year before should have convinced the world that He existed and was not to be trifled with. Yet Jae herself had not known what to make of it and, in spite of all reason, found herself trying to explain it away as some sort of natural aberration.

Well, there would be no explaining this away. Every first-born male in the world who was not a believer in the God of Abraham, Isaac, and Jacob and in God's Son, Jesus the Christ, lay dead. People could rail against heaven; they could shake their fists in the face of the Eternal One, but no one could deny for another second that their enemy existed and that He was powerful beyond comprehension.

If they chose to hate Him for it, after ignoring Him for decades while indeed considering Him imaginary, that was their choice. But Jae doubted a true atheist still existed on the planet.

All this she hurriedly breathed to her mother as the women sat trying to console one another. And Margaret Decenti, to her credit, seemed to agree, despite that she had not had the benefit of all the recorded Scripture Jae had listened to.

That would change soon enough. Jae would get her mother whatever she needed to make it all make sense. As for Jae herself, she prayed silently. *Lord,* she said, realizing it was the first time she had acknowledged God as her Lord, *I have had my mind and heart thoroughly changed. I believe in You with all that is in me. Thank You for Jesus. Forgive me for rejecting You for so long.*

Jae had to admit to herself that, yes, she had benefited—a strange word under the circumstances—from the most dramatic act of God in all of history, and thus her decision seemed to have been made almost too easily. But it was no less real.

• • •

"Bob is gone?" Paul said. Koontz had been his boss and friend for years.

"It happened at closing time, Paul," Felicia said.

Paul could picture the tall black woman on the other end of the phone.

"A bunch of us were getting a head start, streaming toward

the elevators, when the screaming started. We all ran back to our offices. Men were dead everywhere. Bob had been standing in the doorway between his and his secretary's offices. You remember how he liked to do that, just to see if she'd try to leave right at five? She said he just gave her a puzzled look and dropped like a sack of potatoes. Calls came in from bureaus all over the country. 'Member Lester Harrelson from Gulfland?"

"Tick? Sure."

"Dead. Lots of other men you know are gone, Paul. Why didn't you tell me?" Her voice had a bite to it.

"Tell you?"

"Why do you think it's taken me so long to call you, Paul? I've been on the phone too. I lost my son. My husband lost his brother and his father. I lost another brother-in-law. You think I don't know you're an only child? That makes you a firstborn. And I'll bet that sweet child Connor is just fine too, isn't he?"

Paul felt for Felicia. What could he say?

"I know," she said finally. "Who could you trust? I know you were suspected 'round here, so you had to know it too. You didn't know who you could trust, and maybe you couldn't have trusted me. But when this crazy prophecy came out, this challenge to the international government, you had to know it was really going to happen. Even though I was on to you, or was pretty sure, I didn't really think it would happen. But you did. You had to. You knew, didn't you, Paul?"

"I was hoping it wouldn't have to happen."

"And you didn't care enough about me to tell me, to spare me some of this."

"I care about you, Felicia. What could I do?"

"You *know* what you could have done, Paul. You could have warned me. Maybe I'd have laughed. Maybe I'd have ignored you. Maybe I'd have turned you in. But just maybe I'd have believed, and God's hand of death would have passed by my family."

"I'm so sorry, Felicia. I really am."

"Yeah? Are you? Well, so am I. What am I supposed to do now?"

A tone sounded from one of Paul's molars. "I've got another call, Felicia."

"How convenient."

"I'll get back to it later if there's anything I can do for you now."

"No, I guess not. I don't guess I'll be seeing you again."

"Not around there, no."

"I wouldn't turn you in, Paul. And I'd still like to talk about this."

"I believe you, Felicia. We'll make that happen somehow. I can't say when or where, but—"

"Take your call, boss."

It was Straight. "I've been at the hospital," he said. "You can only imagine."

"Are you suspected?"

"Nah. Nobody knows I was a firstborn, and my family's already gone."

"I can't wait to see you, Straight, but I need info. I've got to get to the Columbia Region underground. Jack Pass still running it?"

"Yep. You got a talisman?"

"No."

"I can get you clearance, but you're hot so they're gonna be skittish about you leading anyone there."

Paul filled him in on what he was driving and why, who was with him, and where Jae was.

"Wow," Straight said. "If I were Jack, I'd plead with you to lie low somewhere else."

"Where'm I going to go, Straight?"

"I can't imagine. I'll talk to Jack. Best-case scenario is that they'll come to you somewhere. No way they're going to let you get close, just in case you're already being tailed."

"I don't appear to be yet."

"Paul, do the people you're tailing ever know you're there? You're NPO. You know how to do it. And so do they. I'd recommend staying on the move until I get back to you."

# 5

**IT WASN'T DIFFICULT FOR JAE** to read her father. It never had been. He was a beefy, jowly, red-faced man who should have been long retired. Having been brought back to head the Zealot Underground task force had reinvigorated him, made him a new man.

As always, he wore his feelings not so much on his sleeve as on his face. He had the squint of the suspicious, the pain of the bereaved, and the flush of anger as he slowly entered from the attached garage to the kitchen. "How's your mother?" he said, his voice a low growl.

"Resting. Hurting, as you can imagine. We all are."

"And where's my car?"

"Paul took the kids out. They were getting squirrelly. We just thought—"

"You thought taking children out into this chaos made

sense? You weren't thinking at all. You should see it out there. Reminds me of the war."

He sat heavily and rested his face in his hands. "When will they be back?"

"That's hard to say, Daddy. We didn't set a time."

"He's not running on me, is he?"

"Running?"

"Don't play dumb! Surely his predicament is not lost on you. Is he making a break for it?"

"In an NPO car? What kind of sense would that make?"

"Might be sly. I've faced few adversaries as slick as Paul. I—"

"Now he's your adversary?"

Ranold narrowed his eyes and stared at her. "He'd better be your adversary too, girlie, or we've got big trouble."

She held his gaze and planted herself in a chair across the table from him. "Then we've got trouble, Dad. He's my husband, my first loyalty. Anyway, he said you had changed your mind on all this, wanted to talk, to pray."

"You should have seen through that even if he didn't. I don't suppose he fell for it either, but it was a shot. I had to keep him here. So, what, does he think he's going to find an ice-cream parlor open at a time like this?"

"I don't know where they went."

"But you swear he's not on the run?"

"I'm not swearing anything, Dad. But he's not going far without me."

"Why's that?"

"I told you. Whatever happens, we're in this together."

Ranold stood, trembling. "So you're on the other side now? Is that it?"

"There is only one side anymore, Dad. Can't you see that?

You want to take arms against a Force that could wipe out over a billion men? Now who's not thinking?"

He sat down again and slammed his palm on the table, making the whole kitchen rattle, and Jae jumped. "You lose a battle and you're ready to surrender? Well, not me, sister."

"You're still an atheist?"

"Don't get smart with me."

"I'm not being smart. Are you going to tell me that the Person you've never believed in wins a battle, as you call it, of this magnitude, and you're not ready to concede He exists?"

"I concede nothing. I never give in, never give up."

"What's it going to take, Daddy? Do you have to lose everything and everybody?"

Before he could answer, Margaret padded in, looking as shaky and pale as before she had fainted. Jae quickly rose and guided her to a chair directly across the table from Ranold. Jae was stunned at how frail and bony her mother felt, shuddering beneath a baggy sweater.

"What's all the racket?" Margaret said.

"Guess," Jae said.

"Your daughter is crazy talking," the old man said.

Jae shook her head. "I'm not going to continue fighting you on this, Dad. Your enemies pray God will rain down a curse, an unspeakable, unimaginable horror that not even I believed would happen, and it happens. How could anyone be in such colossal denial as to doubt that God acted?"

"You're a believer now?"

"Who couldn't be, Dad? You may be the only stubborn fool left, shaking your puny hand in the face of the Almighty. Do you need Him to squash you like a bug?"

"Who do you think you're talking to, Jae?"

"I know who I'm talking to, and if ever there was a time to be in your face, it's now, don't you think? If I didn't love you, Dad, why would I risk offending you? I'm way past worrying about that now."

"You're about to make me do something I don't want to do."

"What? Turn *me* in? Bring *me* up on charges? Have *me* put to death? You'd do that to your own daughter and your grandchildren—leave them without parents?"

"We'll take care of the kids, bring 'em up right, sane, not believing in some—"

"Yeah, Dad, whatever you do, don't let them believe in a God who has proven Himself."

Margaret's voice was quavery. "You're not going to turn in your own daughter."

Jae was as surprised as her father had to be. She had never—ever—heard her mother take him on.

"Watch me," he said.

"Maybe you don't care, Ranold," Margaret said. "Maybe you never have. But the minute you do that, you'll never see me again as long as you live."

Jae's father pressed his lips tight and filled his cheeks with air. He stood, thrust his quivering hands into his pockets, as if to keep himself from doing something he regretted, and marched about the kitchen. "Do you not understand the law, Margaret? Do you not respect authority? Do you know the definition of *treason*?"

"Do I need to pack my bags, Ranold?" she said.

"What are you talking about?"

"Have I not been clear? You bring harm to my daughter or my grandchildren and you'll regret it."

"You're *threatening* me?"

"Now you're getting it."

"But what about Paul? A double agent. A turncoat! A Benedict Arnold! He's the epitome of a national security risk. You can't expect me to stand by and let him—"

Margaret placed her hands on the table and tried to stand.

"Mother, please, don't," Jae said.

"I want to stand."

"Let me help you."

Once she was on her feet, the old woman pointed a shaky finger at her husband. "Here's what I expect from you if you care a whit about me and your family: You will leave this alone. The NPO doesn't have time to worry about who's on what side now. This mess of death all over the world is going to take every man and woman left to sort out and clean up. If after all that Paul and his family are determined to be enemies of the state, you don't have to get involved."

Jae could tell her mother, finally heroic after all these years, had pushed Ranold B. Decenti past his boiling point. He leaned directly across the table, his smoldering eyes boring into her, and slammed both fists on the table three times. "How dare you!" he said. "How *could* you? You would harbor criminals?"

"I will protect my family," Margaret said, her breath coming in labored gasps. "Even against you."

"You can't win!" he said. "Who do you think you are?"

"I'm a mother," she whispered, and as Ranold's angry, screwed-up expression changed to a mask of humor and he leaned his head back, guffawing, Margaret sat again. But as soon as Jae let go of her, the woman pitched away from her and fell to the floor, her head thudding loudly.

"You killed her!" Jae screeched. "Look what you've done!"

Her father's face had frozen. He rushed to his wife, whining, "Margaret, don't! We'll talk this through!"

Jae's mother twitched and jerked and suddenly fell still.

"Margaret!" Ranold wailed. "No!"

Jae knelt and pressed her fingers against her mother's neck at the carotid artery. Nothing. Jae slumped to the floor, shaking her head at her father.

"What? What! No! Margaret!" He knelt over her, wrestled her onto her back, leaning close, listening for breathing. He laid his ear on her chest, then straddled her, pounding her chest and administering CPR.

"Daddy, don't," Jae said. "Don't. She's gone."

Ranold turned and reached for his daughter. She allowed him to drape his arms around her, but she did not return his embrace. "What have I done, baby girl? What have I done?"

Jae wished she could say it, wished she could make him eat it. "You killed her" was on her lips, but not even a monster like her father needed to hear that again.

He rocked, sobbing, drawing raspy breaths. "You need to get out of here, Jae."

"What?"

"Just go. If you stay I might do something crazy. Go now before I change my mind."

"Where will I go?"

"I don't care! Just go!"

"I'm not leaving her here like this. Get off her. At least let me put her in a bed or on the couch."

Jae, of course, had never seen her father like this. As she helped him carry her mother's body into the den and stretch her out on the couch, Jae began forcing her grief and anger to a deep place where she could mine it afresh when she had that luxury.

She closed her mother's eyes and mouth and draped an afghan over her, pulling it over the woman's head. Something inside Jae told her she needed to take advantage of her father's largesse and go. There was nothing more to pack. All she had to do was grab her coat and run.

And so she did. She caught a glimpse of her father slumped in a chair near his wife, his shoulders heaving with great sobs. He looked up at Jae as she pulled on her coat, as if expecting a word, a good-bye, an embrace, something.

The sad fact was, she didn't know how long she could trust him. He would be as alone as he had ever been in his life, and he might soon repent of letting her go. Jae hurried out through the garage, trying to think like Ranold when he was in his right mind. He was making a huge mistake. If he wanted Paul, if he wanted to exact revenge, he was letting slip through his fingers the one connection that would have brought Paul right back to him. Jae would have been the perfect hostage, the perfect bait.

But now she was on the run.

The bitter wind hit her face as she pulled up her hood and sprinted down the street toward the main roads. It hadn't been two hours since the global curse, and it seemed Jae was rushing through a war zone. She hit Paul's private number on her speed dial as she ran and, when she got his voice mail, told him where to find her.

• • •

Paul was dialing the number—provided by Straight—of the Washington, D.C., area underground when a tone told him a call was coming in. But he couldn't ring off and get to it in time. By the time he did, he could tell someone was leaving a message. Once it was complete, he pressed his thumb against his middle finger and played it back.

Jae sounded frantic. "Paul, I'm on foot. Meet me in Brightwood Park on Sixteenth heading toward Silver Spring in about twenty minutes."

# 6

**JAE HAD UNDERESTIMATED** the distance from her father's home to where she planned to rendezvous with Paul and the kids. She alternated running and walking, the trauma of the day catching up with her and making her muscles ache. And that atop her burning lungs and labored heart.

Jae didn't want to keep calling Paul. Though he had assured her the connection to him was secure, not a day went by without someone announcing new technology that allowed the tracking of cellular and solar phone systems. Who knew? Maybe he would be safe but she could be tracked. Maybe her father had already changed his mind and had initiated an all-points bulletin.

She hailed a cab, no easy feat. The driver, a husky woman with an eastern European accent Jae couldn't place, tripped the meter and immediately got personal, as if the world situation granted such license. Jae wasn't offended.

"Who you have lost?" the woman said.

"Sorry?"

"Everybody has lose someone. I lose two uncles and brother."

"How awful."

"Everybody suffers," the cabbie said. "You?"

"Half my family."

"Half!"

"My brother and my mother," Jae said.

"Your mother?"

"Heart attack, I think."

"I think it is end of world."

"Do you?" Jae said. "Really?"

"What else one can think? When first I hear about threat, like most, I laugh. Then it happens. End of world."

"You believe in God?" Jae said.

"I do now. How I can not?"

. . .

Jack Pass sounded like the lone switchboard operator for an entire city. "Good to finally meet you, Stepola, even by phone. Sorry about the circumstances. What's your story?"

Paul told him in one long, run-on sentence.

"So you're the spy who wants to come in from the cold."

"I don't want to stay long. Not much for sitting. But I've got to secure my family."

"That's what we're here for, but you can imagine how limited our resources are, especially space."

Paul told him of his family and their ages. "And I might be able to help you with resources. Cash, I mean."

"Seriously?"

"No promises, but I can make a few calls. Well, one call."

"Oh yeah. You were on the Demetrius case in Atlantica, weren't you?"

"Good memory."

"We could sure use the help," Pass said. "Not to mention the extra hands."

"We wouldn't freeload."

"Ah, listen, Stepola, you need to know we've got a situation here. One of our most trusted elders lost a son."

"At 6 p.m.?"

"You guessed it."

"Ouch."

"We don't know what to do with him. He swears it's coincidence, doesn't understand it, says all the right things. We've got him in lockup. We can't risk it."

"If he's an infiltrator, he's probably already reported on your location."

"That's our fear," Pass said.

"You planning an exodus or increasing security?"

"Both. Moving would be a major, major deal."

"Question is who this guy represents," Paul said.

"Could be anybody."

"I'd like to meet him."

"You'll get that chance. We'll come get you."

• • •

After only a few minutes in the cab, Jae thought the temperature had dropped when she disembarked on Sixteenth. She didn't want to appear too obvious, but she didn't want Paul to miss her either. Jae stepped in and out of the shadows near an electronics store at a corner, trying to sort her emotions.

She was exhausted physically and emotionally, of course. Scared. Missing Paul and the children terribly. It hadn't been that long since she'd seen them, but she wouldn't feel safe until they were together again.

Bouncing from one foot to the other, she watched a flickering TV on sale in the window. She couldn't hear, but when "NPO" rolled across the bottom of the screen, Jae stared, waiting for the headline to come around again. The running banners updated death tolls from around the world, and Jae kept peeking away to see if she could spot Paul.

Finally she saw it: "High-ranking NPO official reports wife murdered, government-issue car stolen. . . ."

• • •

Paul took a call from his secretary in Chicago.

"Did you steal your father-in-law's car?"

"I can't wait to hear this, Felicia. I appropriated it, yes. I'm still NPO too, last I heard."

"Not for long. They pressed us all back into service, as you can imagine."

"You're not calling from the office . . . ?"

"Give me some credit, Paul. I said I was running out for a smoke."

"So, how did you know I was—"

"You're a glowing target in that car, Paul. Decenti claims his daughter broke his wife's neck, murdered her, and that you absconded with his NPO car."

"Margaret Decenti isn't dead. I saw her just—"

"I'm just telling you what he's telling the NPO, Paul. If you're in his car, you might as well be waving a white flag."

• • •

When Jae pulled out her phone to warn Paul, a text message awaited. *Peace Park, northeast corner, fast, no calls. We'll be on foot.*

That was eight blocks north and two blocks west! That Paul and the kids were on foot meant he had been warned about the car. What about the luggage? They couldn't handle it all. And if the authorities were looking for a young family, he was going to have to abandon almost everything and keep to the shadows and side streets.

Jae didn't dare try another cab. Who knew if she was implicated? She didn't feel like taking another step, let alone running again. But what could she do? *Rest when you're dead,* she told herself.

•   •   •

Paul left Ranold's car in a secluded spot, holding out the faint hope that whoever picked him up from the underground could swing past it and see if they could retrieve any belongings.

Before tightening the kids' coats and hats, he disconnected every wire he could find under the hood, rendering the car useless.

"We're going to find Mommy about six blocks away," he said.

"I want to stay in the car!" Brie said.

"Me too!" Connor said.

"We can't. And we have to hurry and stay out of sight."

"Why?"

He couldn't sugarcoat it. "Bad people are after us. If you do what I say, we'll be safe."

"And then you'll tell me all about it?" Brie said.

"Promise."

"I'm scared," Connor said.

So was Paul.

•   •   •

Jae entered Peace Park and stayed in the shadows, behind statues and trees, noticing a van, lights off, idling midblock off one corner. It was probably only minutes, but it seemed like hours before she saw Paul and the kids enter the park from the west.

The kids started jabbering as soon as they all embraced in a huge bear hug, but Jae shushed them as Paul placed a call.

"We're here," he said. "Yes, we see it. Brake lights twice, got it."

The van's rear lights immediately shone twice.

"Let's go," he said, and soon they were inside and warm again.

To Jae's relief, the driver—a tall, skinny man in a huge parka— immediately took to the kids and started telling them about other children they were about to meet. That gave Jae and Paul a chance to hurriedly bring each other up to date.

"So she *is* dead?" Paul said. "I'm so sorry, Jae."

"I couldn't believe Daddy let me go, but it shouldn't have surprised me that he's already changed his mind. Paul, what are our chances?"

"I think you know."

"Right now I'd almost be relieved to just have it out in the open," she said. "'Yes, okay, we're the enemy. Do what you have to do.'"

Paul nodded toward Brie and Connor. "And them?"

"Like my mother said, they'd have to kill me first."

# 7

**THE DRIVER FOLLOWED** Paul's directions and swung back past Ranold's car. "I don't see anyone," he said, "but it's your call. Last thing we want is a tail."

"Our whole lives are in that car," Paul said. "Let's risk it."

Jae offered to assist, but Paul insisted that he and the driver, working quickly, would attract less attention. Within seconds they had tossed everything from the sedan into the back of the van.

The driver drove ten minutes, Paul noticing that he was somehow able to monitor his rearview mirrors while distracting the kids. "So, you ready for a real adventure?" he said.

They both nodded, and Connor even smiled.

Paul shuddered. He whispered to Jae, "Any reason the kids have to know about your mother?"

She shook her head. "We're going to have to tell them about Berl. They deserve that."

The driver finally pulled into an industrial park that appeared abandoned. He stopped and threw the van into park, turning in his seat to address Paul and Jae. "There's a secluded alley three blocks ahead," he said. "If I spot a tail or anything suspicious, I won't stop. If I do stop, each of you take the hand of one of the kids and get to the left side of the first building as quickly as you can.

"They're expecting you, and I will radio them that you're here. Knock twice on the side door, which opens out, so step away from it. They'll call out a phrase and you answer it, and they'll let you in."

"What phrase?" Jae said.

"If I have to tell you," he said, "I picked up the wrong people. Now just a warning: This is only one of more than a dozen heavily guarded entrances to our underground, and it happens to be one of the farthest from the actual compound. You will walk more than a quarter mile once you're inside. Don't take any of your stuff. I'll deliver that through another entrance."

• • •

Jae studied Brie and Connor. What kind of a childhood was this? At least they would have companionship. But they knew nothing of God, and all of a sudden they would be surrounded by families risking their lives for Him.

Atheism in the schools for kids their age was more a matter of omission than overt negativity. God was simply never mentioned, never acknowledged. Jae wasn't sure either Brie or Connor even had a concept of God. How she would have loved to begin their education about Him with the story of God's sending His only Son to earth. How could they be expected to understand Him when it was likely that within a day or two of finding out their parents were God followers, they would learn of His fearsome power to kill?

• • •

"See it?" the driver said, stopping and pointing. Paul nodded. "Hurry. Don't hesitate. Go now." The driver spoke into his radio. "*T* minus fifteen seconds and counting."

Paul grabbed Connor's hand and headed directly to a dark, flat door almost invisible in the brick wall. With Jae and Brie right behind, Paul noticed a motion sensor on the ground and a tiny camera on the roof. Hardly anyone outside his profession would have been aware of them.

He knocked firmly and a man's voice called out, "He is risen."

"He is risen indeed," Paul said, stepping back as the door swung open. It was dark until they were all inside; then the man turned on a large flashlight. "Let me get a look at you," he said.

Paul made the introductions.

"Jack Pass," the man said, aiming the beam at his own face. Paul hadn't known what to expect, but certainly not a fortyish man, pudgy and balding. He saw zero resemblance to Jack's late older brother, under whom he had served in the Special Forces years before. Andrew Pass had been a military cliché: crew cut, trim, ramrod straight, all that.

"This is what I call service," Paul said. "The man himself."

"We're all just servants here," Jack said. "Come on. We've got a walk ahead of us."

"I don't like this place," Connor said.

"You will, little one," Jack said, leading them at least two floors down a wood staircase. "Trust me. It's like playing fort all day every day."

# 8

**JAE HOPED THE COMPOUND** itself would be warmer than the subterranean tunnels leading to it. But that wasn't the only thing giving her a chill. She and Paul had not talked about the elephant in the room. Angela Pass Barger, the martyred Andy Pass's daughter and Jack's niece, had to be there.

All Jae knew about the woman was that she was beautiful, a young widow, had two sons older than Jae's kids, and that Paul had appeared to be taken with her when they worked together on a case in Las Vegas. Jae had actually tried to find her there on her way to Los Angeles the year before, only to learn that Angela had returned to Washington.

• • •

When finally they arrived at the end of the labyrinth of tunnels and emerged into the warmth of the underground warren, Paul was struck by how spare and efficient the place was. Jack Pass told him more than a thousand people lived here.

To Paul it appeared as cold and antiseptic as a factory office full of cubicles. He couldn't imagine its original purpose, then discovered it had merely been the far-reaching foundation of several industrial-park buildings. Jack confirmed that it had once been just an empty, concrete-walled space full of water and gas pipes, electrical conduit, and phone and computer lines. "When it became obvious the industrial park was dying, this became more of a dumping ground than active storage, so when we discovered it and took it over, we spent half a year just gutting the place."

It certainly didn't have the intrigue of the miles of salt mines beneath Michigan and Ohio where the Heartland underground was headquartered. And neither was there the dark charm of the catacomb-like, candlelit rooms that housed the Italian resistance in Rome.

This was more high-tech, Paul decided. Every room and cubbyhole seemed to have a purpose. And the brains behind this faction of the USSA underground had taken full advantage of the resources left behind. Besides hundreds of rooms that served as private living quarters for families, larger rooms had been cordoned off for media centers housing discs and computers and phone banks. There were mass kitchens and dining areas, huge restroom facilities. Paul found various schoolrooms for all ages.

And suddenly here she came. Angela. Paul noticed the weariness around her eyes. It shouldn't have surprised him. Someone dedicated to giving herself to this cause, regardless of the cost, had to eventually show the strain. And only the most twisted person would take any joy or find any satisfaction in the "victory" God had wrought, especially when it brought such tragedy.

It was clear Angela was forcing a smile, as it did not involve her eyes. Paul didn't read anything into that but exhaustion.

She took his hand in both of hers. "How nice to see you again. And this must be Jae."

. . .

Jae was taken aback when Angela eschewed her offered hand and embraced her.

"I've heard so much about you," Angela said. "All good, and all, of course, from Paul. Welcome."

"Thank you." Jae wanted to say she had heard a lot about Angela too, but she certainly didn't want to get into the fact that she had seen Angela in NPO surveillance photos.

Most impressive was that Angela immediately knelt and looked the children in their eyes and called them by name. "Bet you can't guess what my job is here, Brie."

"Cook?"

"No!" Angela said, laughing.

"Clown!" Connor said, and she roared.

"You guys are silly! We're going to have so much fun. I'm in charge of kids your age. And I needed one more girl and one more boy. Raise your hand if you're in!"

They raised their hands, beaming, and Jae had to admire how Angela had apparently seen the fear on their faces, distracted them from the reality that they had been uprooted and relocated, and immediately made them feel not just welcome, but also needed.

"If it's all right with your mom and dad, we're having a movie in about ten minutes."

"Where?" Brie said.

Angela pointed down the hall. "About five minutes that way, so we're going to have to get going. Oh, don't worry; I'll take you. You'll be my special guests, and I'll introduce you to the other kids. Fair enough?"

"What's the movie?"

"*The Boy Who Gave His Lunch to Jesus.*"

"To *who*?"

"Oh, you're going to love this. Is it okay, Mom? Dad?"

Jae looked to Paul and he nodded. Jae motioned with her head, and Angela leaned close. "I'm a brand-new believer," Jae said. "The kids have had zero exposure."

Angela raised her eyebrows and nodded. "Good to know. We'll take it slow and just answer questions. I'll keep you informed. This is the perfect movie for an introduction to Jesus. By the time it's over, your stuff will have been delivered, you'll be settled in your quarters, and I'll bring the kids to you."

In spite of herself, Jae already loved Angela. How could she not? She had been prepared to be defensive, to look for something to envy, to dare Paul to show some flicker of familiarity.

As the kids eagerly walked off with Angela, Jack introduced to Jae another woman who would take her to their quarters and help gather their belongings. "I need to borrow Paul for a few moments," Jack said. "If that's all right."

Despite the welcome and the security she felt, Jae hesitated. The fact was, she didn't want to be apart from Paul and the kids again so soon. These strangers seemed wonderful, and she was eager to see where the family was to land and get off her feet, but still she shot Paul a desperate look.

"I won't be long," he said. "They want me to meet a prisoner, an infiltrator."

There would be no keeping him from that, but naturally Jae wondered: if there had been one turncoat, were there more? Did she have to suspect everybody down here, regardless of their smiles and friendliness?

• • •

"We thought it would be good to locate our makeshift lockup as far from the general population as possible," Jack said, pointing Paul to the passenger seat of an electric golf cart. They rolled several hundred yards past half a dozen checkpoints, where ersatz security guards nodded to Jack and couldn't hide that they were sneaking peeks at Paul.

Jack finally stopped outside a heavily reinforced door with a window replaced by plywood and wire mesh. Inside a sweating man with short brown hair sat at a cafeteria-style table, eating a substantial meal with one hand. His other was handcuffed to a pipe on the wall.

"He's our only prisoner," Jack said, "but we made an executive decision to feed him the way we do the general population. We don't treat him bad, don't torture him. We just ask questions. He swears he's one of us, and for a long time we thought he was. Said all the right things, helped out, all that. He was here with his only son, and when the curse hit, that son dropped dead. Meet Ernie Marmet."

Marmet looked up but kept eating, which Paul knew was no small thing, because he had to recognize Paul. "That's not Ernie Marmet," Paul said. "That's Roscoe Wipers from western Gulfland, specifically Louisiana, Baton Rouge NPO bureau. How you doin', Roscoe?"

"Been better, Doc."

"Bet you have. So have you already made this place to the NPO?"

"Me?" Wipers said, a cheek full of food. "No, man. I'm like you. Converted. Playing both ends against the middle."

Despite fuming inside, Paul smiled. "Nice try. Difference between us is that everybody in the underground knows about me.

I don't hide my identity from the side I'm really loyal to. How long you been here?"

"About four months."

"Six months and three weeks," Jack said.

Paul shook his head. Part of him wanted to attack the defenseless Wipers right there. One two-step maneuver and the man would be dead in seconds. He could tell Wipers knew that too, his eyes darting and his breathing accelerating as he seemed to try to maintain composure by slowly eating.

Ironic, Paul thought, wanting to kill a man for doing well a job that Paul had done for years.

"This is bad, Jack," Paul said. "NPO has to know exactly where you are by now." Then, to Roscoe: "What's your daily check-in time?"

Wipers just stared.

"C'mon, Roscoe," Paul said through clenched teeth. "You're a prisoner of war, man. We're not people of violence, but you've put everybody in this place in mortal danger. At some point these nice people are going to ask me whether it makes sense to let you live. You know what I'm going to tell them?"

"Pray tell." Wipers shoved his tray aside and slurped a juice box.

"You and I both know procedures are in place in the event you don't check in at your assigned time. If you're willing to check in, mislead the NPO, take the heat off this place, I might decide you're worth more alive than dead."

Wipers scratched his forehead. "It's all just business with me, Stepola. I'm out of options. I can't make contact unless you want me to, so I'm stuck. I got to play ball."

"So, when do they expect to hear from you?"

"Two hundred hours on the dot, every day."

"Uh-huh. And your contact person?"

"You know her."

"Balaam? Bia Balaam?"

"She's the one."

"So at two in the morning, you're willing to check in, tell her this place is no more, everybody cleared out, and you're just following the crowd to a new location that hasn't been announced yet?"

"I'm easy, man."

# 9

**JAE WAS SOON ALONE** in a den of two rooms with a bath-room down the hall. When their stuff arrived, she busied herself unpacking and making a makeshift home of the place. It wasn't spacious and hardly opulent, but there was privacy, ample bed-ding, and seating. When she was finished, she followed direc-tions and left the empty luggage and boxes outside in the hall. Soon they were hauled away for storage.

Jae stretched out on her back on one of the beds. When she felt herself drifting she prayed for her kids and for her husband. She even prayed for her father and for Aryana. Jae rolled to her side and wept for her mother, her grief quickly moving to great sobs. She lay on her stomach and soon slept.

• • •

"I'll be back to walk you through that call, Roscoe," Paul said.

Maybe in the meantime Paul could talk himself out of doing
what he wanted to do to the man.

Wipers nodded resignedly and saluted with his free hand.

Outside in the hall, Jack Pass whispered, "I was never military or law enforcement, Paul. Education was my game. So correct me if I'm wrong, but all that seemed a little too easy."

"No, you're right. All he has to do is call in at the wrong time,
leave out one code word, or say something cryptic, and NPO
knows he's been made. They'll be on you like Elvis on felt."

"And so?"

"I'm assuming you have secure phones."

"Of course. We have everything. Wait till you see what we're
doing with cars and dead people's clothes."

"With what?"

Jack looked at his watch. "In due time. You need a phone?"

"I could call with my own connection, but I hate to compromise my contact. I think I'm secure, but I'm calling Chicago
NPO, and they have the latest in tracking and recording capabil-
ity."

Paul rode with Jack to a massive communications center,
where he was directed to a padded booth that eliminated surrounding sounds.

"Any one of these units," Jack said, gesturing toward a bank
of cell phones, "has flying, centrifugal, random-code technology
that could not be matched in a million years' worth of a million
digital combinations per second."

Paul shook his head. "Good enough for me." These people
were somehow on a par with the NPO. What Jack meant was
that the phone unit threw out a digital code in an ever-
accelerating manner that, in essence, spun the numbers in a circle, not unlike a line of crack-the-whip skaters. Duplicating the
scrambled code was virtually impossible.

Paul dialed the Chicago NPO office, disguised his voice, and asked for Felicia. He pictured her, scared, weary, probably working at his desk.

"This is Felicia," she said.

"Oh," he said in his own voice, "I must have the wrong number," and before she could say, "Paul?" he hung up.

Not two minutes later she called his molar-implanted personal phone. "Okay, cowboy," she said. "I got the hint and am out for another smoke break. What do you need?"

"Something that will put you on my side," Paul said.

"It's too late to be talking in code, boss."

"There was a reason I left you out of this for so long, Felicia."

"You couldn't trust me."

"It wasn't that. I didn't want to assume you would flip like I had, compromise you."

She sighed. "Like I said before, Doctor, you apparently didn't care enough about me to try to spare me what has happened."

Paul didn't know what to say. Yes, he had believed the sword of death would smite firstborn males and, yes, that many of his friends would suffer. "What would you have said or done if I had tried to warn you, Felicia?"

"I don't know. But I wouldn't have turned you in; I know that. And then, when it happened, I would have been grateful that you tried to spare me. And who knows? I might have flipped. I mean, c'mon, Paul, widespread death is pretty hard to argue with."

"I'm sorry. I care about you and your family; you know that. I didn't know what to do, and doing nothing certainly wasn't the right thing."

"All right," Felicia said. "So we still love each other in spite of it all. What do you need?"

"This is going to make you take sides."

"You already made that clear. I've spent a lot of years here, Paul. And I've also spent a lot of years letting the government convince me there's no God. Well, if there's no God, who killed all the men? I'm not saying I'm ready to become a devotee. I mean, I finally find out God is real, and this is the kind of a person He is? But I sure don't want to be on His bad side either."

"And so?"

"And so I'm now in this for myself. If helping you earns me points with Him, count me in."

"I don't think it works that way, Felicia."

"Well, someday I'll let you tell me all about it. All I know is, you've been suspected around here for months. I didn't know what to think. I thought maybe if you were a double agent, you might tell me, but then why would you? The fewer who knew the better, right? Did Bob know?"

"Of course not. Nobody inside knew."

"Well, that makes me feel better. So now I know, and scary as this all is, I'd rather be on your side than where I've been; know what I'm saying?"

"Uh-huh."

"So you want something. You want me to be your inside contact. I get caught and I'm in the same boat with you. But if I don't do it, maybe I'm in trouble with God. Right now I'm more afraid of Him than I am of the NPO."

"I'm not sure that's the best motive, Felicia, but I do need your help and have to trust you."

"You could have always trusted me, Paul, but how could you know that? Just tell me what you need. I'm going home in a little while no matter what. I'm so tired I can hardly see straight."

"Okay, you want to write this down or you going to trust that memory of yours?"

"Just fire away, Paul."

"All right, there's an encoded file that Bob Koontz and I share. It's invisible until you bring it up with the following code. The code changes every day, based on date and time, so here's the calculation." He recited it for her. "Once you're in it, you'll find a list of NPO infiltrators, their code names, their passwords, their contacts, their reporting times. I need everything you can find on Roscoe Wipers out of the Gulfland bureau."

# 10

**JAE AWOKE** to a light tap on the door and rose to find Angela Pass Barger with Brie and Connor. The kids looked tired but also wired. They eagerly told her all about the movie and the miracle of Jesus feeding thousands of people with one small boy's lunch.

"I never even heard of Jesus before," Brie said, and Jae wondered how old she herself had been when she first heard of Him. Probably junior high school.

She sent the kids down the hall to get ready for bed and sat with Angela. "Thanks for watching out for them," she said.

"They're delightful. And how are you doing?"

Angela seemed to say that with such compassion that Jae was immediately overcome. And when Angela laid a hand on her arm, Jae broke down. She found herself gushing her life story, telling Angela of her upbringing, her marriage, how she had seen a change in Paul, how she herself had come to faith, the loss of her brother and then her mother. "I prayed with her just before my dad got home," she said. "I'm so sorry to lay all this on you."

"Not at all," Angela said. "You've sure had more than your share."

"I feel so guilty about the children," Jae said. "Have we started too late? It isn't that we told them God or Jesus was bad or even a myth. We simply never mentioned either of them."

"And of course neither did the schools," Angela said.

Jae nodded.

"Actually, Jae, they're at a perfect age. It would have been good to have them younger, of course, but at eight and six they have no guile, no cynicism. We'll take it slow, but it won't be long before they realize all the other kids love Jesus. And imagine all the great stories they have yet to hear."

"I can't wait to hear them myself," Jae said. "I'm embarrassed at how little I know about the Bible and the stories of Jesus."

"I could use an assistant," Angela said. "You can work and hear the stories all at the same time, and no one will be the wiser."

• • •

Paul sat across the table from Roscoe Wipers while Jack Pass stood behind Paul.

"So your contact person is Bia Balaam and you call her every twenty-four hours at two in the morning."

"Right," Roscoe said.

"And what's your code?" Paul said.

"Catcall."

"And your password?"

"Git mo."

"Uh-huh. And if something's wrong, what's your catch-phrase?"

"I'm to say, 'Everything's going fine here, just fine.'"

Paul planted his elbows on his knees and buried his face in his hands. "Oh, Roscoe, what am I going to do with you? You can't be so stupid as to not realize your life is in my hands. You think these people would have a problem with my breaking your neck right now?"

"Trust me. Why would I lie? I got nothing to gain and everything to lose."

Paul rested his chin on his fists, then turned and gazed at Jack. "I don't know. You want my professional opinion?"

"'Course."

"You ought to let me put him out of his misery."

"It's your call," Jack said.

Roscoe cocked his head. "It's *his* call. Why is it his call? Isn't he new here?"

"This is war, Roscoe," Paul said. "We're people of faith, people of redemption, people of second chances. But you're an enemy of God. We believe your lies, and we could lose our whole population. You're willing to be responsible for that and yet you think we'd have qualms about eliminating you?"

"I'm not following."

"Sure you are. The only thing you've told me so far that rings true is that Bia Balaam is your contact. But you don't talk to her directly because she's an early-to-bed, early-to-rise type."

"Okay, so I talk to her machine. So what?"

"You think I just fell off a turnip truck, Roscoe?"

"What? No!"

"You underestimate me. You don't think I'm highly enough placed within the NPO to have access to your information?"

"What are you saying?"

"First, your call-in time is four hundred hours, not two hundred hours."

"Point taken. That was a slip of the tongue on my part."

"Oh, fine then. As long as it was just a mistake. That little two-hour error could have cost everyone here, couldn't it? Your code word is *boomerang*, your password is *Cuba*, and your red-flag catchphrase is *same old same old*."

"Can't blame a guy for trying."

Paul rubbed his eyes. "I don't have the time or energy for this, Jack. Do you?"

"Don't believe I do, Paul. But if we kill him and he doesn't report in at four o'clock, then what happens? If we're already made, we've got to move."

# 11

**SOMETHING UNIQUE** was happening with the kids, Jae decided. Angela had bid them good night, and Jae was convinced they would immediately begin badgering to know all that was going on. Jae had promised. She owed them that much. And she could remember herself at their ages, feeling always on the perimeter, never really knowing what was happening among the adults.

Maybe it was fatigue, maybe excitement, the new surroundings, the movie; she didn't know what. But they came back from the bathroom in their pajamas and carrying their toothbrushes, looking so weary they could have dropped right there.

Jae put them down in single beds pulled together, and neither seemed to feel like talking. "Tired?" she said. Brie nodded and turned onto her side. Connor stretched and yawned. "Guess what I'm going to do before I go to sleep?" Jae said.

"Eat," Connor said.

"No. Are you hungry?"

He shook his head. "Only for bread and fish. It sure looked good in the movie."

"I'm going to pray," Jae said.

The kids stared at her. "Like Jesus prayed?" Brie said. "He blessed the food before He made it stretch to feed all those people. Miss Angela said He was talking to His Father."

Jae nodded. "That's who I'm going to pray to. Jesus' Father. He's God."

Connor rolled up onto an elbow. "Where does God live?"

"In heaven."

"Where's that?"

"We don't know. Somewhere far, far away."

The kids fell silent. "Is it a fairy tale?" Brie asked finally. "A make-believe story?"

Jae shook her head. "It's real. God lives in heaven, and Jesus is His Son. God sent Him to the world to love us."

"Jesus loves us?" Connor said. "He doesn't even know us."

"Yes, He does, because He's God's Son."

"He's still alive?" Brie said. "That story looked like it was from a long time ago."

"More than two thousand years ago," Jae said. "But you know what? Jesus is still alive. He will be alive forever. And we can be too."

"We can?" Brie managed, her eyes slow and heavy.

Jae knew if she just quit talking, the kids would fall off to sleep. And so she did. And so they did.

•  •  •

Paul found Jae dozing when he returned, and he tried not to wake her as he took off his shirt, shoes, pants, and socks and lay back on the bed.

"How was your prisoner?" she mumbled.

He turned to see her eyes still shut. "Sleep," he said.

"I want to know," she said.

He told her who it was and that he would have to leave her again at near four in the morning for the phone-in to the NPO.

"I'm sorry," she said.

"Me too. I'm dead."

She told him she had prayed with her mother before her father had arrived home.

"She was a believer then?" he said.

"I think she was, Paul. And I believe the kids soon will be too, though I worry about them."

"How so?"

She told him how they had forgotten all their questions, didn't bug her about promising to tell everything.

"That *is* strange."

"They're going through a lot, Paul. Too much. I feel guilty. As if it's my fault. As if I should have somehow been able to shield them from all of this."

"We both know it's my fault," Paul said. "Of course, I wouldn't have it any other way and can think of no alternatives, but it was my choice that put our whole family in jeopardy."

She didn't respond. He was grateful. She needed sleep as badly as he did.

At ten minutes of four, the alarm feature embedded in Paul's teeth sent a tone only he could hear through his cranium. He immediately sat up, as clouded and heavy lidded as he had felt in a long time. Slipping out of bed, he dressed quickly. Jae and the kids lay stock-still, breathing deeply.

Paul grabbed a small set of wires with a suction cup and earpiece from one of his cases and found Jack Pass at the end of the hall in the golf cart. "How is it you look so chipper?" Paul said.

"I'm a night owl. Can hardly tell day from night here any-way. Besides, I've got an idea."

"Uh-oh."

"Yeah, I know. It'd be like you trying to give me educational ideas. I'm not in espionage, and I—"

"Just spill it, Jack. I'm not territorial, and I'm wide-open to any suggestion. I'm going to go crazy cooped up down here for long, but unless one of us comes up with a plan, I'm stuck. I have to be the most recognizable and vulnerable fugitive in the USSA."

Jack zipped past the security checkpoint and finally pulled up outside the holding room for Roscoe Wipers. "Where'd he get a name like that anyway?" Jack said. "Sounds like a retail shop."

Paul stared at him. Surely Jack wasn't expecting an answer. *Where does a man get a name like Jack Pass either?*

"Anyway, here's what I'm thinking. This gun—" and he pulled out one of the heaviest, ugliest, oldest .357 Magnums Paul had ever seen—"uses high-speed hollow-point tips and will wake the dead."

"Tell me about it. You're not planning to kill this guy, are you?"

"Not for real. But I should ask you the same, Paul. I could see in your eyes you'd have liked to have dropped him yourself earlier."

"Let's just say you'd better handle the gun," Paul said. "But for what, if you don't plan to actually use it on him? Pretend?"

"Exactly. We get him connected, make sure he says the right stuff, have him tell this woman's machine that we have moved out of Washington. Then, just as he's starting to tell her where we've gone, we interrupt him, tell him he's been made, fire off the gun, he drops the phone, end of threat."

Paul thought a moment. "I like it," he said. "I think. The

question is whether we let Roscoe in on the fact that he's not really going to be killed."

"I say let him wonder. Then he won't pull anything."

"You're going to shoot the weapon regardless, and maybe more than once?"

"Right," Jack said.

"Better tell your people, unless you want them to come running, guns out."

"Right again. And here's Roscoe's phone."

A minute later Paul and Jack stood before the door of the darkened room. "We've got to put him on the defensive right off the bat," Paul said. "Unlock the door and open it just a quarter inch."

Jack knelt by the doorknob. When the door was unlocked he signaled Paul, and Paul waved him out of the way. "Follow me in with the gun," he said. Paul backed up a step and drove his foot into the door. It flew open, crashing the wall as he turned on the lights. Roscoe Wipers, stretched awkwardly on the table with a woolen army blanket and a pillow and wearing only an undershirt and shorts, raged and swore and thrust out both arms, shrieking as the handcuff at his wrist reached its limit.

"What'd ya have to do that for?" Roscoe whined.

"Time for your phone call," Paul said, "if I can talk my friend here out of just plugging you right now."

Roscoe's eyes widened at the sight of the gun. "I said I'd cooperate, didn't I?"

"You also lied to us first, gave us phony code words, all that. Why should we trust you?"

"Well, for starters," Roscoe said, pointing at the .357, "that."

Paul attached his listening device to Roscoe's phone with the tiny suction cup and secured the earpiece in his own ear. "One mistake, intentional or not, and all I have to do is nod at Wyatt Earp here."

Roscoe sighed. "Listen to me, Stepola. I don't want to die, all right? You'll see. I'll do this good, the way you want it."

Jack sat facing him four feet away, the pistol in his hands. The wires on Paul's bugging device were but three feet long, so he sat closer. He told Roscoe exactly what he wanted him to say. "I hear anything close to 'same old same old' before you're supposed to say it, and you're a dead man."

Roscoe punched in the numbers. He looked as surprised as Paul felt when Bia answered.

"Balaam," she said.

"Code word *boomerang*, password *Cuba*," Roscoe said.

"I recognize your voice, Wipers," Bia said. "Everything okay?"

"Oh, you know, same song, different verse."

With the sound of the *s* in *same*, Jack rose, loudly cocking the gun and pressing it against Roscoe's temple, so hard that the man cringed and tried to pull away.

"If you don't mind my asking, ma'am, what are you doing awake?"

"Can't sleep. I lost my son, you know."

"Sorry."

"Yeah, thanks. I know I'm not alone, but . . . you lose anyone?"

"Yes, ma'am. A few relatives. I have no kids."

"But that young man we planted with you. What about him?"

"He died, ma'am. Six straight up."

A long pause. "Well, but, then . . . you, you've been made, haven't you?"

Paul narrowed his eyes at Roscoe as if to remind him his very life depended on his answer.

"I must be pretty good, ma'am, because I convinced 'em

it was a coincidence. At least so far. They're performing an autopsy."

"That's not good, Agent Wipers. The common denominator of these deaths is that they make no pathological sense. Cause of death is being reported as the irreversible cessation of vital functions. No heart attack, no stroke, no aneurysm. They simply die. What're you going to do when they come back to you with that news?"

"I don't know. Hope you guys extract me, I guess."

"What did you mean by 'different verse,' Agent?"

"Ma'am?"

"You said, 'Same song . . .'"

"Oh yeah. Lots of talk around here about a mass exodus. Everybody's packing. We're leaving within the hour."

"Where to?"

"They're too smart for that, ma'am. They don't even tell the long-timers here where they're going. I hear rumors of the new place being a couple of hours north, though, but that's all I know."

"You ever figure out where you are? I'm not saying we've got forces that can get there before the move, but obviously we'd have to have some idea."

"I told you, they bring even the ones they know and trust a long, convoluted way, with blindfolds and hoods on."

"Well, your info has been good and the names invaluable. As soon as you know where the relocation site is, get back to me."

"Will do . . . oh no."

"What?"

"Same old same old!"

"What's the problem, Agent?"

"I've been made!"

"How do you know? Ditch the phone!"

Paul removed the suction cup and smacked the phone out of Roscoe's hand, and it clattered to the table and then to the floor. Paul prayed it was still connected to Bia Balaam.

"Marmet!" Jack hollered.

"What?"

"Who are you working for?"

"Nobody! What?"

The gun exploded twice, and Paul reached down to slap the phone shut.

# 12

**JAE'S EYES POPPED OPEN** at about nine in the morning Wednesday, January 23, but she felt no compulsion to rise. She had not even heard Paul return, and the kids were still dead to the world. She felt hungry, but she was convinced her body needed rest more than food.

Through the tiny slits in the shades at the windows to the hallway, she saw shadows passing from both directions. The Washington, D.C., underground was alive with activity, but everyone had assured her no one would bother the Stepolas until they emerged from their cozy warren.

So this was what it meant to be a believer. Grief over her brother. Mourning her mother. Horrified at the unspeakable magnitude of the loss around the world. And yet a deep sense of peace. She wasn't happy. Jae couldn't call it that, not with

everything that had happened. But there was a bedrock content-
ment that God was somehow in control.

She didn't need to understand Him. It wasn't her place to
judge His actions. Had the curse, the plague, seemed excessive?
Yes, to her human mind. But ever since she had made the transaction and placed her eternal destiny in the hands of the God
she had only recently come to believe in, her own intellect felt
puny. From the Bible discs she had listened to, she resonated
with verses that said such things as the fact that man's wisdom
was not God's wisdom and that His ways were beyond finding
out.

Jae didn't know how long her fragile, fugitive family would
last on earth, but part of her couldn't wait to meet God and Jesus
face-to-face in heaven and have myriad mysteries explained. Her
goal the next time she strapped on the earphones and drenched
her soul with the soothing truths of the New Testament was to
find the verse that said God provided a peace that passes all
understanding. Truer words had never been spoken.

Two hours later Jae had risen, taken the kids to breakfast,
and was on her way to her first day as Angela's assistant. On her
way out, she had found a note slipped under the door from Jack
Pass to Paul: *Call me when you're ready for breakfast. Roscoe's desperate to talk.*

•  •  •

Paul had long been grateful that he had the ability to recover
from extended exhaustion with one good night's sleep, as long
as he got in enough hours. As he showered and dressed, he felt
invigorated. The underground was already beginning to feel
confining and even claustrophobic, but he sure felt better about
having Jae and the kids hidden away.

He was encouraged to see dozens of adults jogging the endless corridors as he made his way toward Jack Pass's office. So that was how people stayed in shape and kept their sanity down here.

"Hope you don't mind scrambled and links nuked," Jack said, pulling a Styrofoam plate from a small refrigerator, removing the foil top, and sliding it into the microwave as Paul sat.

"Well, I was hoping for the all-American buffet."

Ninety seconds later they were eating and talking across Jack's cluttered desk. "So what's up with Roscoe?" Paul said.

"You'll see. He's kind of weepy this morning. Didn't sleep well."

"I can't say the same," Paul said. "Slept like a gravestone."

"Nice image," Pass said. "But I know what you mean. Slept pretty well myself. You gotta know you scared me good when you recognized Marmet as NPO. I figured we'd all be toast soon."

"You could have been. But I believe in God's timing, don't you?"

"I oughta by now," Jack said.

When they were finished, Jack asked if Paul wanted to visit Roscoe.

"Nah, let 'im stew. He's not going anywhere."

"He's pretty agitated."

"That make you feel guilty?" Paul said. "Think you owe him putting his mind at ease? He was willing to sacrifice every soul in here just a few hours ago."

Jack shrugged. "Hard to argue with logic. He'll wait. You want to be brought up to speed on job number one around here?"

• • •

Jae had never met anyone like Angela. The woman had her own sorrows, being a single mom with two young boys, living underground, uncertain of her own future. But it was clear Angela had learned to take the focus off herself. It was as if she lived to serve others.

And where had she learned so much about the Bible? Jae had been enriched, filled, nearly overwhelmed by what she had heard on all the discs, but she had to admit she found more than half of it confusing. She hated to acknowledge, even to herself, that she feared she was at the level of these young children in her knowledge of the Bible.

That meant she was in the perfect place. Questions the kids asked were questions she had, and Angela explained things so clearly and simply that Jae was drinking it in. She felt as if she had learned more in a couple of hours than she had known in a lifetime.

What she loved most, of course, was that she could read her own children's faces. They were enamored of all the stories, fascinated with Jesus, and had a ton of questions. She and they would all learn together, and she prayed it wouldn't be long before Brie and Connor shared her faith.

• • •

"I think you'll find this a pleasant surprise," Jack Pass said, handing Paul a protective mask and coveralls.

"You've got my attention."

They sped to the other end of the compound, Jack checking the security checkpoints near the various entries. Finally they arrived at a cavernous area with what appeared to be miles of exhaust hoses running from cars to the ceiling. "They're all connected to hidden vents at the surface," Jack said.

The room was full of men and women working on the cars. "I hate to say it," Jack said, "but in many ways, this latest catastrophe is the best thing that has happened to this kind of work."

"And what kind of work is this?"

"Appropriating cars, clothes, and identities."

Paul narrowed his eyes.

As if reading his question, Jack said, "No, we don't steal their money. We assume they have left families who need their resources. But if they're dead, they certainly don't need their clothes, their driver's licenses, that kind of stuff. Yes, regrettably we're leaving some bereaved families without vehicles, but that's the price of war."

"Summarize it for me, Jack," Paul said. "What's the scope of this operation?"

As they walked, Jack explained. "The whole Columbia Region, but for our purposes, the D.C. area, which is littered with cars, many with bodies inside. Trust me, we respect those bodies, even though we're stripping them of clothes and IDs. We leave the corpses where authorities and families can find them."

"And you abscond with their stuff, including their cars."

Jack nodded.

"But won't there soon be a database filled with vehicle identification numbers of cars stolen?"

"Of course. We're not just tuning up these cars, Paul. VINs are being traded, plates—you name it. If you were to need a car, for instance, we would find one owned by someone with your height and weight and build, give you his ID, your VIN and plate would match the car make and color, and if you behaved yourself behind the wheel, you should be safe. Let me show you the paint shop."

That's where Paul recognized the real need for the mask. A dozen cars were in various stages of sanding, preparation, taping, and spray painting. Nearby, body damage was corrected too. Jack signaled Paul to follow him out.

They climbed back into the golf cart, but Jack stopped in the middle of a long corridor, far from any ears. "You look a little nonplussed, Paul."

Paul cocked his head. "Processing it. You're just doing what I've been doing with NPO for years, but I guess I didn't expect it from this side of the conflict."

"Well, we don't kill people except in self-defense. And we *are* on the right side, after all."

"Of course."

"I don't see how we could compete, keep ourselves alive, stay in the battle, if we didn't fight with creativity."

"What do your elders think? Anyone have a problem with the stealing?"

"Sure," Jack said. "We pray a lot. Talk a lot. Argue a lot. I'm in charge, so I have to face the music on this. If I've been all wrong, God will hold me accountable. I don't know what else to do, Paul. I can tell you this: I never go against a majority vote of the elders."

"But it doesn't have to be unanimous?"

Jack shook his head. "We don't have time to find our way to that kind of a consensus every time."

"I'd like to meet your elders."

"And they'd like to meet you. They see you as some sort of a spiritual giant, you know. They're eager to sit at your feet, have you bring them great spiritual insights."

Paul shook his head. "Your tone tells me you know better. I'm newer at this than most of you, probably all of you."

Jack nodded. "I know. But you've been on the front lines, a true double agent."

"But God blew my cover. I'm nothing but an international fugitive now."

Paul looked at Jack as if to ask why they were still sitting in the middle of the hallway and to give tacit permission to move on, but it was clear Jack had something on his mind. "Got another minute? 'Cause I've been consumed by something."

"Well, my calendar is pretty full today, Jack, but I'll make time for you."

"I've got a good—really good—right-hand man here, Paul. Like me, he is single, no family. Frankly, I think he's interested in my niece, and that's okay, as long as it doesn't distract him when I give him the reins."

"The reins?"

"You mentioned you'd go squirrelly down here, and you just got here. Imagine being here as long as I have. I gotta tell you, Paul, I took my brother's death pretty hard. He was the one who was always venturing out. I held down the fort. I couldn't even go to his funeral, because I would have become a known quantity to prying eyes and they would have likely followed me right back here.

"But you know there is a family of undergrounders around the country that communicates via e-mail and phone regularly. We've become friends and comrades even though we've never met."

"You know what the NPO calls all of you, don't you?"

Jack nodded. "The zealot underground. I know they mean it pejoratively and want to liken us to Nazis, Al Qaeda, extremists, and all that. Tell you the truth, I kind of like the name. We're not extremists. We're not murderers. But in the biblical sense, yes, we are zealots. And the Lord knows we're underground. I think it describes me and my friends pretty well."

"I've met a lot of them."

"I know you have. And I want you to introduce me."

"That could be a very risky, very pricey social exercise."

"Oh, believe me, Paul, it's more than just to get me topside and meeting new people."

"What then?"

"How about I tell you after we drop in on Roscoe Wipers?"

# 13

**THE MEETING WITH WIPERS** had to be delayed yet again as Paul talked longer than he expected with Arthur Demetrius of Demetrius & Demetrius in New York.

Arthur, the surviving brother and one of few believers in the colossal precious-metals conglomerate, didn't even ask what Paul was calling about. He just jumped right in to his own agenda. "Paul, I miss you, man. Wish you were here, counseling me, teaching me, guiding me."

"I miss you too, Arthur, but I don't have much to offer in the way of—"

"So what do you make of the big curse? I've never seen any-thing like it. I don't know how it is there in Chicago, but in a—"

"I'm in D.C."

"Whatever. In a city like New York, you can imagine we have a mess. An unbelievable mess. I lost a huge percentage of my employees. A lot of companies have. People are still trying to sort it all out. I can't for the life of me figure how anyone can doubt God now; can you?"

"Hardly. I—"

"I mean, what are they, blind? Listen, Paul, tell me something: how much time do you think we have?"

"Time?"

"You know, on earth. How long will God put up with this? Doesn't He have to intervene, even more than He has, if you can imagine that?"

"Jesus told His disciples that not even He knew when the end would come, but that only the Father knew."

"But there have to be signs. He sure seems to be asserting Himself lately, wouldn't you say?"

"Can't argue with that. The signs are wars and rumors of wars and nations rising against nations, but even then, Jesus said that would be only the beginning of the end."

"Well, let me go out on a limb here, Paul, and see what you think of this. You got time?"

"For you? Sure."

"I can't imagine God letting this go on for even another year, but let's give Him the benefit of the doubt. You once told me that to God a day is as a thousand years and a thousand years as a day."

"Did I say that?"

"Pretty insightful, I'd say."

"It's hardly original. It's biblical."

"Well, of course it is. All right, I've been doing some figuring. For some reason God has made me ridiculously wealthy. I mean, I could set aside half my means and still have more than enough to do what I'd like to propose for the next twenty years. And regardless of God's economy of time, as you call it, I'd bet my life none of us is going to be around two more decades. Curious?"

"About what you'd like to propose? Are you kidding?"

"Okay, here it is. You've got underground factions in every one of the seven regions, right?"

"Right."

"I know these represent lots of different cells and groups, but they're pretty much centralized by state."

"Right again," Paul said.

"Okay, get this. I know some regions are bigger, needier than others, but for the sake of argument, I'm treating them all as equal entities. Say I put a sea of money in a protected Swiss account. If every state underground withdrew five million dollars a month for the next twenty years, it would not exhaust the fund."

Paul was speechless. How was that possible? He thought he had a hint of the expanse of Arthur Demetrius's holdings, but he had underestimated by perhaps a hundredfold.

"Are you there, Paul?"

"I'm here, Arthur. What has put this in your head?"

"Practicalities. The market could change overnight, so if I put away a portion of my net, it's protected. And I certainly don't need it, especially if our time is limited. How much does a man need? I spent my entire life trying to acquire things for myself, and I'm sick to death of it. Besides, even doing this, as I say, I still have way more than anyone could ever spend in a lifetime."

"Arthur, this would even the playing field between the international government and the zealot underground."

"Even it? With this last curse, I'd say things have swung our way already."

"Maybe," Paul said, "but Chancellor Dengler has a way of digging in his heels."

"Well," Arthur said, "then I say let him try to compete with these kinds of resources."

• • •

Jae saw the signal from Angela and followed her gaze to Brie, who sat in a storybook-listening circle quietly weeping. The girl looked embarrassed and appeared to be trying to stanch her tears.

Jae went to her and asked if she was tired and would like a nap. With that, Brie burst into sobs, embraced her mother, and followed her back to their quarters.

Jae sat with her at a table. "What is it, honey?"

"I don't know," Brie said. "I guess I just don't know what to think. Everything's different. We were at Grandma and Grandpa's, and Uncle Berl and Aunt Aryana were supposed to come over. Then something really bad happened and we left and came here. Aren't we going to go home to Chicago? What about my real school?"

"Don't you like this place?"

"'Course I do, and I love Miss Angela, but what is this place and why are we here?"

Jae prayed silently. She was in a spot. How much to say? She wanted to tell the truth, but a lot of this was way too much for an eight-year-old.

• • •

Paul was still reeling from Arthur Demetrius's plan when he and Jack finally sat across from Roscoe Wipers.

Here was a haggard man. His hair was greasy and mussed, his eyes bloodshot. His face was red and raw from where he had rubbed it with his free hand. The wrist on his cuffed arm looked tender.

"I told them to get you a shower this morning," Jack said. "That not happen?"

"It happened."

"The way you look, all this mess, has come since then?"

Roscoe nodded miserably. "You got me; you win; I'm done."

"What're you talking about?" Paul said.

"You pulled off a good plan, Stepola. You too, Pass. I never did figure out where I was. You scramble the GPSs down here, just in case. So NPO doesn't know where we are, thinks we're moving anyway, thinks I'm dead. My partner *is* dead. I know I'm next. Why don't you either put me out of my misery or give me that sidearm you deafened me with in the night and let me do the deed myself?"

"You really want to die?"

"'Course not, but you have no use for me now. Be serious. Trading places, believe me, I'd off either one of you."

"Thanks, Roscoe. We appreciate the thought."

"Just being honest."

"Yeah," Paul said. "That's your style: lying to us until we prove you wrong. Do you really have a death wish, or do you just want to be reassured we're not going to kill you?"

"Well, that would be nice."

"We're not going to kill you," Jack said.

Roscoe looked truly surprised. "You're not? Promise?"

"Scout's honor."

The tension seemed to drain from Roscoe's face and neck, and he appeared to relax. His voice fell weak and became whiny. "May I ask why?"

"You've been with us all this time and you still don't know what we're about?" Jack said. "I'm insulted."

Roscoe studied him. "No, I know," he said. "I don't doubt you guys are sincere and all that. Thing is, I was a liar, a double agent, out to get you, would have had you all obliterated if I had the chance. You're not going to try me, fry me, nothing?"

"We're going to keep you confined, if that's what you mean. But no. We don't kill people we don't have to. It's not what we're about."

Paul was surprised to feel the stirrings of actual compassion for Roscoe. That could come only from God, but still Paul couldn't fight the conviction that it was premature. "Fact is, Wipers, part of our whole faith thing is that we believe there's always hope for everybody. We kill you, that's the end of the hope."

"You're not going to see any jailhouse conversion," Roscoe said.

"That's up to you and God," Jack said.

"God!" Roscoe spat. "Don't put Him and me in the same sentence."

Paul glanced at Jack. "Maybe we *ought* to kill him."

Roscoe's head bobbed as he traded off staring into the eyes of each man.

"Don't worry," Paul said. "That's just our flesh talking. God would have us spare you. So be careful how you refer to Him around us."

"Sorry."

"That's for sure."

• • •

Jae felt like a failure. She couldn't for the life of her find a way to explain Uncle Berl's death to Brie. She said he and Aunt Aryana had a car accident. That made Brie cry all the more, of course, but it didn't answer any questions. Something in her little girl's demeanor, however, persuaded Jae that she was ready for at least some modicum of explanation about why the family seemed to be on the run and in hiding.

Jae started slowly, telling Brie that she had been born into a country and a culture where very few people believed in God. "In fact, the leaders made it against the law. If people chose to believe in God and Jesus or any religion, they had to do it secretly, in hiding."

"Like here? Is that why we're here? We're breaking the law?"

"Yes."

"But I thought Daddy worked for the government."

"He did. But when he decided that God was real and became a believer in Jesus, we had to hide."

"I'm scared, Mommy."

"I am too, honey, but I believe in God too and that He will take care of us."

• • •

Greenie ("Please don't ask") Macintosh was standing outside Jack Pass's office when Jack and Paul returned. It was clear to Paul that the man was a bundle of nervous energy. He looked like anything would be preferable to waiting, and he was bouncing from foot to foot, studying his little notepad, searching for something on his PDA, and generally trying to stay productive— or at least busy—until he found out what Pass wanted.

He was a small, thin, wiry man in his late thirties with very short black hair, a prominent nose, slightly bucked teeth, and buggy eyes. He looked eager. To do what, Paul couldn't guess. But this was clearly a man of action, maybe ideas.

Greenie wasn't much for fashion either. He wore what Paul would have described as a janitor's outfit and scuffed, sensible shoes with inch-thick rubber soles. His pants and shirt were green denim and were missing only the name patch above the pocket.

And, of course, despite the plea during their introduction and handshakes, Paul had to ask. "Greenie?"

"Okay, listen, I'll tell ya, but then that's the end of it, deal?"

"Deal."

"I'm Irish, sure, but my ma saddles me with a first name you'd kill your best friend over. Get this: Grenadier. Yep. Grenadier. Somebody who lobs grenades. We're a warring people in a warless world. I complain and moan so much about it when I start school that she tells me all along she meant to give me a normal nickname, like Greg or Gil, something like that.

"I like Gil, so I try that out on my friends, and what do they say? They tell me I've always looked like a fish and a little green around the gills. So nobody calls me Gil. It's Greenie."

"And you've accepted it. That's good."

"I didn't say that. Resigned to it is more like it. Anyways, I'm Jack's right-hand man, assistant chief elder, and heir apparent— though there's precious little to inherit in this hole. He wanted us to meet. I mean, I wanted to meet you too."

# 14

**JAE WATCHED CAREFULLY** as Brie rejoined the kids and sidled up to Connor. On one hand Jae worried how such news would hit him, but on the other she trusted Brie to share it better than she herself could.

Connor looked nothing short of amused and ran to Jae. He leaned close to her ear and said, "Is it true? Are we bad guys?" as if nothing would give him more pleasure.

"If it's wrong to believe in God and Jesus," Jae said, "yes, Mom and Dad are bad guys."

He nodded and ran off. There would have to be a lot more talking.

• • •

Greenie moved as if his head were on fire, sat as if he'd rather be standing, and talked as if he'd rather be acting. Paul decided to be forthright. "People respect you around here?"

"I think they do," Greenie said.

"They do," Jack said. "They know he speaks for me, and nobody ever sees him loafing. That carries weight."

"You want the responsibility, the head job?"

"No," Greenie said quickly, leaning forward. "No, sir, I don't, and I would suspect any man or woman who did. This isn't about head anything. This is about serving people and getting a job done, so let's just say I'm willing. Reluctant, but willing."

"Reluctant?"

"I'd rather not see Jack out of here, frankly, and I think his scheme is harebrained, if you want to know the truth."

"We tell each other the truth around here," Jack said.

"So I gather," Paul said. "Better remind him I haven't heard your idea."

Greenie wheeled to face Jack. "You haven't even told him yet? Aren't we getting ahead of ourselves then?"

Jack raised both hands, palms down. "First things first. Tell Dr. Stepola what our techies are finding."

Greenie scratched his head and wiped his face with his hand. "Okay, we're seeing some evidence that someone might be hacking into our server."

"How can that be?"

"We don't know. We don't see any evidence of their threatening our phones, but that would be next."

"What are they finding exactly?"

"I don't know, and you wouldn't either if I told you, would you?"

"I don't suppose I would."

"But we trust our people, and they don't like it."

The three fell silent.

Paul stood. "I can get to the bottom of this." He excused

JERRY JENKINS • 85

himself and stepped into the hall. His own phone was not part of the underground system and, as far he knew, was still secure. Paul called Felicia and indicated cryptically that she should call him from an outside line, which she did a few minutes later.

"I was about to call you anyway," she said.

"Oh no."

"Underground's catching on to what we're up to?" she said.

"'Fraid so. How close are you to totally contaminating us?"

"Within hours. Columbia Region is wholly compromised."

"Already? Really?"

"Uh-huh. Most of the others are pretty well exposed, and inside people here are telling us they'll be monitoring every transmission in and out in all seven states by the end of the workday today."

Paul sighed. "I know how hard this is for you, Felicia. I don't know what to say."

"You owe me, Paul."

"How well I know. What can I do for you?"

"Well, I'm pretty well committed to your side now, aren't I? I'd like to know I've made the right choice and, frankly, what's in it for me."

"For risk at your level, I'd do anything for you; you know that. What do you need?"

"You think I'm thinking about money?"

"We've got it," Paul said. "Just say the word."

"You don't know me. After all these years."

"Sorry?"

"Paul. Please. What I need is God."

# 15

**EXHAUSTED AS HE WAS,** Paul had trouble sleeping. He had left an important message for Felicia, whom he wished he could talk with one more time.

Then Jae had brought him up to date on where she was with the children, how much they knew, how little they understood. For now they considered this an adventure, and while Brie was more skittish than Connor, Jae believed they were on board and would be cooperative, if not cooped up underground too long.

It was Jack Pass's harebrained scheme—and Greenie Macintosh's caution against it—that rattled in Paul's mind and kept him awake. It had been like mining spaghetti to get Jack to reveal it, especially with Greenie interrupting every few sentences to try to keep the idea locked in the sedimentary rock of Jack's mind.

Finally Paul had struck the mother lode.

"Operation Noah," Jack said.

Paul blinked. He glanced at Greenie, who shook his head, raised his eyebrows, and shrugged. "See what I mean? Hey, I'm no scholar, but even I know God promised to never do that again."

"Do what?" Paul said.

"Noah!" Greenie said. "Hello! Flood the earth."

Paul made a face at Jack. "He's got you there, bro. God's not gonna violate His own word. The rainbow was a promise, remember? Never again."

"Okay, selective floods then," Jack tried. "God washes away the NPO, your father-in-law, Chancellor Dengler, our enemies in high places."

"That *would* be a worldwide flood again," Paul said. "The enemies are everywhere."

"Then why not? Maybe God spares Los Angeles, keeps it a drought. Believers can flee there. For anybody else who tries, it's feast or famine. Get washed away in a flood or die of dehydration in L.A."

Now Paul lay with his hands behind his head, grateful for Jae's deep breathing. Was she finally sound asleep, feeling secure, warm, and fuzzy at the thought of her family under one roof? The comfort of being among fellow believers was scant consolation for living in hiding in this claustrophobic den beneath the nation's former capital.

It had been not that long ago, Paul realized, that he would have pooh-poohed Jack's suggestion out of hand. The idea of trying to rally the various governing members of the zealot underground to pray down a judgment on the enemies of God would have hit him as ludicrous just over a year ago. Before the curse of the drought on Los Angeles. Before the angel of death slew the firstborn sons of unbelievers.

Now Paul feared that God might actually hear and honor the fervent prayers of His oppressed resistance. Paul had to admit he was weary of judgment, of mayhem, of chaos. When God acted, it reminded him of the old joke about why lightning is reputed never to strike the same place twice: because it doesn't have to. When God acted, there was no doubt— even in the minds of the enemy—that He was real. Once He decided to intervene on behalf of His people, there was no fighting back. Retaliation maybe, but no head-to-head competition.

• • •

Felicia Thompson hated working late, but that was nothing compared to risking her life to join the resistance. For years she had thought working for Paul Stepola in a high-security-clearance job in the Chicago bureau of the NPO was the very definition of stress. When she first suspected Paul had flipped to the other side, then became convinced of it, she knew who was really living with stress.

Well, now she had joined him. There could be no playing at this, no touching a toe over the line. If she hadn't become thoroughly convinced, she would have had to turn Paul in and let the chips fall. How anyone could still be on the other side of this battle, however, Felicia could not make compute.

Yet many still lived in denial. The remaining brass, mostly men who had not been firstborns, seemed not only entrenched against the enemy and against God, but also livid. They strode purposefully around headquarters with red, pinched faces. In some ways Felicia was grateful there was no longer the banter that accompanied this type of work. Too many had lost too much—herself included. Losing a son—a bright, beautiful, overachieving, in-love twenty-seven-year-old—had doubled her over with grief. And her husband. Well, Felicia feared for him.

Years of teaching and coaching at a middle school, one of the more upbeat people she had ever met, and now Cletus seemed suicidal.

She had left several messages for Paul before he had finally called her back, just before she was to leave for home in north suburban Deerfield. At that time of night she could make it from the Loop in less than an hour, despite debris decorating the shoulders of the Edens and 294 North from what the media was now calling The Incident.

"Either tell me what I need to do to join your side," Felicia told Paul in one message, "or point me in the right direction." She waited none too patiently for his callback, then discovered he had left her a message, most likely while she was on the phone with Cletus, promising she would be home in a few hours.

Paul had informed her of a secret file, something he had kept even from her, which surprised Felicia. She thought she had known all his secrets, codes, passwords, hiding places. He told her where it was in his credenza and what code would open it. "It appears to be random notes about the crazy believers," his message said, "but it is a prescription for receiving Christ."

Felicia's fingers trembled as she found the file and stuffed it into her oversize purse. She pulled on her full-length mink—not as expensive as it looked but still a reminder of how good the NPO had been to her, a longtime employee. How she had once loved that coat, and how merely functional it seemed now.

On her way out Felicia was joined in the elevator by Hector Hernandez, a late-twenties computer whiz who had briefed her and others on her floor about the progress his team had made in hacking into the system of the underground resistance. "The zealot underground is in trouble technologically," he had announced, giving her pause.

She wasn't sure why the phrase had bothered her so. Maybe it seemed too obvious, too overt for what was at stake. Everyone knew what the techies were up to and what was at risk for both sides. Merely presenting an update, a progress report, would have been sufficient. No one had to be told the consequences.

Felicia nodded at the young man. "Hector," she said.

"Ma'am."

"You must be near the age of my son," she said.

"Thirty next month, Mrs. Thompson."

"Danny was twenty-seven."

"I'm so sorry, ma'am. Truly, I am."

"With all your *ma'am*s and *Mrs.*s, you're talking to me like I'm your mama."

"I apologize. But I was raised to respect my . . . you know . . . to not call you Felic—you by your first name. And I'm sorry, but I couldn't even if you asked me to."

"Would you do me a favor, Hector? Would you walk me to my car?"

As their shoes echoed in the concrete chamber, Felicia could see her breath. The young man kept holding his, then letting it out in great clouds. She sensed Hector steeling himself to say something. Finally he slowed and whispered, "Would you greet Agent Stepola for me?"

She gave the young man a long look. "Surely you know his status. . . ."

"Of course. I also know the high regard with which you held each other, and I just thought—"

"I will," she said. "If I hear from him."

Hector drove out of the garage behind her until their paths split and they waved. As soon as he was out of sight, Felicia pulled in front of a dark store and tore into the file. There it was. Paul had written:

*These people believe their eternal destiny is sealed when they
'receive Christ.' They base this on verses from the New Testament that seem to claim that every person is born in sin and is
thus separated from a Holy God. Romans 3:23 says that all
have sinned and fallen short of the glory of God. Romans 6:23
says that the wages of sin is death but that eternal life is God's
gift through His Son, Jesus Christ.*

*Later, in the Gospel written by John (1:12), it says that to
as many as 'received' Him, to them He gives the right to become
the children of God.*

*People 'receive' Christ by what they call the A-B-C Method.
Accepting this truth. Believing in God and Jesus and what He
did on their behalf—dying on the cross for the their sin. And
Confessing this, or telling someone else. The transaction, as
some like to call it, happens when they acknowledge this in
prayer—that they are sinners, need God's forgiveness, and
receive it and Him.*

Prayer. Felicia had older—much older—relatives who still
prayed. Two aunts and an uncle were judicious and careful in
public but made no secret that they had never bought into the
government edict against God and faith. Felicia herself had been
ten when the ban on religion had been instituted, and while she
couldn't remember having practiced any religion before that,
she had to admit to herself that she had believed there was a
God. Until it had been all but shamed out of her in elementary
school.

But prayer? Perhaps she had never prayed, unless railing
against God for taking her son could be considered such. She
had cursed Him. Raised her fist at Him. And, she knew, by doing
so, she had acknowledged something she hadn't considered
since childhood: that He was there and had acted.

Felicia checked her rearview mirror. The last thing she wanted was to attract attention, particularly that of a cop. How would she explain sitting there in the dark, reading a top-level-security-clearance federal file by the tiny car ceiling light, and weeping?

All she saw were emergency vehicles and wreckers here and there, moving and loading abandoned cars, as they had been doing for days. The disabled vehicles were moved out of the roadways first. The abandoned cars were moved to central lots as there was time. And the wee hours of a weeknight was the best time.

Felicia found herself overcome—by what, she didn't know. She felt an urgency to get home to Cletus, and yet something about that foreboding house of death repelled her. It wasn't that anyone had died in the modest two-story where she had raised a family a block and a half from the tracks. They had bought it years before in the only section of Deerfield they could afford, and they wouldn't be able to afford their own house today.

But memories were bound up in that two-story brick with the postage-stamp backyard. It was there her children had gone from infancy to gap-toothed smiles, and from awkward puberty to first dates and dances. It was where she had met Danny's girlfriend, the one who had become his fiancée, the one who had placed a hysterical call just a few hours ago to tell Felicia that Danny had died in her arms.

Felicia raised her collar, wishing the car would warm quicker, and stared at Paul Stepola's notes through watery eyes. Did it matter, she wondered, how little she understood? This was all so new, so foreign. Accept? That there was a God? Who could not now? He had bludgeoned His way into everyone's consciousness, into everyone's life, into everyone's family. The Los Angeles business from the year before had sobered her, stopped her, made her wonder. This latest attack—what else could she call it?—had pushed her over the line.

Did she believe? That was no longer a question. Did she feel like a sinner? Could she acknowledge that to a God she felt was her enemy? And could this Enemy save her soul? She felt puny; she knew that. Defenseless. Insignificant. What kind of basis was that for this "transaction," as Paul called it?

What Felicia wanted, she decided, was a God who loved her, cared about her, could comfort her. But was He not the one who had caused this pain? Somehow she had to reconcile that. She tried praying, tried apologizing for having cursed Him. Yet that very memory washed her anew in resentment and anger. "Why? Why?" she railed. "Why did You have to do that to me, to Cletus, to Danny, to my friends, to everyone?"

Felicia sat silent as the interior of the slow-warming car fogged over. How bizarre to have gone from a thoroughgoing, docile atheist to praying and expecting an answer! She really wanted to know, to hear a response. And she fully expected one. Anyone powerful enough to slay His enemies in one terrible act could answer the sincere challenge of a grieving mother; could He not?

Felicia put the folder back in her handbag and folded her arms, feeling her body slowly warm. She set her jaw and settled in, waiting. She could not be convinced that hers was other than a fair question, a legitimate challenge. The niggling need to get home to her husband abated as she nestled there, resolute.

She had made her decision. There would be no more pretending God didn't exist. And she had already put her career and her very life on the line to serve the resistance through Paul. But to personally make the transaction? That would require some answer. It was one thing to feel disenfranchised. In many ways that cliché had been her lot for as long as she could remember. But it was another to be made to feel responsible for the terrible act of God that took one's own son.

# 16

**CHANCELLOR BALDWIN DENGLER** emerged from his limo in the underground parking facility beneath the International Government of Peace headquarters in Bern, Switzerland. As his two bodyguards flanked him and headed toward the elevators, he paused.

The men stopped and turned. "Forget something, sir?" one said. "Can I get it for you?"

"I'll be a moment," he said.

Tall, graying, and elegant, Dengler handed his leather port-folio to one of the men and reached deep into the pockets of his cashmere coat and pulled on calfskin leather gloves. He grabbed the ends of his scarf and tucked them into his coat, buttoning it to the neck. He'd heard on the radio that the day-break temperature was zero degrees Fahrenheit. "Fitting," he said.

"Sir?" one of the bodyguards said, and Dengler noticed he caught the eye of the other.

"The temperature," Dengler said. "Fitting."

The chancellor had turned and moved toward an exit.

"Where are we going, sir, if I may ask?"

"I want to walk on the river," the older man said. "You stay here and stay warm."

"You know we can't do that, sir."

"Suit yourselves."

In his abject grief over the loss of his son, the father of three of his grandchildren, it was not lost on Dengler that everything about him had changed. Not just his voice, which had gone from a crisp, forceful baritone to a hoarse whisper, but also his gait. He had long been amused by press reports that his stride was half again longer than a normal man his height's. He was sure it wasn't true, but something about his walk—at least once he had been elected chancellor—produced wonder, if not awe, in observers. Perhaps it was a stride of confidence that caused his expensive brogans to announce each purposeful step.

But now he shuffled along, bent. What had reduced him to an old man but mourning? He wore the same clothes, bore the same appendages. And yet he felt like a shell of a man. He would not shirk his duties, despite sleepless nights, would not turn over the reins—even temporarily—to the vice chancellor, who was dealing with her own son's death. And he would somehow cover his personal turmoil when the cameras rolled. But now, just now, he could not face the palatial office, the marble floors, the teak and mahogany he had once accepted as the trappings of his station.

Now he simply wanted to walk alone on the Aare. Its sterile, icy surface matched the temperature of his soul, and—who knew?—maybe he would simply veer into the frigid water itself and let it take him to wherever his beloved son was.

"You mean the bridge, I assume," his bodyguard said, following Dengler out the door and signaling the other to wait.

Dengler didn't want to speak. He shook his head. "I mean the river," he said.

"It's not frozen all the way over," the man said. "And there's a foot of snow on either side."

Dengler stopped and faced the man, as weary and resigned as he had ever felt. It was as if he had to muster every last ounce of strength to meet this challenge. He sucked in an icy breath. "Please," he said. "Please. Wait here for me. I will return presently."

"Sir, I—"

Dengler held up a hand to silence him. "Not to worry." He wasn't so sure about that, especially if the man was truly worried about his safety . . . or his sanity.

The chancellor turned and trudged through the snow, his shoes darkening from the moisture. As he neared the fast-flowing river, encrusted with ice to just six or eight feet from the shore, the snow grew deeper and he felt the freeze in his socks and on his shins.

Incongruously, the sun peeking over the horizon made the scene sparkly to the point of being festive. Dengler felt hollow—had not eaten yet felt no hunger. He could tell by the looks of those in his orbit—his family, his driver, his bodyguards and aides—that they worried he might be self-destructive.

True, life seemed worthless, hopeless, pointless. And yet a lifetime of civil service had made him who he was. He was responsible for billions of people, and—much as he wanted to retreat—he would not shirk. Somehow he would power through this black hole, despite the fact that he had let down his family. They had mustered in his mansion, grieving the eldest brother, grieving the firstborn male grandchildren, grieving a dozen other firstborns in the extended family. And they had looked to him for strength, for character, for perspective.

Not only had he had nothing to say, but neither could he force himself to comfort anyone, no one, not even his wife of more than forty years. His very countenance, he knew, had exacerbated the situation. They had not been seeking much from him, had clearly not expected that anything he said or did could assuage such staggering bereavement. But it was clear that neither had they expected to see the leader of the world pushed back on his heels, reeling, stunned, helpless. Silent.

Strangely, none had tried to comfort him either. Dengler had felt needy, even weepy—though he steeled himself against tears—yet something about him fended off help.

The chancellor had not even tried to sleep, pacing all night. His wife had risen occasionally and come to him, but he would not look at her. And somehow, over the years, she had apparently learned that if he was not looking, he was not engaged, and there was no sense trying to communicate with him.

A shave and a shower and his world leader uniform—an exquisitely tailored gray suit with a subtle pattern—had made him look the part. But as he had gazed into the full-length mirror in his closet, he could see everything but his own face. He stared into empty eyes and could not conjure an expression. It was as if he had become invisible.

And now, as he neared the edge of the Aare, Baldwin Dengler hunched his shoulders, thrust his hands deep into his pockets, and stepped gingerly onto the ice. He did not know himself what this obsession meant. He simply had to walk the river. Not far. He felt the worried gaze of his bodyguard and heard the parking-facility door as the other peeked out to be sure all was okay.

Paul Stepola. That was who Dengler needed to speak with.

The man had warned him—under the guise of expert consultation—that the underground believers had beseeched their God for this calamity. And the word from the United Seven States of America was that Stepola, himself an only child and thus a first-born male, had been spared. He was now an international fugitive, exposed as a zealot.

Chancellor Dengler's initial response had been anger—a bitter, deep rage that tempted him to throw the entire force of the international government into league with the USSA to bring down this turncoat.

And yet Stepola had been right.

Could Dengler fault Stepola for not convincing him he truly believed God would act? The chancellor could not have envisioned a scenario that would have made him believe. Until now. That angel-of-death scenario certainly worked. What could Stepola have done to prove it, to preclude it? Dengler did not want to be a hero. He wanted Stepola to have been one, to have somehow pleaded his case so convincingly that Dengler would have had to have paused, reconsidered, backed away from his threats.

Dengler shook his head. God had needed to act in this dramatic fashion to get his attention. It had been his own fault. He stood as the emblem of international thought. No one other than the underground resistance had believed this would actually happen.

The cold finally reached the chancellor, and he stopped. He turned and moved off the ice, through the snow, back toward the bodyguards, who had begun moving toward him. He raised a hand to stop them. There was no need for them to venture farther.

Dengler found his sleek cell phone in the breast pocket of his suit coat and flipped it open. The platinum, having rested near his chest, proved warm against his frozen ear. He reached his chief of staff. "I'll be at my desk in five minutes. I want NPO agent Paul Stepola on the phone as soon as possible."

"It's anywhere from six to nine hours earlier in the USSA, sir, depending on where he is."

Dengler stopped, feeling his management chops returning. "I'm sorry," he said, "were you under the impression I had asked what time it was in America?"

"Right away, sir."

# 17

**STUART "STRAIGHT" RATHE** had seen the doctor around, of course, but he couldn't have told you the man's name, let alone his area of specialty. Come to think of it, he *had* seen the man in surgical greens and booties, so he was an operating-room man.

The surgeon had sought out Straight; that was clear. Straight had been on his rounds, visiting new patients, doing his volunteer welcoming thing, trying to keep people calm, amusing them to get their minds off their troubles. That had become more difficult overnight because of the reason for the new wave of patients. Families who might have been spared a loss because they bore no firstborn males were just as likely to suffer because of what had happened in the aftermath of all those sudden deaths.

Straight found himself hurrying from floor to floor, wing to wing, department to department, visiting the injured of all ages. The surgeon had caught him in a corridor between buildings.

"Rathe, is it?" he had asked, his unusually blue eyes—probably the result of designer contact lenses—darting about to be sure they were alone.

"Yes, sir, Doctor. Call me Straight. May I help you?"

"You might," the doctor said. He was broad and thick with black, curly hair. He carried a leather portfolio and wore a suit. "Gregory Graybill," he whispered, slipping a business card into Straight's pocket. The taller, older black man nearly put it out of his mind as the surgeon hurried off.

Straight remembered it when he was disrobing at the end of the day, after midnight, in his drafty apartment. The card was standard issue, identifying the doctor as a surgeon with Chicago's PSL (formerly Presbyterian St. Luke's), but the personal scrawl on the back made it unique.

In tiny, neat lettering, giving the lie to the adage that all physicians have poor handwriting, Dr. Graybill had penned:

> *If you would be so kind, please call me at 2 a.m. within the next three days. This number is secure.*

•  •  •

Felicia Thompson sat waiting. Did she dare believe the all-powerful God of the universe actually owed her an answer? owed her anything? Maybe *owed* wasn't the right word, but she was going to sit here until He responded or delayed long enough to convince her He never would.

Fogged into her own world, she suddenly felt her shoulders relax and realized she had hunched them against the cold until she was painfully cramped. The tension seemed to ease out of her body, and she sat warming.

*I'm here.*

No one had spoken. She had not been tempted to look in the backseat or check the radio or lower a window. *I'm here* had been communicated directly to her heart, to her inner being, and she would not have been more certain it was God if He had appeared in the passenger seat.

"You're here?" she whispered.

Apparently He didn't feel the need to repeat Himself.

*I love you.*

Okay, it might be God, but if it was, they were going to talk.

"You love me? And You show me this how? By taking my son? By turning my boss and friend into a fugitive and leaving me on my own? By wounding my husband until he is not the same man he once was?"

*I lost a Son too.*

That stopped her. She had heard this story. Was it possible He knew how she felt? But hadn't He choreographed that whole scenario? Couldn't He have prevented it? Did His loss really count?

It was as if God read her mind, and, she decided, that only made sense. *Had I prevented His death, there would have been no payment for sin.*

"My sin?" Felicia said, wondering if she really wanted God to give her an inventory. She hadn't ever felt like a sinner. She tried to be a good person, to treat people nicely. But somehow, in the presence of God, or at least in the presence of His voice in her heart, she felt microscopic, unworthy, filthy.

Why should she feel filthy? She didn't understand it, but she felt so far removed from God, even though He was clearly communicating with her, that she wished she could run and hide and cover herself.

*My Son died so that you might have life.*

With that, it all seemed to come together for her in a flash. If she had been perfect, if she had never sinned, the very fact that she had ignored God was sin enough. She had rejected Him and

His Son and His plan. The whole world had. It was a wonder He hadn't acted in such dramatic fashion before.

Felicia lowered her head. "I'm sorry," she whispered. "I'm so, so sorry."

It was as if the presence, the voice, left her. Was it because she was hopeless, or was there merely nothing more to be said?

"I *am* a sinner," she said, remembering Paul's outline. "I accept You. I believe in You! I'll confess it to somebody. I'll tell Cletus."

And while she sensed no more words in her spirit, the feeling of the presence of God returned, and it was she who felt accepted.

Felicia arrived home a few minutes after 1 a.m. and pulled into the attached garage. She noted a dim light burning in the living room and hoped it didn't mean her husband was still up. With any luck, Cletus would be in bed, sleeping away his grief and depression. She used the remote to close the garage door before getting out of the car, trying to keep the frigid temperatures at bay.

That didn't help much, as the garage seemed as cold as the street, but at least she was out of the wind. She entered through the kitchen and found her way to the living room, where Cletus sat wringing his hands in his recliner. The only light came from the lamp over the piano. If he had been even trying to watch TV, she'd have been encouraged. But no.

The room reeked of beer. "Are you awake, sweetheart?" she said, knowing he was but hoping to gauge his mood and sobriety from his response.

He nodded, and as she turned on a light next to his chair, making him squint, she noticed the mess on the opposite wall. "Have you been drinking, dearie?"

He shook his head. "Trying to kill God," he said, and she shivered.

Felicia sat on the arm of the couch not far from him. The

house was warm, but not warm enough for her to shed her coat just yet. "You don't believe in God," she said. "You told me so yourself."

"Do now," he said.

A six-pack of beer sat next to him on the floor, four bottles gone, two remaining. He had heaved the four against the far wall, three of them breaking and splashing. The fourth remained intact but had put a serious hole in the drywall.

"Come to bed, darling," she said. "Let's talk."

"Done talking," Cletus said.

"Don't do this to me," she said. "We've both suffered. We've both lost. Don't shut me out. We have to share this to survive it."

With that he reached for one of the two remaining bottles and flung it wildly. It slipped from his hand as he followed through and hit the ceiling, dropping to the carpet and spinning to the wall. He sighed and sobbed. "Can't even break a bottle of beer," he said.

"Give me that other one," Felicia said. "Let me have a crack at it."

He looked at her, cocking his head, and she believed she had finally connected with him. Was he smiling? impressed? He handed her the bottle, as if eager to see what she would do.

Felicia had played a little ball in her day. She unsnapped her coat and spread her arms, giving herself room. She held the bottle over her head like a pitcher would, then stepped while pulling it low behind her. With everything that was in her she put her whole body behind the heave. That bottle soared high to the wall, smashing to pieces and showering fizzy beer all over the room.

But her heel had caught when her foot should have been sliding on the carpet, and her momentum carried her down in a heap. That made her laugh in spite of herself, in spite of her pain, in spite of her anger and remorse and grief.

And apparently Cletus couldn't help but laugh too. "That was a bit high!" he said, chortling. "But I got to call it a strike." He swore loud and long, and his laughing turned to wailing.

Felicia pulled her tall frame from the floor and found her way to his lap, shedding her coat as she did. She collapsed into his arms, and the recliner leaned so far back she feared they would topple. But it held, and they held each other, and they sobbed the sobs of the forlorn, the devastated, the nearly destroyed.

They held each other tight and took turns caressing each other and sharing their grief. When Felicia sensed Cletus was spent and had calmed some, she said, "I need to tell you what I did tonight, hon."

• • •

It was all Straight could do to stay awake, and he knew he should not have stretched out on the bed. He dozed for seconds at a time, starting and jerking to read the clock, certain he had slept past the appointed hour. But he had not.

Finally, at 2 a.m., he dialed the number on Dr. Graybill's card.

The surgeon picked up immediately. "Mr. Rathe?"

"Straight, yes."

"I can't thank you enough for calling. I must see you privately."

"How can I help you?"

"Not by phone, sir. Can you meet me tomorrow?"

"When?"

"I see patients in my office until noon; then I'm not due to the hospital until two. I could meet you at 12:30."

"That works for me. Where?"

• • •

"You *received* Christ?" Cletus said, with so much emphasis on the verb that Felicia knew she had an inordinate amount of explaining to do.

He sat up and Felicia stood, gathering her coat. "I'll clean up the mess in the morning," she said.

"My mess, my job," he said. "Now tell me."

She told him everything, dug out the file and showed him that too. Cletus had the same questions she had had: How did what God had done make Felicia feel like a sinner? Wasn't God the sinner?

"We were warned," she said. "We were all warned. You can't legislate God out of life and then wonder where He is when everything goes wrong. There was a solution to this, a way out of it. But in our pride and ignorance, we didn't listen, didn't believe it. Los Angeles should have been a clue, but no, we knew better."

Cletus sat shaking his head. "I'll grant you that God proved Himself, but I still don't know how you got from that to where you surrendered to His side. You did this why? Because He left you no choice? He bullied you into this?"

"I still have a choice, Clete. I can shake my fist in His face, throw bottles against the wall, try to kill Him. But if it's true, if all of this is real, if He does have power over life and death and to give and take, the rest of it has to be real too."

"The rest of it?"

"That He's been trying to get our attention for decades. He offers forgiveness and life, but we—all of us—pushed Him away, made Him illegal, denied He even existed. It's a wonder He didn't wipe all of us out."

"You're on His side now. You're a traitor to your country, to the NPO. You're a turncoat, a double agent, a fugitive as soon as you're found out."

"I am," she said. "Are you with me, Cletus?"

# 18

**"GOD *SPOKE* TO YOU?"** Cletus said. "Like audibly? You heard Him?"

Felicia was back on the arm of the couch, leaning toward her husband. He had to think she was talking insanities, so she was trying everything in her power to be earnest, credible. If ever there was a time when crazy talk had to be taken seriously, this was it.

"I didn't *hear* Him hear Him. I heard Him through my heart, my soul, my mind."

"You heard yourself, what you wanted to hear."

"Hardly. Listen, Clete. I waited and waited, and every time I was about to explode, to curse Him anew, I sensed Him—or something, or someone—urging me to wait. I was to sit, to listen. I had asked a question, and not only did I deserve and expect an answer, it seemed I was about to get one."

"So He talked to you, to your inner being." Cletus was clearly not buying this. "What did He say?"

Felicia's voice caught. That surprised her, but it shouldn't have. The message had made her cry when first it came. She didn't know why she thought she could just relate it to her husband without it overwhelming her again. "He reminded me," she said, forcing a whisper though her constricted throat, "that I was not the first or only parent to lose a son. He had lost one too."

Cletus stared, blinking. "Yeah, but . . ."

Felicia waited. *Yeah, but what?* What could Cletus say? That it wasn't fair because God was God and had the power to bring His own Son back to life? That it wasn't fair because Danny would not be returning to them?

"Did that make you feel better?" Cletus said.

She shook her head. "Nothing makes me feel better, sweetheart. Sometimes I feel I'll never get over this, that I won't survive it."

"I'm not sure I want to."

"Of course you do, Clete. I need you to. You're my rock. I can't do this without you."

He buried his face in his hands. "Some rock," he said. "Crazy old man sitting in the dark flinging beer bottles at the wall."

"We do what we gotta do," she said.

"What does that mean?" he said. "I throw bottles because it gives me something to do?"

Felicia put a hand on his knee. "Let's stick together, buddy. It's been you and me all these years, and we've gotten through everything else."

"Yeah, but—" here it came again— "this is in a whole different league, baby. You can see that. I've about gone mad here, and you're hearing God talk to your soul."

"But I did! He told me He loved me! He loves everybody!"

"Strange way of showing it."

"That's just it. He's been trying to show His love for centuries, and His creation has rejected, rejected, rejected. We worship everything but Him. We worship stuff. Worse, we worship ourselves. We worship our minds; we satisfy our wants and needs. We decide He doesn't even exist. He hears the prayers of His true believers and rains judgment on Los Angeles, and we quickly explain that away and go back about our business."

"He told you all that?"

"I got it; that's all I know. God is more than love and goodness and patience. He's also righteous and just. And His patience has limits."

"Obviously," Cletus said. "Did He say anything about killing a fly with a nuclear bomb?"

"I'm not following."

"He overreacted, wouldn't you say? Wasn't there some other step in there, between drought in L.A. and slaughtering a billion men and boys and babies? Couldn't He have tried again to get our attention before unloading His whole arsenal?"

Felicia was suddenly awash in fatigue. She had thoughts; she even had arguments. She just couldn't utter them. She shook her head. "I don't know. And I don't guess I'll know till I see Him face-to-face."

"I'd like to see Him face-to-face right now," Cletus said.

"Careful, love. We have a way of getting what we ask for . . . what's coming to us."

"This was what we had coming?" he said, rising.

Felicia hadn't noticed how he looked, how he moved like the old man he claimed to be. *Poor Cletus. He's at the end of himself.*

"Listen," she said. "All I know is we paid a high, high price for God finally getting our attention. And now that He has it, I want Him to know He's got it. I accept that He's God, that He's in charge, that He did what He had to do. I don't like it. And at times I don't like Him. But I believe in Him. How can I not? Did I receive Him and confess it to you because I don't want anything else bad to happen to me? to us? Maybe. That was part of it, sure. But I'm in, Clete. Whatever more it costs, whatever else it means, I'm in. I'm on His side. I'll fight for His cause. I'll fight His enemies."

"Your employer. Your government."

"You bet," she said. "We are the ones who have tried to shut Him out, to ignore Him, to pretend He doesn't exist. You know anybody still saying that? They may be fighting Him, may be furious with Him, but only a fool would still claim He's not there."

# 19

**RANOLD B. DECENTI HAD A ROUTINE,** and he stuck to it. One privilege of his station was access to emergency services the common man did not enjoy. He had been able to get the bodies of both his son, Berlitz, and his wife, Margaret, transported to a government morgue. Funerals and burials were beyond even his control, however, with the sheer numbers service personnel had to accommodate.

But Ranold drew some modicum of satisfaction from meeting his obligations. He had done all he could for the time being, and if his dead loved ones had to lie in repose in refrigerated chambers— even for months—so be it. He was, frankly, glad to not have to worry about the bodies and felt no sense of urgency to do more.

Aryana, Berl's widow, was already proving a nuisance. He had been kind to her at first, matching her grave tones word for word, commiserating that between them they had lost a husband, a son, a mother-in-law, and a wife, and wasn't it just the worst thing that anyone could ever imagine.

Well, of course it was. Yet Ranold had been able to swallow his true assessment of both his wife and his firstborn son. Margaret had been a facile, if boring, mate lo these many years. And while he had chastised his son-in-law, the rogue Paul Stepola, for infidelities, Ranold had enjoyed countless dalliances himself, with Margaret, to his knowledge, none the wiser.

Would he miss her? He couldn't imagine. He could pay for the services she rendered, in the home and in the bedroom. And with his power and income and prestige, for some of that he would not have to fork over a cent. He found himself thinking about Margaret occasionally; they'd made their memories. There had been trips and high-level ceremonies, introductions to and banquets with heads of state. And the raising of the kids when they were young enough to be malleable, pliable, less than disappointments.

But Berl had matured—strange word for it—into a life-sized regret. The women, the money, the marriages. The jobs. The hopes and dreams or lack thereof. *Oh, face it,* Ranold told himself. *Berlitz was a loser.* And the emotion Ranold had felt when Berl died? Natural. He was shocked, surprised, repulsed. But in a strange way, losing the boy—the middle-aged boy—was no great loss. In fact, alive Berl had been a complicator, as his widow was now.

Ranold's patience with Aryana had run out earlier Wednesday evening when she called for the umpteenth time. "It's left to you and me," she said, "to plan the service."

"There'll be plenty of time for that," Ranold told her. "You have no idea the backlog of bodies in that facility—"

"Well, but . . . yes, but, Dad, I'd rather we not refer to Berl as one of the backlog of—"

"And I would prefer that you not call me Dad, Aryana."

"Sorry. But just now I feel so close to—"

"We've been over this ground before. You're hardly Berl's first wife, and so frankly it's been hard for me to even view you as family. I mean, I hope I've been nothing short of cordial, but—"

"No, you have," she said, but her tone indicated the opposite.

Ranold considered himself a trained observer of human nature. He knew when people were lying, when they were deceiving even themselves. "I'd prefer you call me Mr. Decenti or—"

"That seems so formal. I mean, *my* last name is Decenti now, you know. It would be like my calling Berl Mr. Dec—"

"—or Ranold, I suppose, but you know what, Aryana?"

"Sir?"

"I say, do you know what?"

"No, what?"

"I'd prefer you not call me at all."

"Sir?"

"Did you not hear me or not understand?"

"I heard you, sir. I hope I did not understand."

"I'm not trying to be unkind, Aryana. But we have nothing more to talk about. My son—your husband—is dead. There is the matter of the funeral, which I will of course attend and will look forward to seeing you there."

"Look forward?"

"You know what I mean. Please don't parse something negative from every word. We will do the right thing by the man, and—"

"The *man*?!"

"He was a man, Aryana. Maybe not a man's man; let's not mince words. But now he is gone, and I will do the right thing, as I know you will."

He had silenced her. He wasn't sure how and didn't care. It was just good to hear nothing from the other end of the phone, especially when he considered the alternative: the plaintive, whiny, throaty pleading. But the silence was short-lived.

"You're family, Mr. Decenti. I need—"

"Oh no. No you don't. Don't start with this. We were barely family when you married in. And Berl's death ended all that. You know, of course, that technically you're not my daughter-in-law anymore."

"But I want to be! It doesn't have to be legal, official, whatever. You're my last tie to him. I loved him. I—"

"You think being married to him for a season entitles you to something? Let me tell you, young lady, he had a negative estate, as you well know. And not a penny of mine will find its way to your grubby little—"

"Ranold! This is your grief talking! Your anger! I want nothing from you. I would never presume—"

"Aryana! Aryana! Would you then do me a favor and return to my earlier statement. I am not trying to be rude or insensitive. My wish is that you not call me. How about I call *you* when I hear from the morgue that a time and place has been cleared for the funeral. There we can be cordial, share a memory or two, and get on with our lives."

The click of the receiver surprised Ranold, but it was certainly not unwelcome. Best of all, he assumed it meant the end of these incessant calls.

That evening Ranold changed into his silk pajamas and floor-length robe, watched an hour of news—all of it bad, of course—and retired to bed with his favorite newsweekly. He read until he fell asleep.

This morning he shaved and showered and dressed in a suit tailored for his massive frame. The tie cost more than he once paid for shirts, but by the end of the day he knew he would be eager to shed the whole outfit.

The pilfering of his NPO car by his son-in-law and its becoming evidence proved a mixed blessing. Ranold had to use his own car for personal errands after hours, but he had been assigned a car and driver to get back and forth to work, despite that personnel were stretched far past their capacities since The Incident.

Ranold saw the car approach, knowing the driver would not make the same mistake twice: The day before he had pulled to the curb and waited. And so Ranold had waited him out. Then came the courteous tap on the horn, which Ranold also ignored. Finally the driver called Ranold's home number from his cell, and Ranold refused to answer. The message said, "Thought I was to pick you up at your house, but I don't guess you're here."

As the car had pulled away, Ranold phoned his office and told his secretary to "get on the horn to that motor-pool fool and tell him to get his can back here, come to the door like a gentleman, carry my briefcase, open the car door for me, and do his job if he wants to keep it."

Today the man pulled into the driveway early and jogged to the door. He rang the bell and reached for Ranold's briefcase as soon as the man opened the door. The driver was obsequious and deferential, but Ranold neither responded to any comment nor made eye contact.

On his way to the office his secretary called and informed him that International Chancellor Baldwin Dengler's people had phoned to arrange for a private call within an hour of Ranold's arrival at his office. Ranold knew The Incident had decimated the intelligence workforce around the world, and especially within the NPO. But the world chancellor wanting to talk with him personally? That could mean only one thing: promotion. Perhaps he was to ascend to his rightful place as head of NPO USSA or—who knew?—even NPO International.

# 20

**DESPITE THAT CLETUS WAS RESTLESS** and probably had not slept, Felicia found herself rested Thursday morning. She had awakened every hour or so, checking to be sure he was still beside her. Usually he was. Sighing. Tossing and turning.

Once she had found him gazing out the window. "Are you all right?" she said.

"Of course not, Felicia. Are you?"

"Yes and no. My heart aches. I'm scared. And yet I have a deep peace. I can't explain it."

He pointed to his head and twirled his finger.

"I'm crazy?" she said.

"Of course. We both are, or we would be dead."

Felicia had fallen back to sleep, somehow confident Cletus would make it to the morning sun. Her own grief was always at the edge of her consciousness, and yet she sensed she had made a decision that had altered the rest of her life. Her choice was made; the die was cast. She had committed herself to the resistance at the risk of her safety, not to mention Cletus's. And yet she knew there had been no other choice. No other decision would have allowed her to sleep and truly rest with everything going on in her mind.

It made no sense, she told herself. All the way into the office Thursday morning she repeated that, sometimes aloud. She had talked Cletus into calling in sick, trying to get some rest, and planning to get back to his teaching and coaching within a week. Felicia had sensed in him a flicker of life. All she wanted was that he somehow distract himself from their loss. That he might one day share her faith was too much to dream for now. Her top priority was keeping him alive.

The office was abuzz with the search for Paul Stepola. Chancellor Dengler himself wanted to talk with Paul, and the brass had directed his people to Ranold B. Decenti in the Columbia branch. The place was also hopping with news of Bob Koontz's replacement: Harriet Johns of the L.A. bureau. She had been reassigned to San Francisco after the drought, and now a nationwide game of musical chairs put her in Chicago.

The first person she wanted to speak with? Felicia Thompson.

"I might have thought you would be on time every day," Ms. Johns began, "this soon after The Incident."

Felicia had just hung up her coat and was fewer than twenty minutes behind schedule.

"Forgive me," she said. "My husband and I lost a son."

"You have my sympathies, but of course you know that we in positions of trust must separate our personal and professional lives, and that you are hardly alone in your grief."

Felicia nodded.

"And so I expect you here on time from here on out, at your desk and ready to go at starting time."

"Yes, ma'am."

"That said, Mrs. Thompson, I need to know whether, during all the years you worked side by side with Agent Stepola, you ever suspected him of being a double agent."

"Didn't we all? Didn't you?"

"You're not interrogating me, ma'am," Harriet said. "I'm interrogating you."

"You are?"

"Questioning you, yes."

"Am I being suspected of something? charged with something?"

"Certainly not. I just need your input. Naturally you would have been closer to Agent Stepola than anyone else."

"Naturally."

"And so?"

"Yes, I suspected him. And for a time he was under heavy scrutiny. Then he solved the European terrorist attacks and deflected all suspicion. He had me fooled."

Felicia found it hard to reconcile this stranger in Bob Koontz's office. The woman was forthright, not unlike Bob; she had to give Harriet that.

"Do you know where Agent Stepola is now?"

"I do not."

"Do you have any idea where he is?"

"I do not."

"You haven't thought about it?"

"Sure I have."

"And your guess?"

"I suppose I would be surprised if he was far from where he was last known to be."

"At his father-in-law's home," Harriet said.

"Correct."

"If he's hiding in Columbia, he ought to be easy to find."

Felicia smiled.

"You disagree."

"I do."

"You remain loyal to Agent Stepola?"

"I remain an employee of the National Peace Organization."

"And if you hear from Agent Stepola?"

"I will do the right thing."

"Very good. And have you heard from him?"

"If I had, I would have done the right thing."

"Excellent."

• • •

Ranold Decenti hung his hat and coat and visited his private lavatory, primping before the mirror, even though his appointment with Chancellor Dengler was by phone.

He buttoned his suit coat, tugged at his sleeves, straightened his tie, and ran his hands through his hair. Dengler might not be able to see him, but the chancellor ought to be able to sense he was talking with a man of prestige and power, a man of accomplishment. He ought to be able to detect a peer—there was no other way to say it.

Ranold let his secretary talk with Dengler's people until it was time for the two of them to converse over a secure connection. Ranold reminded himself to curb his proclivity for dominating a conversation. He must come across respectful and deferential, especially if he was in line for an important assignment.

"General Decenti?"

"Yes, sir."

"Baldwin Dengler from Bern, bringing you greetings from international government headquarters."

"Good day to you, Mr. Chancellor." Ranold at first wondered if it was really Dengler. Where was the sharp, clear voice, the air of confidence? Dengler was formal and professional, but the power was gone.

"I understand you have suffered as many of us have, General."

"Please, call me Ranold."

"Ranold, you have my condolences on the deaths of your son and your wife."

"Thank you, sir. I'm managing."

"I understand Agent Paul Stepola is your son-in-law."

"Regrettably so."

"I need to speak with him. Can you help me with that?"

"Sir?"

"I assume you have a cell number on him. Bottom line: I would like him to call me."

"Um, sure. I should be able to get that message to him. Or I could just give you that number. . . ."

"General, please. I think we both know he is not likely to accept a call originating from Bern."

"I have stopped trying to predict his behavior, Chancellor Dengler. You know he brainwashed my daughter into murdering my wife."

"Terribly sorry to hear that."

"Oh, and forgive me, sir, for not acknowledging your own loss. You had a son die too, did you not?"

"We're all coping the best we know how, General. Thank you. Please get a message to Agent Stepola that—"

"He's certainly no longer an agent, sir."

"Well, of course. See if you can get him to call me, would you?"

"I'll do my best. An honor to speak with you, sir."

"Likewise."

"Nothing else I can do for you?"

"That's all, General."

"But I—sorry."

"Was there something else, General?"

"Well, I—forgive me, sir, but may I assume your reason for wanting to connect with Stepola aims at his eventual capture and prosecution?"

A long pause signaled Ranold that he had overstepped the bounds of propriety. "I'm sorry, Chancellor. That is none of my business. I—"

Dengler sighed. "No, that's all right. I suppose if anyone has a right to know, you do. Sure, the law enforcer in me wants to bring Stepola down. On the other hand . . . do you have a minute?"

"Certainly."

"General, we're of similar ages and backgrounds. We have seen our share of tragedy. I know your history."

"Thank you, sir."

"Perhaps Stepola was still being coy with you," Dengler said, "right to the end, but the fact is, in his own way, he tried to warn me."

"Warn you?"

"Of what was coming. He urged me to carefully consider the warning from the resistance."

"The underground zealots," Ranold said, a hard edge to his tone.

"At the time," the chancellor said, "I thought he was just being a good soldier, in the NPO sense. Consider both sides; cut losses; play it safe; keep an eye on the long term, the big picture, the greater good."

"All that, yes," Ranold said. "And no, he didn't take that tack with me. Made me believe he was loyal until it became obvious he wasn't. Of course, you know I was on to him. Had been for some time."

Another sigh from the chancellor. "Well, the point is, we're all on to him now, aren't we?"

"Yes, and that's why I'm curious about your intentions."

"To be perfectly frank, General, I want to know more about what he knows. It's clear which side he's on, and like it or not, he's cast his lot with the side that is winning."

"What are you saying?"

"Come now, Decenti. You can't admit we got a whipping this week? Denial can be worse than defeat."

"But you don't lose a battle and concede the war, do you, sir? I find my back is up; I'm on the offensive. I want to retaliate, to take no prisoners, to win."

"Well, don't we all? But if history has taught us anything, it's to know when we're outmanned."

Ranold couldn't help himself. "Outmanned? You believe we are outmanned?"

"You don't?"

"Absolutely not. I'm willing to admit I may have underestimated the enemy. But the only thing Tuesday did was make me more resolute."

"Well, good for you, General. I guess that's what we want at your level of the intelligence community."

"But that's not where you are, Chancellor?"

"Where I am is facing reality. We oppose a force with the power to slay a billion males in an instant. That should give us all pause and make us plead for an audience with the other side."

Ranold found himself standing, fuming. When the conversation ended he returned to the lav and kicked the door so hard the knob drove a hole in the paneling and brought his secretary running.

"Are you all right, sir?"

Ranold bent over the commode and vomited.

"Do you need me to call someone?"

"I'm fine!" Ranold managed, gasping. He wiped his mouth and faced himself in the mirror again. He felt puffed with rage. Who'd have guessed Chancellor Baldwin Dengler would prove a wuss? Was Ranold going to be forced to fight this battle alone? If the world needed anything right now, it was a leader.

• • •

Paul awoke to a raft of messages on his phone: three from Felicia, six from his father-in-law.

Felicia filled him in on all the activity in Chicago and warned him not to call her. She would call him when she had a chance. The messages from Ranold were full of expletives and invectives and warnings, in essence commanding him to call Dengler.

Now that was interesting. Paul would let the man—yes, the chancellor—wait. He had to be sure there was no way Dengler could trace the call. But what could the man want beyond talking about God and what He had done? There was little else to say. Surely Dengler wouldn't congratulate Paul on duping him. The time for talking directly with the chancellor might come, and it would be crucially strategic, but for now it would have to wait.

• • •

Dr. Gregory Graybill told Straight that he had learned the best place for a clandestine meeting was in plain sight. So they arranged to meet in the cafeteria. "People can think we're talking patient strategy," the doctor said. "And perhaps we will."

They loaded their trays with institutional delicacies and set about pretending they were old friends. As soon as they were seated, the doctor opened a cup of pudding and leaned forward so only Straight could hear him. "We need to trust each other," he said.

"Do we?" Straight said. "Why is that?"

"Because I know you are a believer."

"You know nothing of the sort," Straight said. "You risk your freedom and your life by even talking like this, so I urge you to tread carefully."

"The time is long past for that," Dr. Graybill said. "If it makes you feel more secure, I'll declare myself first. I am a believer. I work with like-minded physicians to determine who's with us and who isn't. When the enemy is under our care, we slow them a bit."

"You slow them?"

"We do not violate the Hippocratic oath, but let's say it takes these people longer to get back to work than some others. Did that with a blind patient you worked with last year, for one."

Straight shuddered. Is this what The Incident had accomplished? It made the underground reckless? "What if you have misread me, Doctor?"

"I'll know that soon enough, won't I? You'll turn me in, and when the decimated government forces get around to it, I'll be arrested, tried, and—I presume—executed."

"That simple, eh?"

The doctor nodded. "I would not have made this contact if I wasn't sure about you, but it would set my mind at ease if you would assure me we're on the same side."

Straight sat back and studied the man. Bravado or desperation? He didn't know how to read the doctor. Surely the man couldn't suspect Straight was well connected with the underground. If Graybill had figured that out, Straight could be in deep weeds. "For the sake of discussion, let's assume you've not just committed suicide. What could you possible want with me?"

Dr. Graybill rushed to chew a saltine cracker and followed it with a sip of iced tea. "Patient information," he said. "You know before we do whom we're dealing with. All we get are names—some we recognize, of course—and medical histories. I'm guessing you have a better handle on who's who, whom we should target for, shall we say, more deliberate care."

Straight sipped his coffee, then rubbed his eyes and wiped his face, realizing he had forgotten to shave. If he were a poker player, that would have been a tell, and Dr. Graybill would have known he had found his man.

"Let's leave it this way," Straight said. "If you get news about an incoming patient or two, you can breathe easier and act accordingly. If, instead, you are arrested, you'll know how grievously you have misread me."

• • •

Felicia waited until most of the suits, including Harriet Johns, were gone, before she found her way to Hector Hernandez's cubicle. The young man was deep into something on his computer, so when she tapped lightly on the wall, he jumped and spilled coffee on his desk.

"Sorry, sorry," Felicia said. "Didn't mean to—"

"No, it's okay, ma'am. Come in, please."

Hector wiped his glass desktop with a small napkin, and as Felicia moved to help, he held her wrist with one hand and used the index finger of his other hand to draw opposing and intersecting arcs in the residue.

He quickly wiped it all away, but the significance was not lost on Felicia. "Seafood fan, Hector?" she said.

"I love fish. You?"

She nodded. "You're taking a great risk," she whispered.

"When rumors began about your boss, I wondered how you could keep working for him. Unless . . ."

"Unless I was a fish lover?"

He motioned her close with a nod. "You know there's a network of other, ah, fish folk here and at other bureaus."

"Why didn't anyone tell me? I sure could have used the support."

"No other fish friends?" Hector said.

She shook her head. "A relative or two, but they're not close."

"Let me show you something," Hector said.

She leaned over his shoulder to see his screen. "This secure?" she said.

"Think I'd risk it otherwise? I design the security systems here."

Felicia started when a throat cleared behind her.

"What are you two up to so late?"

# 21

**WAS IT POSSIBLE** Felicia's ruse was over this quickly? How had Paul lasted so long? She was an amateur; that was sure. Two days into her new life on the edge and she had been found out.

The interloper was Trudy Nabertowitz in gray-on-gray security fatigues. Stocky and short-haired, she had been at the Chicago bureau nearly as long as Felicia. In fact, Felicia remembered the woman's first day. She had been young and thin, smiling and energetic. She sure seemed to love that uniform, the leather belt, the handcuffs, the baton, the assumed authority. And she hadn't seemed to harden over the years, as happened to too many security guards.

"Oh, yeah, hi," Felicia said. "We're just—"

Hector interrupted. "Finalizing a report for General Decenti in Washington on—"

"Listen, Mrs. Thompson," Trudy said, her voice barely above

a whisper. "Here's the deal. My chief sees you on the monitor, says you can't be too careful these days, can't trust anybody, blah, blah, blah. He's going to swoop down and give you what for for bothering a techie who likely has after-hours clearance. I tell him I know you; he says who doesn't? I say I need to stretch my legs and will bring him a coffee. He lets me come."

Hector seemed to take this in stride, but Felicia's heart was doing Tae Bo against her ribs. She wasn't cut out for this. Frantic to invent an explanation, she froze, staring first at Trudy, then at Hector, imagining herself in prison orange.

"Me?" Felicia managed, her voice squeaking. "I'm on my way home, saying good-bye to—"

Trudy's eyes danced. "Well, which is it, Mrs. Thompson? Hector here hectoring you about your former boss so's he can put it in the big report to Washington, or you just saying good-bye to your friend who nobody knew was your friend till right now?"

"I," Felicia said, "that is, we—"

Had Trudy just winked at Hector? Had Felicia been set up? Could she have been that careless? that stupid? She clammed up, resolved to say nothing until she had a lawyer.

"Didn't see you at Wilson's last month, Hector," Trudy said.

"I'll be there in two weeks," Hector said. "Everybody'll be there. Probably even Mrs. Thompson."

*Monthly meeting? Wilson's?*

"You know Wilson's," Trudy said, "don't you, Felicia?"

"I know *a* Wilson's," she said, her voice cracking. She felt like one of The Three Stooges playing spy. "The restaurant in Joliet?"

Hector peeked at her knowingly. "More specifically, a *seafood* restaurant in Joliet."

"Monthly meeting there," Trudy said. "Of real seafood lovers. So, is Hector right? Maybe we'll see you there next week?"

Felicia couldn't control her pulse. "Maybe."

"Peace be with you," Trudy whispered.

"And also with you," Hector said.

Trudy turned to face Felicia. "Peace be with you."

Felicia hesitated. Clearly this was some code. She looked to Hector, who nodded and mouthed the response. And Felicia said, "And also with you."

Trudy smiled, but Felicia was nonplussed. "All right, I'm totally confused," she said. "How did you—?"

"I came down here to protect a brother," Trudy said, "but I could tell from Hector's face he felt safe with you. Since The Incident, more and more of us have been coming out of the woodwork. That's why next week's fish fry is going to be the biggest yet."

"That'll make it more dangerous," Felicia said.

"More dangerous than what? You been readin' the papers?"

"Newspapers? No. Who's had time?"

"Take time. Editorials, opinions, letters to the editor—everybody's ready to cut the underground some slack. Huge groundswell."

"That doesn't mean it'll happen," Felicia said. "These people are just foolishly identifying themselves to the authorities."

"I'm telling you," Trudy said, "even unbelievers are getting on the bandwagon. Nobody wants a repeat of what just happened. Now, please, tell me you have after-hours security clearance like Hector does, so I don't have to lie to my boss."

"Of course," Felicia said.

"Good. Carry on."

"Want to know what we're really doing?" Hector said.

Trudy raised a hand. "The less I know, the better."

• • •

By Monday, January 28, Paul had still not called Ranold, let alone Baldwin Dengler. The hacking into the underground computer system continued unabated, and there wasn't a techie in any underground who could assure Paul the entire communications system—phones included—had not been compromised. He asked Jack how that was possible with the seemingly impenetrable security system in place.

"You don't want to know," Jack said.

"Of course I do."

"Has to be an insider. No one could crack that code otherwise."

Jae seemed settled and pensive at the same time, worried about the children yet thrilled with her work with Angela. The kids were eager to tell Paul what they were learning every day. He listened closely, as did Jae. They were learning too. Stories from the Bible and the life of Jesus—fascinating, moving, insightful stories they should have known for years.

Jack Pass seemed more eager than ever for a road trip, one that would take him and Paul to the other undergrounds to encourage them, tie them together, and rally them to pray for one more dramatic act of God. Paul was fighting him, agreeing with Greenie that if the slaying of firstborn sons around the world had not reached the hard hearts of the people, nothing would.

But Jack would not be dissuaded. He spread half a dozen dossiers on the table before Paul, showing him how he could appropriate any one of the identities of men his age and build who had died in The Incident. Some were black, some Indian, some Hispanic.

"I have people who can make you look like any one of them," Jack said. "Skin dye, hair color, contact lenses, dental prostheses, clothes, you name it. Your own wife wouldn't recognize you."

"She wouldn't want to. If I left her now, she probably wouldn't want me to come back."

Paul's molar phone chirped, and he pressed his fingertips together, making the caller ID communicate directly to his inner ear. "Number classified and private." He whispered a code and was informed the number was government issued. Good that he had resisted the urge to merely answer. He waited until the end-of-message tone, then excused himself and moved down a long, empty corridor.

Dengler? Ranold? Felicia? Harriet Johns?

He couldn't have been more surprised to hear the unmistakable voice of Bia Balaam. They had history. Boy, did they have history. His surreptitious research had uncovered that she had been behind the martyrdom of Andy Pass, his former special-ops commander and Jack's brother. She had suspected Paul early on and made no secret of it, following him around the world and trying to trip him up.

Nearly six feet tall, rawboned, and with eerie silver eyes that matched her hair, Bia was everything the former Paul Stepola would have admired in an NPO chief: ruthless, cold, cruel, ambitious, condescending, sarcastic.

But that's not what he heard on this message. It was her voice all right, but in a tone and with a timbre he had never heard. He didn't trust her. Of course he didn't. But she certainly pulled out every trick in her bag to convince him she was sincere.

"Paul," she said, "you must call me. Please. You have my private cell number, and it is secure. Ignore your father-in-law if you must. Blow off the chancellor too, if you don't trust him. But do call me. Here's how deadly serious and transparent I am: Before I even tell you what I want, I am going to betray the NPO, betray my government, and go against everything I ever knew, was ever taught. I am going to tell you what we know about where you are and what is planned for those in league with you in the Columbia underground.

"You may choose not to believe it, but you will have to wonder how I know and why I am telling you this. There is only one reason. I'm conceding. You win. Your people and your God have proven themselves, at least to me. I have lost my son, my everything, and I have nothing more to lose, nothing more to offer. No way I'll risk my daughter's life for a cause I no longer believe in.

"Paul, I know where you are. I know who you are with. And I know the danger you are in and how long you have to get out of there. When I give you the details, you will know I am telling the truth and, I hope, know how patently sincere I am. I must hear from you. Please."

# 22

**FELICIA STOPPED** for a *Chicago Tribune* before heading out of the city. She would save it to share with Cletus—they had to do something together besides cry and commiserate, eat and try to rest. But she couldn't help glancing at the headlines, and sure enough, Trudy Nabertowitz had been right. Something had emboldened the populace, even people who described themselves as anything but religious.

This must have been the way it had been nearly forty years before, Felicia decided, when the world was so devastated by the gruesome war and the pandemic loss of life that even well-meaning people agreed the banning of religion would be a good start to eradicating war.

Now the sentiment had finally seemed to reverse itself, and as she and Cletus sat next to each other at the kitchen table, forcing themselves to nibble and keep their strength while leaning shoulder to shoulder as if they would otherwise topple, they read to each other from the paper.

The many stories of brave people speaking out, even full-page ads signed by dozens unafraid to declare themselves, made Felicia and Cletus turn on the news. And from around the globe beamed stories of demonstrations, parades, speeches, harangues. "Underground believers, zealots, extrem-ists, whatever anyone chooses to call them," one man railed in Chicago's Bughouse Square, "they are the new minority, the new oppressed."

"How are *they* oppressed?" a heckler raged. "They did not suffer! We are the ones who lost sons, brothers, fathers."

"God is on their side!" the speaker said. "I was an atheist who is now an agnostic. But that sounds foolish even to me when the promise of a curse, a plague, has been carried out be-fore my eyes. Hear me: I will not worship this vengeful God. But neither will I ever again pretend He doesn't exist and has not the power to squash me like a bug. All I'm saying is that the world will not come to an end if we beseech the government to lift the ban on the practice of religion. But it could very well end if we do not lift the ban. Do we want another judgment? another show of power from beyond the heavens? I don't!

"The people of faith have played their trump card, and we have lost the hand. Let's not risk losing the entire game."

That diatribe and the back-and-forth of the masses was typi-cal all over the globe. "We need not concede anything, believe anything, or even change our way of life," a Frenchman opined in an open letter to the world. "Have we not learned to live and let live? Our provincial laws have oppressed these people in ways we would never allow ourselves to be oppressed. We don't have to agree with them. We don't have to like them. We don't even have to acknowledge them. Just let them be; let them live as they wish. It's such a small price to avoid a repeat of what we have endured . . . or worse."

•  •  •

Ranold Decenti threw himself into his work. He had gone from semiretirement to full-time Zealot Underground task force chief and was now pressed into service as the ersatz director of the stateside NPO. Not only was it a job he had always relished, but he also found great satisfaction in filling his whole day, from early morning until late at night, with real work. No more dragging himself home for dinner at the end of a long day. He could have food delivered and keep working.

The former general checked and rechecked his budget, pleased—though he would not have used that term—to find that the sheer reduction in salaries due to The Incident would soon overcome the payment packages due the survivors. Decenti had millions transferred from glutted budgets into his own and had his secretary schedule a personal audience with Chancellor Dengler in Switzerland. Someone had to talk sense to the man or muscle him out of the way. The resistance consisted of paper tigers who understood one language: a dialect of intimidation that Ranold B. Decenti still understood, even if Baldwin Dengler did not. Dengler had made Ranold physically sick. Now he would set the chancellor straight.

"Does the March 22 deadline on signing the oaths of loyalty still stand, or does it not?" Ranold asked Dengler on the phone.

"I'll speak to that in a moment, General. First tell me whether former agent Stepola has gotten my message. I have heard nothing from him or you."

"I have done my part, Mr. Chancellor. I cannot make him call you."

"Yes, I understand."

"Now, about that deadline."

"Well, as you can imagine," Dengler said, "everything is up in the air now. Everything is conditional, under review."

Ranold could not even respond, so afraid was he that he might explode.

"You understand," Dengler said. "Don't you, General?"

*Oh, do I ever.*

•  •  •

"Something's missing from all these stories," Felicia said.

"Pray tell," Cletus said.

"They fall short of telling what the underground resistance is all about. I mean, they acknowledge it's made up of people of faith and that they called upon God to act on their behalf, and He did. But no one is acknowledging the other side of God. His love. His mercy. His interest in getting our attention."

Cletus shook his head. "He got our attention all right, Felicia. Nobody's gonna buy that He didn't accomplish that."

"Well, I've got an idea."

"Uh-oh."

"Why not broadcast Paul's notes—the explanation of how to receive Christ—to everyone who has a computer?"

"That's redundant, Felicia. Everyone has a computer. Most have more than one."

"There you go."

•  •  •

If there was one call Paul wanted most to return, it was Bia Balaam's. He had considered her message, prayed about it, noodled it for hours, and he couldn't come up with an explanation for it aside from what she had claimed.

If it was true that she was violating every NPO protocol by

telling him so much, what motive could she have other than a personal one? Paul didn't know, but he didn't want to get duped either.

The ball remained in her court. She wanted to talk with him, not vice versa. Well, in fact, the opposite *was* also true, but she needn't know that. Leave the burden on her, he decided. Let her come to him.

She tried. And she tried again. Every time she missed him—his choice, of course, to not talk with her—she left a more detailed message. Finally, she said, "All right, if this is what it takes to convince you, I'll throw caution to the wind and leave myself vulnerable to treason." And with that she proceeded to tell Paul she knew he had his family with him; precisely where the underground was located; the names of Jack Pass, Angela Pass Barger, and even Greenie Macintosh; the extent of the encroachment of NPO techies into the computer system; and the timing of the attack that would decimate the Columbia underground.

Paul couldn't get to Jack fast enough. Dare they seek help from other regions? And how were they to go about that with their computer communications compromised?

• • •

Hector Hernandez told Felicia he loved her idea of disseminating Paul Stepola's instructions on how to receive Christ, and he immediately set to work at home on a construct that would allow him to pull it off remotely. No trace of Hector's work would appear on the NPO mainframe, but if everything worked correctly, every computer in the world would get Paul's notes.

In an instant, everyone interested in how a person switched teams would be without excuse.

# 23

**STRAIGHT BELIEVED** there was wisdom in many counselors, but for now he wanted just one: Abraham, code name for the leader of the Watchmen—an elite squad of undergrounders, largely from the Michigan/Ohio salt mines. And despite the complication of traveling at a chaotic time like this, Abraham was apparently sufficiently alarmed by Straight's story to suggest a face-to-face in Chicago.

"The man sounds credible to me," Abraham said as they sat on a cold bench near Buckingham Fountain, idle during the frigid weather. "But that insight is not from God, merely from me."

"And if he's credible, how much do I give him?"

"How much do you know?"

"Enough. I get a printout of new patients. I recognize a lot of names from the news, and my contacts help me with others. Stepola knows the most, naturally, but others are helpful."

"And what do you get out of this?"

"Sir?"

"It ought to be reciprocal, Dr. Rathe. Don't you think?"

Straight shrugged. "I hadn't considered that."

"Consider it. Even in the best case, you and this surgeon are on the same side, and there is benefit to what he is doing. But you are every bit as vulnerable as he. Let's say you give him a name or two, confirming you are part of the resistance, and he is not who he says he is. You've implicated yourself. At least make the risk worth your while."

"And what do I want from him?"

Abraham offered a weary smile. "Think, man. What do we most need?"

"Brother, I haven't thought clearly for days. Forgive me and tell me."

Abraham sighed. "You say this doctor assured you he doesn't do any real harm to these patients, which would violate his oath. But surely a percentage of his cases are terminal nonetheless. It would seem a small thing for him to let you know who those are early enough that you can take advantage of the information."

"And appropriate their IDs."

Abraham clapped a hand on Straight's knee. "See, you're not so tired that it has completely clouded your judgment."

• • •

After days of frustration, the governor of the Columbia Region, Haywood Hale, officially named Ranold B. Decenti interim head of NPO USSA. Ranold secretly wished the governor would visit him in his office at headquarters, but of course protocol required the general to visit the West Wing of the old White House.

The longer Ranold waited, the more agitated he became. He considered showing his pique and even bad-mouthing the international chancellor, but he felt the wind leave his sails when he was finally granted an audience.

The Oval Office certainly proved a thin representation of what it had been when presidents resided there. Governor Hale had actually installed cubicle walls and two clerical workers where beautiful furniture had once graced the place.

The tall, reedy governor was elderly now—in his late eighties, having been the last vice president in the old system before being assigned his current role by Baldwin Dengler's predecessor. Despite tissue-paper skin and dark age spots on the backs of his hands, Hale still seemed sharp and none the worse for wear—despite a slight tremor, though his largely ceremonial duties were hardly taxing. Still, Ranold thought, he seemed more forthright and decisive even than Dengler.

"Two things I need to clarify for you, General," the governor said. "One is that this is only an interim position. We are actively seeking a man of more appropriate age to lead the NPO. You have all the tools, of course: the reputation, the experience, and the respect of your colleagues—all of whom will be subordinates after today. But neither of us is a young man anymore, Ranold."

"Granted." Ranold was smiling but also seething. He hated when the obvious was paraded as novel. "And the second? Sir?"

"You may be wondering a bit at the delay."

Now there was an understatement. "Oh no," Ranold said. "I understand these things take time."

"Well, this took longer than it should have, and I apologize. But the fact is that Chancellor Dengler himself sat on it a few days. You know he lost a son and other family members, and—"

"As did most of us." Ranold regretted that as soon as it came from his mouth, because he could see he had offended, or at least irritated, the governor merely by interrupting him. "Forgive me, sir. I cut you off."

"I was saying that besides the turmoil of his personal losses, I believe he had some hesitation about your appointment."

Ranold feigned surprise. "Because of my age? I—"

"No, I don't believe so, General. Apparently you have pressed the chancellor on certain issues. . . ."

"I won't deny that," Ranold said. "But I was under the impression he appreciates forthrightness—"

"Of course he does. As long as it's—"

"Deferential and respectful, naturally."

The governor stood and moved to sit on the corner of his desk, and Ranold was immediately insulted by the obvious attempt to intimidate. He had used the technique himself.

"General Decenti," Hale began, "you of all people—with your military background—know that absolute adherence to the chain of command is indispensable. The chancellor, as your ultimate superior, has the right even to be wrong. You should feel free to steadfastly argue your positions with him, until he—"

"Announces a directive, naturally. Yes, I know that."

"General, please allow me to finish a thought before—"

"I apologize, Governor."

"If you do that with Chancellor Dengler, I could understand his reticence—"

"I don't believe I have, sir, but let me suggest this: how about I make my first priority a personal visit to Bern where I assure the chancellor that we are on the same page."

Hale reached to shake Ranold's hand, and the latter was struck by the fragility of the man's grip. "Now you're talking, General. On the other hand, don't make the mistake of assuming I didn't know those arrangements have already been made."

Decenti felt himself redden. "Do I need to fire my secretary? She's been with me for more than—"

Hale shook his head and held up a hand, smiling broadly. "Your secretary has not betrayed you, General. Chancellor Dengler's has betrayed him."

• • •

Paul knocked and slipped into a meeting of the elders where Jack Pass stood at a flip chart and Greenie Macintosh sat in the front row. Paul signaled Jack that he needed to see him, but Jack merely nodded and kept going. He had written *Isaiah 59* on the board, and when Paul sat, the elder near him slid a Bible his way.

Paul turned to the passage and speed-scanned it:

*Behold, the LORD's hand is not shortened, that it cannot save; nor His ear heavy, that it cannot hear.*

*But your iniquities have separated you from your God; and your sins have hidden His face from you, so that He will not hear.*

*For your hands are defiled with blood, and your fingers with iniquity; your lips have spoken lies, your tongue has muttered perversity.*

*No one calls for justice, nor does any plead for truth.*

*They trust in empty words and speak lies; they conceive evil and bring forth iniquity. . . .*

*Their feet run to evil, and they make haste to shed innocent blood; their thoughts are thoughts of iniquity; wasting and destruction are in their paths.*

*The way of peace they have not known, and there is no justice in their ways; they have made themselves crooked paths; whoever takes that way shall not know peace.*

*Therefore justice is far from us, nor does righteousness*

*overtake us; we look for light, but there is darkness! For brightness, but we walk in blackness! . . .*

*Justice is turned back, and righteousness stands afar off; for truth is fallen in the street, and equity cannot enter.*

*So truth fails, and he who departs from evil makes himself a prey. Then the LORD saw it, and it displeased Him that there was no justice.*

*He saw that there was no man, and wondered that there was no intercessor; therefore His own arm brought salvation for Him; and His own righteousness, it sustained Him.*

*For He put on righteousness as a breastplate, and a helmet of salvation on His head; He put on the garments of vengeance for clothing, and was clad with zeal as a cloak.*

*According to their deeds, accordingly He will repay, fury to His adversaries, recompense to His enemies; the coastlands He will fully repay.*

*So shall they fear the name of the LORD from the west, and His glory from the rising of the sun; when the enemy comes in like a flood, the Spirit of the LORD will lift up a standard against him.*

"Do you see what that's saying, gentlemen?" Jack said. "People fear the name of the Lord from the west because He brought the drought upon Los Angeles. They will fear His glory from the rising of the sun, which happens where?"

"The east," someone said. "Where we are."

"Where we are," Jack echoed with such gravity that Paul feared he had lost his mind.

"You're proof-texting!" Greenie said. "Be careful, Jack. You can't tell me that when this was written, the writer was thinking of California and Washington, D.C."

That seemed to stop Jack, but not for long. "Listen to Amos

5:24," he said. "'Let justice run down like water, and righteousness like a mighty stream.'"

"Now you're going to tell us that's a prescription for Operation Noah," Greenie said.

"Well, what would you call it?"

"I agree with you, Jack," one of the younger elders said. "If we were to vote right now—"

"We're not going to vote right now," Paul said. "We have more pressing business."

Jack shot him a look. "What could be more pressing than this, Paul? We have to act."

"We have to get out is what we have to do. And we have ten days."

# 24

**IT WAS QUIET TIME FOR THE KIDS,** and a couple of high schoolers were watching them. Jae got Angela alone.

"You're out of sorts today," Angela said. "What's up?"

"Do you realize I can't go to my brother's or even my mother's funeral?"

Angela nodded. "I wouldn't have been able to go to my father's if it were today," she said. "Horrible as it was, at least I was not known as part of the underground when he was murdered. It did help to be there."

"I can't even talk to my father," Jae said. "Who knows whether he'll even have funerals for them?"

"Oh, surely . . . his wife and son?"

"You don't know him, Angela. I'm going to have to call my sister-in-law to find out."

"Sad," Angela said. "Could you use some good news?"

"Could I ever."

"I think your kids are close."

"Really?"

"Yes. In fact, so close that my sons think Brie and Connor are already believers. They were telling them that the next step is getting out of here and telling their friends about Jesus."

"I wonder if Brie and Connor have even made friends at school here yet," Jae said, "even if they could get out. They couldn't, by the way, could they?"

"Have friends? Why not?"

"No, not that. They've been here such a short time. If they wanted to tell somebody about Jesus, it would be their friends in Chicago. But I mean they couldn't get out of here, right?"

"Without your permission or knowledge? No. It's as hard to get out of here as it is to get in."

* * *

All eyes were on Paul, so it was time to put up or shut up. But before he could even get into Bia Balaam's warning, a junior techie from the computer area rushed in and thrust a printout at Jack.

Jack read it and looked up. "Where'd this come from?"

"Obviously nobody knows. But it looks like a universal broadcast."

"So what is it?" someone called out.

"Yeah, come on. Read it."

Jack did, and Paul immediately recognized it. "Those are my notes on salvation," he said. "Which tells me where it came from. I just hope the person who did this was careful."

"If this went to the whole world, we could see a revival," Greenie said. "We wouldn't even have to talk Jack out of Operation Noah."

"Let's not get ahead of ourselves," Jack said. "Now, Paul, what on earth were you talking about?"

. . .

As soon as Ranold was back in his car he was on the phone to his
secretary, instructing her to marshal his crack team of operatives.
By the time he reached his office, the six, led by Bia Balaam, were
waiting in a conference room. When he hurried in, they stood.
Was it just his imagination, or had Bia been the last to stand?

She looked terrible. Dressed impeccably, as usual, she still
cast an imposing image, but her naturally olive skin appeared
washed-out. Her eyes looked tired, her face drawn. It was as if
she wore no makeup, and yet he knew her better than that. No
way Commander Bia Balaam would appear in public, especially
at work, looking other than her best. On the other hand, if this
was her best . . .

Clearly she was taking the loss of her son hard. That was the
trouble with women, but Ranold had to admit he had not noticed compassion or sentiment in her before. She had been a top
leader because she had the instincts of a man; Ranold was sure of
it. He himself wasn't beyond emotion, or at least a little melan-
choly, over the losses in his own family. But if he was honest
with himself, he felt the estrangement from Jae more than any
grief over Berlitz or his wife.

He had already pretty much forgotten Berl. At least, he didn't
think about him much. Margaret was a different story, of course,
but he chalked that up to the decades they had spent together,
interacting every day. In truth, he had not found Margaret exciting or even attractive in the way, for instance, that he found Bia.
In fact, if she could get beyond this preoccupation with her own
troubles and regain that spark she once had, now that they were
both available . . . perhaps she would not think him too old. He
believed women were drawn to power and money, and he had
plenty of the former and more than enough of the latter.

# 25

**PAUL'S NEWS** devastated the elders. Jack Pass dropped into a chair near Greenie and faced the group, addressing Paul in the back. "I believe that's why God sent you to us. How would we have known otherwise?"

Greenie was on to more practical matters. "I understand you can't reveal details about this contact person, but you say they are in a position to know?"

"Absolutely. Exposure to the highest levels of the opposition."

"And they're aiming at a February 8 D-day, a week from this Friday. That begs the question: if they know where we are, what are they waiting for?"

"The new NPO chief has another priority. A visit to Bern."

• • •

Felicia was as giddy as Hector was scared. At least, he looked
scared. She had run into him on the elevator at the start of the
day, and he had immediately put a finger to his lips. His black
eyes looked wide and terrified. She had found a reason to stroll
by his cubicle on her way to a meeting, but as soon as he saw her,
he looked away.

Felicia wanted to tell him that his idea of also sending the
missive to all the NPO computers had been no less than genius.
Really, what a stroke! Besides taking the suspicion off anyone inside, it was already the talk of the place.

Harriet Johns had called her in first thing. "Seen this yet?"
Harriet said, waving a printout before Felicia had even sat.

"What is it?"

"Zealot underground propaganda. If you're thinking about
getting saved, here's how."

Felicia looked at it and shook her head. "It's nothing I need,"
she said.

"Me either, but it *is* a complicator. You'd be amazed at the
number of people who will be influenced by this. I wouldn't
have thought so a month ago, but now? With all the unrest?
With the turning tide of public opinion? I can't think of worse
timing for something like this."

"What will we do about it?" Felicia said.

"Not much we can do but put our people on trying to trace
it. The damage has been done though. There's no trying to
repack the parachute while you're in the air."

Felicia shot the woman a double take. "Now there's one I
haven't heard before."

"You like that? It's yours."

"No thanks. You keep it."

• • •

"You six have the highest level of security clearance in the history of the NPO," Ranold said, watching for the bright-eyed response of pride. Seeing none, he pressed the point. "There are those who would advise me to interrogate you individually, to administer truth serum or lie-detector tests, to put it to you directly and be sure you're still fully on board with the international loyalty initiative. But I don't need that. I know you all well enough, personally and professionally, that if I didn't trust you implicitly, you wouldn't be here."

Finally, finally, a shuffling, some movement, posture changes, especially in the five men. They sat up straighter. They were the elite, the chosen, and they reveled in it. *Well,* Ranold thought, *they ought to.*

"I have been invited to Bern for a private meeting with Chancellor Dengler, wanting to officially welcome me to this new position. I tell you only because this is your accomplishment as much as mine.

"We're still on schedule for the annihilation of the Columbia zealot underground complex, and I want from the attack side a full report of your plans, needs, timetable, and the like by a week from today. I will meet with the chancellor Friday and will be back in this office Monday, bright and early.

"My understanding is that we have lost two men there, and that—if for no other reason—is enough justification to strike hard and fast and completely. One died, as he was a firstborn son, and the other, Commander Balaam tells me, was caught while reporting in and assassinated. Besides the death blow their side struck worldwide, we will have vengeance for our own."

Bia nodded wearily, and Ranold wondered if she was about to topple. During a break he took her arm and drew her close.

"Here's what else I need," he said. "I understand there is a talisman related to being a member of this branch of the resistance. I want one of those, whatever it is."

"It's a flat, white stone," Bia said quietly.

"And we have access to those?"

"Of course. We have confiscated a few over the years."

"I would like that today."

Bia merely gazed back at him.

"Is that doable, Ms. Balaam? Are you still with me?"

"Yes, certainly. Sorry, sir. By the end of the day."

• • •

"Well," Greenie said, "I think that's the end of Operation Noah *and* my plan."

"What was your plan?" Paul said.

"Can we not get into this?" Jack said. "If you're right, Paul, we've got to mobilize fast. We've got, in essence, a thousand men, women, and children to relocate, and to who knows where?"

"Salt mines are the only option," Greenie said. Many nodded, including Paul.

"The question," Paul said, "is whether they're willing to take us. If not, we've got to parcel these people out to undergrounds in other regions."

"We're going to need a lot of vehicles," Greenie said.

"The Demetrius money should make that easy," Jack said. "No 'appropriating,' no changing VINs, no repainting. Just buy 'em under assumed names, do wonders for the Columbia economy, and get these people out of Dodge."

"I still want to know what Greenie's plan was," one of the men said.

Jack shook his head and exhaled loudly. "He wanted to use all our vehicles to create gridlock in the district."

"For what purpose?"

"That wasn't all," Greenie said. "I also wanted to plug the Potomac, create our own little drought."

"Just to bug the authorities?"

"C'mon! Give me a little credit. I had a whole plan, a whole scheme. It involved Fort McNair, which has a loading dock for the cars and service tunnels for all manner of mayhem. Isn't there something in the Bible about how having faith without doing anything is like death?"

"Something like that," someone said. "But your plan still sounds like just a nuisance."

"Fine!" Greenie said. "Forget it! Can't do it now anyway. Our priority has just been handed to us on a silver platter."

Paul couldn't argue that. The time had come to return Bia Balaam's call.

# 26

**PAUL STAYED AFTER THE ELDER MEETING,** along with Jack and Greenie. Jack looked as if he hadn't slept for days, but then he always looked that way. He rested his elbows on a table and cradled his head in his hands. "So this is it then, eh?"

"'Fraid so," Paul said.

"I mean, this contact is solid, right? Good as gold?"

"This contact told me where we're located, Jack."

"And are you sure it's correct? You were rushed here during a personal crisis yourself."

"Please, Jack. I used to work in this city. I know where we are. My biggest worry is that we've got another infiltrator here, maybe more."

"Isn't that something your contact can tell you?"

"Let's hope."

Jack put Greenie in charge of coordinating the mass exodus,

still without knowing where they were going. "Isn't that sort of important?" Greenie said.

"Not yet," Jack said. "We have to leave here—that's certain. Which way we turn when we pull out of here isn't crucial until the last minute. And if even we don't know yet, it's unlikely to leak, isn't it?"

Greenie nodded. "What do you need from me?"

"Everything. All the logistics. How many vehicles, how many people, how we will account for them all, where we will send them—all that."

"And are we moving heavy stuff, equipment, computers?"

Jack looked to Paul.

"Only what we can manage," Paul said. "Obviously, people are our priority."

"Obviously."

Jack sped Paul to the tech center, where the chief guy brought them up to date on the threat to the mainframe and examined Paul's molar implants. "I'm 99 percent certain you're clear," he said.

Paul glanced at Jack. "Normally I don't like having even one percent hanging over my head, but under these circumstances . . ."

"It's your call," Jack said. "Time's a-wastin'."

"Borrow your cart?"

"I've got business here anyway."

Paul raced to the end of the corridor, dialing Bia Balaam as he went. He was disappointed when her machine picked up. He hoped if she was there she would recognize his voice.

"Commander Balaam, I'm finally getting back to you. You know where to reach me. Obviously, we need to talk soon."

"Don't hang up, Paul."

"I'm here."

"Thanks so much for getting back to me."

"No problem, at least on that score. But I need to know—"

"How and why you should trust me, I know."

"I'm listening."

"Was I not specific enough?" she said. "Were you not convinced? Would you rather take your chances?"

Paul heard weariness and resignation in her voice, but there was still that edge that told him if he chose to cross her, he could regret it.

"As I said, I'm listening. Of course, if I were a suspicious man, I'd wonder if you misled me on timing. That would be a tragic mistake."

"You said it, Doctor. I'd wonder about that little detail. How long will it take to get a thousand people to safety?"

Paul hesitated. How could she know so much? "Tell me, Commander, are there others inside I need to worry about?"

"Fair question. If I were playing games with you, I'd let you wonder. Truth is, Agent Wipers was better than many ever gave him credit for."

"So you knew before you last talked to him."

"Yes. Did you like my question about whether he had ever figured out where he was? I assumed someone might be listening. Wasn't sure it would be you. Please tell me his killing was a ruse."

"It was. Roscoe's alive and well. Well, alive anyway."

"And our other man?"

"If you knew where we were, Bia, Roscoe had to have already filled you in on the well-being of your other man."

"Yes, and knowing he was a firstborn, I figured as much. The only way he would still be alive would be if he had flipped on us."

"You understand more than I gave you credit for," Paul said. "Now we need to talk."

"You're wondering what's behind all this."

"Only if there's more than the message you left. Otherwise, you were pretty clear."

"Oh, Dr. Stepola."

Bia sounded so wounded, Paul didn't know what to say. He waited her out.

"I've never been a huge fan of your father-in-law, you know," she said finally.

"No, I didn't know. You could have fooled me."

"He has his gifts; don't get me wrong. But no. Scuttlebutt around the office is that he has pleaded for an audience with Dengler in Bern, but he tells us the chancellor has summoned him, ostensibly to congratulate him on his promotion to interim head of the NPO."

"Interim head? As of when?"

"Today. This morning. But that isn't the point."

"Yeah, I know. I got it. I've endured the man for years. So he's going to see Dengler when?"

"This Friday."

"How I'd love to be a bug on that wall."

"Wouldn't we all? When he gets back he wants the attack stuff in place. I'll keep you posted in the event he gets impatient. Here is one more tidbit though." She told Paul about Ranold's request for an identifying talisman.

"You need me to get you one?" Paul said.

"We've got 'em. Believe it or not, I still have Andy Pass's."

"Seriously?"

"He tossed it out during the chase, and some of my guys recovered it. It's been a sort of keepsake. I thought I might offer it to you or to his daughter or brother some day. It would mean a whole lot more to one of you."

"Do me a favor, would you?" Paul said.

"I guess we're trading some fairly dire favors already."

"I guess we are. Could you put an identifying mark on whatever talisman you give Decenti? Put a scratch on the back of it so I know when it turns up here."

"What makes you think it's going to turn up there?"

Paul was taken aback by the question. "Well, what do you think he's planning on doing with it? He isn't trying to get someone else past our guards?"

"I don't know. Maybe you're right. But we don't really need anyone else down there. We just need for no one to leak to you that the end is near so we can have everybody in one spot at the same time."

"I suppose you realize that if you're to be trusted, you're saving a lot of lives."

"It'll never make up—"

"Bia, tell me. Is it the loss of your son that's caused this flip?"

"That and a lot of other stuff. I have a brain, Paul. How can I come to any other decision?"

"You know what you need to do now, don't you?"

"Of course."

"You do?"

"I do. I got the e-mail like everybody else in the world."

"And . . . ?"

"I may call you for clarification."

"You know where to reach me."

# 27

**THIS WAS A STRANGE,** new experience for Paul. Keeping top-secret stuff even from his wife had never been an issue. He had not been tempted. She didn't need to know, wouldn't want to know, and there was nothing but downside to telling her anyway.

But now, now that they shared a common faith and were truly in love with each other as never before, well, this was different. And yet Paul had agreed with Jack and Greenie and the rest of the elders that no one else was to know the true situation yet.

There were too many elders to expect it to remain a true secret, and suspicion would grow when Greenie and his assignees started asking logistical questions. Who wouldn't wonder what was going on if they were asked what might be crucial to take along and what might be left behind in a pinch?

Paul found his first inclination was to pull Jae aside and start her thinking about their own details. How lightly could they pack? How would they keep it from the children? Was it possible the kids could embrace this as an adventure too, or were Paul and Jae asking too much?

But Paul resisted even mentioning it, and he was stunned at how difficult that was. He wasn't worried about Jae being offended later when it *would* come time to tell her. She had simply become his most trusted confidante nearly overnight, and it frustrated him to keep her out of this loop.

It became doubly difficult for him when she told him of her phone call to Aryana. Jae was just short of purple with rage. "Daddy allowed Aryana to have a memorial service for Berl, and I was not even informed."

"You couldn't have gone anyway, hon."

"I know that, Paul, but he was my brother! I would like to have known, to have been thinking about him when they were. And Daddy has my cell number. He could have called, could have tried to say the right things."

"Now you're dreaming."

She shot Paul a look, and he realized she didn't need his editorializing. She didn't want this fixed. She wanted to be heard.

"I'm sorry, babe," he said. "You're right. It's unconscionable that you were not at least told. Why didn't Aryana call?"

"Dad told her he had called and left me a message and that I called back to tell him, in no uncertain terms, that I no longer considered myself a Decenti and that he could go to you know where."

Paul shook his head. Just when he wondered whether Ranold could sink lower . . . "Then Aryana must have been surprised to hear from you."

"You're telling me! She was frigid when I called. I asked her what was wrong, and she asked what did I care. I said, 'Aryana, I love you. I care about you. I'm hurting for you because of your loss, which is also my loss.' That's when she told me the service had already taken place and what Daddy had said. Honestly, Paul, if he'd been in my presence, I can't say I wouldn't have tried to kill him. How awful is that?"

Pretty awful, but Paul was through trying to make it better. He might have tried to throttle the general himself, under the circumstances. This man was going to push too far someday, and Paul just might have to take him on. It wasn't a matter of physically fighting an old man. Ranold was trained in combat, and because of his size might have bested Paul in his prime. But not now. That wasn't the issue anyway. Paul had worked around his father-in-law for so long, it had become second nature. But now the man compounded his lie about Jae's breaking her own mother's neck with this invention about divorcing herself from the family.

On top of all that, Ranold was behind the directive for the destruction of the Columbia underground, intending to annihilate a thousand people. There were days, like this one, when Paul wished it was just him and Ranold, mano a mano, kill or be killed.

"What are they doing about remembering your mother?" he said.

"That's a whole 'nother story, as Connor would say. Do you know Daddy had Aryana convinced you had brainwashed me into killing Mom?"

"Can't say it surprises me. That's the story he's told the media."

Jae's hands were balled into fists. "To her credit, Aryana never bought that story. I told her exactly what happened, and she said she figured as much and that she had never seen me treat my mother with anything less than love and respect. She said, 'Now if someone had told me you strangled your father . . .'

I had to laugh. I mean, I was crying, but I had to chuckle, Paul. Aryana is new to our family and barely knows me, but she knew there was no way I killed my own mother.

"As for a service, Dad assured Aryana that Mom had always been quite clear that she didn't want a funeral of any kind."

"That doesn't sound like her."

"No, but it sure sounds like him, doesn't it? You know, in the middle of all this, Aryana says Dad's going to Bern on Friday."

"You don't say."

"Guess he's been invited by Chancellor Dengler to welcome him to his new job—director of NPO USSA."

"Interim."

Jae started. "You know this? Of course you do. You know everything. So it's just interim?"

"Of course. They don't hand out jobs like that to old men, even as undermanned as they are."

"Then does it make sense that Dengler would fly him all the way to Switzerland for a handshake and a picture?"

"You tell me, Jae. I mean, the NPO is important to the international government, and Dengler has to approve the move, but they really are separate bodies."

"So it's more likely this trip was Daddy's idea, and the rest is just his spin."

"Mrs. Decenti didn't raise no dummies. Hey, Jae, why don't we have our own memorial services for Berl and your mom? The kids need to know she's gone too, and they need some closure."

• • •

Straight was finally feeling his age. Ever since he'd been sober and alone, he had not had to admit that. And while sixty was younger than it used to be, the stress of living a double life wore on him. The news out of Michigan that the underground had been asked about making room for a thousand soon to be displaced from Washington left Straight depressed. Especially the reason . . . which he chose not to even think about.

He sensed, however, that Paul needed to hear from him, and so Straight called.

"What are we going to hear from the salt mines?" Stepola wanted to know. "Can they accommodate us?"

"Hard to say yet. It won't be easy. But most seem to like that idea above parceling you out here and there. You know I would take Jae and the kids."

"Yeah, that's all you need."

"I would, Paul."

"I know you would, brother. You know enough to stay away from our house, right? The Chicago bureau has it under surveillance, as if I'd be dumb enough to try to sneak in there for a few things."

"Figured as much."

"Straight, you sound terrible. You okay?"

"I guess. Tired. Old, you know."

"Yeah, you're old. I should be so old."

"Feelin' it, that's all."

"How's your inside guy working?"

"The surgeon? Looks legit. I told him I needed something from the deal. You know, as Abraham suggested. Within forty-eight hours we had traded info. I put him onto two government guys who are now sleeping longer and more soundly than they have in a long time. I mean, they're fine, just logy and slow to perk up. And he's put me onto a couple of terminal patients, both of which could provide great identities for you."

"Don't think I need 'em just now, Straight, but I'll let you know."

"I'm starting a database. It'll let your people know what's available. I've got a hunch you'll need these sooner than you think."

• • •

Wednesday evening, January 30, Paul and Jae sat the kids down after dinner and told them that not only was their uncle Berlitz dead, but so was their grandmother. When Paul saw their faces, he wondered whether he and Jae had made the right decision.

"How did she die?" Brie said. "Car wreck too?"

"Heart attack," Jae said quickly.

"What's that?" Connor said.

"Your heart stops beating. She was so upset when she heard her son had been killed, and with everything else that was going on— our having to come here, all that—it was just too much for her."

"Where is she now?" Connor said. "Will we see her again?"

"We won't see her here on earth again," Jae said, "because they have to bury her and we have to stay here for a while."

"Is she in heaven?" Brie said.

Paul felt Jae's glance. Despite their recent growth spurts, the kids had never seemed so young. Paul said, "You know, not everyone who dies goes to heaven."

"They do if they have Jesus in their hearts," Brie said. "Did Berl and Grandma?"

"We don't know," Jae said. "We hope so, don't we? I'm pretty sure Grandma did."

"What happened to Jesus when she had the heart attack?" Connor said. "I mean, if He was in there?"

Where was Paul supposed to go with that? Did he need to get into the fact that Jesus wasn't physically inside a person's body, let alone their heart?

"Because I've got Jesus in my heart," Connor said. "Brie does too."

"You do?" Jae said. "Tell us all about it."

# 28

**IT HAD COME TO RANOLD** in the middle of the night, two days before he was to fly to Bern. Normally he was a sound sleeper, but his eyes popped open at about two in the morning, and he realized deep in his gut that something was wrong with his most trusted inner circle.

He swung his feet off the bed and sat in the darkness, trying to put his finger on the pulse of the problem. Bia was tired and wounded, fine. She was his most trusted aide. But the five men. What was it with them? Eye contact? He watched for that instinctively. Had it been missing or even inconsistent? Two of the men were in their fifties, and he had known them for years. Two were in their early forties with the résumés younger men would kill for. But what about the younger one? The tall, thick man with the smooth face and short blond hair.

He wasn't so young, really. Dick Aikman had worked his

way up through the NPO and was in his late thirties, a family man. He had suffered no close losses in The Incident, but that was because he had only daughters. Ranold recalled some mention that he may have lost an aging uncle.

Why did Aikman stand out to Ranold? Just a hunch? He tried to replay their meetings in his mind. He could see through sycophants too, and while he enjoyed deference and respect—even admiration—as much as the next guy, he knew better than to surround himself with yes-men. They could make you feel good, but in the end, a leader needed the truth. Once he made a decision, then he wanted yes-men. But during the planning process, he needed hard, honest input.

And Ranold believed he was getting that. From all his people. But was he getting the eye contact and the body language to go along with it? Were team members catching each other's eyes during meetings and communicating with looks and other nonverbal cues? Could he have a turncoat, even at this level? More than one? A mutiny?

Ranold didn't want to make more of his discomfort than he should, but he was fast changing his mind about exempting his inner circle from signing the loyalty oath, and he wasn't beyond insisting on lie-detector tests. Perhaps he would have Bia administer those immediately to put his mind at ease before his trip.

Ranold padded to the kitchen for a snack and then left a phone message for Bia, instructing her to get the oaths signed and polygraphs administered by noon. He was finally able to sleep, and soundly.

But when he arrived at the office, Ranold was surprised to find Bia waiting in his outer office. It was clear she was piqued. He invited her in.

She began before she had even sat. "I have long appreciated your openness to the truth, hard as it may be and even when it initially contradicts your wishes. As you are fully aware, I have always been a loyal subordinate and have followed directives to the letter."

"That is why I chose you for this most crucial—"

"Forgive me, sir, but it's a mistake. The message you left was tagged with a wee-hours-of-the-night time frame, and I'd like you to consider that your idea was the result of something you ate or dreamed."

"I'm listening."

Bia pursed her lips. "You say you're listening, but you look as if you're not."

For all his confidence in his own ability to read physical cues, Ranold suddenly became aware that he was sitting rigidly, leaning back, arms folded uncomfortably over his barrel chest. "Well, you may be right about that," he said. "I'm listening but I'm not liking where this is going."

"Let me assure you, Chief, that as long as I am your subordinate, I will follow your orders, but I request your indulgence in at least attempting to talk you out of this."

"Fair enough."

"I fear this is going to reflect poorly on you and put serious questions in the minds of your most trusted people. You chose them from the entire organization for their skill and experience and because their loyalty is unquestioned. Am I right?"

He nodded.

"If you direct me to force them to sign the oath of loyalty—not unlike what we all signed when we were hired—"

"But which might have changed in their minds since then," he said.

"—and then follow it with polygraph tests, no one will ever again be able to say that their loyalty was unquestioned. Will they?"

Ranold pressed his lips together and shrugged. He could still overrule her, but he was beginning to see that she had him.

"It will put doubt in their minds about your view of them. . . ."

"Especially if they all pass."

"Of course. They're proven loyal and you look paranoid. How will they ever forget that you had a question? If you can't trust these people, you're in trouble."

Ranold was fast weighing his nagging doubt against Commander Balaam's counsel. What if they were both right? What if he had a bad apple but didn't pursue his suspicions because of how it would reflect on Ranold himself?

"I need a traveling companion and bodyguard for my trip. Perhaps I should take one of the men."

"Perhaps you should."

"Let's all meet at one today."

"Can do." She pulled from her pocket a shiny white stone. "You wanted this."

Ranold weighed it in his palm, then turned it over and over. It was cool to the touch and smooth, save for a one-inch scratch on one side. "What's the significance of this?" he said.

She shrugged. "Just normal wear, I think. Some have scratches; some don't."

"And this thing identifies an underground zealot."

"In Columbia it does," she said. "Different states use different talismans."

"That's right. Sunterra used that old Lincoln-head penny, didn't they?"

She nodded. "Do you mind if I ask—"

"What it's for? 'Course not. Just a souvenir. Don't you keep souvenirs?"

"I do actually," she said. "I have one of those myself."

Ranold chuckled. "You'd do well not to be caught with it."

"By whom?" she said, and he finally saw her smile. "I doubt I'm under surveillance."

"Yeah, that would be the day."

Later in the morning, when Ranold called to confirm something with Bia, her secretary told him she was in a meeting with Dick Aikman. "With just Aikman?" he said.

"I believe so, yes, sir."

"Have her call me immediately."

When Bia called a few minutes later he demanded to know what she was talking with Aikman about.

"Sir?"

"You heard me. I let you talk me out of my suspicions and you run to him right after. What am I supposed to think?"

Silence.

"Well?"

"Sir, I was informing him of the one o'clock meeting."

"Then why not the others?"

"I'm doing it one at a time, sir, as has been our protocol. We don't want the rest of the staff knowing about these meetings, so we eschew e-mail or phone. I invite them face-to-face. Now if you'd rather I change procedure—"

"No, no, it's all right. Forget I mentioned it."

Ranold was embarrassed, and that angered him. He knew he was being irrational and, yes, perhaps paranoid. But hadn't that aspect of his character put him in the position he found himself today?

At the one o'clock meeting, though breathing heavily and feeling logy after too big a lunch—delivered from a local ribs place—Ranold found himself studying the eyes and body language of his charges all the more. Was it only his imagination, or did Dick Aikman look both relieved and shaken? The man was pale, his light blue eyes darted, and he seemed to be watching Bia.

"Mr. Aikman, what sidearm do you carry?"

"Same as you, sir, being former military. Nine millimeter."

"How many rounds in your magazine?"

"Ten, sir."

"But it holds fifteen."

"Which has been known to stretch the spring."

"Excellent. You remain proficient with it?"

"I'm at the range at least once a week. Still shoot competitively."

"You win?" Ranold said.

"Occasionally, but as you know, Chuck Finney remains on the team."

"Enough said. He was beating *me* years ago."

Ranold asked Aikman if he would accompany him to Bern and serve as his bodyguard.

"I'm at your service, General. I shouldn't think you'd need a bodyguard at international headquarters, but—"

"You never know. Due to the reduction in workforce, we'll be flying commercial."

"I always fly commercial, sir," Aikman said, and everyone laughed.

# 29

**AT THEIR LEVELS OF SECURITY,** neither Ranold nor Dick Aikman had a problem boarding the flight to Bern with their sidearms in their checked luggage and their ammunition in their carry-ons.

"We're not expecting threats in Switzerland, are we, Chief?" Aikman said.

"Nah. But these days you can't be too careful. Now listen, if international-headquarters personnel make any move toward steering us through their metal detectors, it falls to you to shame them out of it."

"Sir?"

"You know how midlevel security people can become: nobodies trying to be somebodies. Running an executive of my level through security on our way to an audience with the chancellor himself would be an egregious breach of diplomatic protocol that would embarrass Dengler to no end. For his sake, you need to ensure it doesn't happen. I could squawk, of course, but again, such a tiff should be beneath me. Not beneath me *personally*, you understand. I don't lord my position over yours, for instance. But beneath the dignity of my office. Understand?"

"I think so," Aikman said, but Ranold wondered. He was pleased when the commander pursued clarification. "You just want me to take the lead with whomever appears to be in charge, should they try to—"

"Should they insult my office by attempting to process me—or you, for that matter—through security. A well-placed word of advice, hinting at the person's own dignity, should suffice. Just remind them who I am and that it certainly shouldn't be necessary."

"Which it shouldn't, if I recall international protocol correctly. We both have high enough clearance levels that we should not have to be processed. All we need do is—"

"Prove we are who we say we are," Ranold said. "I know."

About half an hour from touchdown in Bern, Ranold asked a flight attendant to invite Commander Aikman to join him in first class. "With this seat empty, General," she said, "we would have been happy to have accommodated him for the entire flight."

"Why, thank you. I should have thought of that." *Silly woman.*

When Aikman joined him, Ranold had more instructions. "You packed your nine millimeter in your smallest bag, right?"

"Per your instructions, yes, sir."

"Good. Before deplaning, slip your ammunition magazine from your carry-on so it's on your person. Obviously, keep it hidden, as we don't want to alarm any passengers. When we get our luggage, we will likely be aided by someone from the chancellor's staff who has been assigned to drive us to headquarters. Once we have everything, let's leave our carry-ons with the aide and each take our small piece of luggage into a stall in the washroom, where we can retrieve our sidearms and load them. You see the point?"

"To avoid loading our guns in public, yes, sir."

"Or even in front of the chancellor's aide. It's just tacky."

"Understood."

"I offered to rent a car, but Chancellor Dengler insisted on sending someone. He knows how to roll out the red carpet."

"So I've heard. It will be an honor to meet him. Thanks for the privilege."

"You've earned it, Commander. Now, I have a small gift for the chancellor that I would like you to keep in your pocket until I ask for it. It'll be a nice touch. It happens to be something I know he has heard of and will appreciate receiving."

Ranold pulled the stone talisman from his pocket and slipped it to Aikman. The younger man rubbed it between his palms. "These are unique, aren't they? Wonder where the zealots get them."

"Never thought of that," Ranold said. "They must have to manipulate them—by hand or machine—to make them so smooth and shiny, don't you think?"

"They must. And so you'll ask me for this during the meeting?"

"Probably near the end. I'll play it by ear. Just keep it where you can retrieve it quickly."

• • •

It was after midnight in the States when Paul was awakened by a tone in his tooth. He slid out of bed, hoping not to disturb Jae, and padded into the hall to take the call.

Bia Balaam brought him up to date on her machinations with his father-in-law. "He was getting suspicious, but not of me for some reason."

"You're good, Bia."

"I ought to be after all these years. I learned the game from him, after all. It's just that I've never used my abilities against him before."

"He's the best."

"Well, he was once. Let's hope—for both our sakes—that we're better than he is now."

"I hear you," Paul said. "What are you doing up, if I may ask?"

"Taking calls from various moles planted here and there."

"Can't they leave messages?"

"Sure, but I don't sleep anymore anyway. The truth is, Doctor, I've been studying this document of yours, the salvation thing."

"Yeah?"

"I don't get it. It looks too easy. I thought these people—you people—were all about being good and trying to be perfect and stay in God's good graces so He wouldn't punish you."

"What do the verses say?"

"Well, you've got this passage about being saved by grace through faith. . . ."

"And not by works so no one can boast that they did it for themselves."

"So how do you qualify? How do you earn this?"

"What do the verses say?"

She sighed. "Okay, I get the point. Whatever the verses say, you buy. This is your rule book, and what it says is what goes."

"Exactly."

She read it aloud, softly, as if to herself. "'For by grace you have been saved through faith, and that not of yourselves; it is the gift of God, not of works, lest anyone should boast.'"

Paul was tempted to explain, but he knew he couldn't do better than to let the words speak for themselves, especially for someone as bright as Bia Balaam.

He heard her breathing. Finally, "Like I said. Too easy."

"You want to earn it."

"Of course I do. I've earned everything else I've ever gotten in this life."

"And what will you do to accomplish that?"

"Change my life. Be nice. Play for the right team. Thwart the NPO, work against the USSA, expose the atheistic international government that brought this judgment on us."

"And that will make up for all the other stuff, the rest of your life? How old are you, Bia?"

"None of your business, but you know well I'm a good bit older than you."

"Ever killed anybody?"

"What do you think? I've lost count."

"How many good things will it take to make up for each of those?"

• • •

Felicia Thompson was sleepless in Deerfield as well.

Cletus was up and pacing. "I want to believe," he said, clearly in agony. "I just can't shake this anger."

"I'm angry too, sweetheart," she said. "Angry at myself for being so blind and stupid all these years. We brought this on ourselves. The whole world did."

"So you're not angry with God?"

"I don't know," Felicia said. "I suppose part of me is."

"Part of you. All of me is."

• • •

Ranold enjoyed the attention from not one but two aides from Dengler's office. They could have been twins, quiet men in their late twenties wearing matching woolen trench coats and black gloves.

Ranold had traveled light, checking a bag only to separate his weapon from his ammunition and packing a change of clothes only in case weather forced him to stay overnight. His return flight was scheduled for late that afternoon, and he had arrived at eight in the morning.

Ranold considered the aides appropriately quiet and attentive. The loading of the weapons went off without a hitch, and he let the men carry his and Aikman's bags—though Aikman looked as if he'd rather have carried his own. He'd learn.

Bern was an ironic name for a city that flirted with zero degrees Fahrenheit even with the morning sun riding high in a cloudless sky. Ranold felt it, strangely enough, in his ankles. And they didn't warm in the car, though it had been idling with the heater running.

"We're prepared to give you a talking tour along the way," the driver said.

Aikman perked up. "That would be—"

"No need," Ranold said. "Been here before. At least I have."

"Would Commander Aikman care to hear—"

"We need to talk," Ranold said, rolling his eyes at Aikman. That finally bought the aides' silence, and Ranold made up small talk he whispered to his subordinate.

The Americans were delivered to the entrance of international headquarters. They were greeted by a squat black woman in a gray-and-navy uniform that may have fit in her younger days but now made her look like a toddler in too-small hand-me-downs. She proved the epitome of the security chief Ranold had predicted.

"I bring you greetings and welcome from Chancellor Dengler," she said with a Caribbean lilt, "who eagerly awaits you. It will be my pleasure to usher you through security and up to his office."

Ranold nodded and Aikman thanked her. But when she led them to a metal detector, Ranold gave him the eye and the younger man went to work.

"Surely you won't require the head of NPO USSA to be processed," he said.

"Just routine," she said. "You can see we're in private here."

"Be that as it may," Aikman said, "you don't want to embarrass General Decenti. Surely Chancellor Dengler would not want you to circumvent diplomatic protocol."

"Look," she said, stopping to face Aikman, "my job is to process you through security. Now—"

"And my job is to protect the dignity of the office of the chief of NPO USSA, not to mention your reputation with your own boss."

"Do you have something to hide, sir?"

"Certainly not, and I'm offended at the suggestion." He looked to Ranold, who put his hand to his ear.

"Please get the chancellor's office on the phone for me," Aikman said, "so I can inform him of our levels of security clearance."

"Security clearance in the USSA does not necessarily translate to clearance—"

"Even at this level?" Aikman said, flashing his ID.

The woman had already pulled out her cell phone. She flipped it shut. "That's internationally sanctioned," she said. "Forgive me. My mistake."

As Aikman and the woman spoke, Ranold removed his gloves and put them in his suit-coat pockets.

"Gentlemen," she said at last, "follow me, please."

When the woman handed the men off to Dengler's staff upstairs, she started a little thank-you speech, to which Ranold turned his back. It sickened him to hear Aikman making nice and thanking her. They were introduced to a small cadre of staff, the last a tiny Japanese woman, the vice chancellor, Madame Hoshi Tamika. She bowed slightly, and Decenti returned the gesture, but just to make sure she knew her place, he shed his coat and handed it to her with a thank-you. She hesitated and Dengler's secretary quickly stepped forward and retrieved the coat.

Within a minute, Chancellor Dengler appeared in his doorway with an exhausted smile and an extended hand.

Ranold was stunned at the man's appearance. He had that height, that willowy, dignified air, but the power seemed to have seeped out of him. Dengler was grieving, of course, but who wasn't? He looked as if he hadn't slept in days, though he was typically nattily dressed, coiffed, and shaved.

After meeting Aikman, Dengler said, "Would he care to wait for you? You certainly don't need a bodyguard in here."

Ranold hesitated, his mind racing. This was Dengler's turf and protocol made this his call, but still . . .

"Oh, he's much more than my bodyguard, Chancellor. Commander Aikman is one of the highest-ranking members of my inner circle, and I'd appreciate it if he could sit in with us."

Dengler's face went slack and he exhaled loudly. "Certainly," he said flatly. He led the way into his massive, gleaming office. Ranold turned to signal Aikman to close the door behind them. That brought another look from Dengler, who busied himself drawing an extra chair next to Ranold's.

The general knew for sure he had pushed Dengler past his comfort level when the chancellor settled in behind his desk. He knew it was Dengler's practice to sit with guests, not across the desk from them. Ranold didn't want Aikman to know this meeting was not really about his being officially welcomed into his new role. So rather than wait for Dengler to ask what he could do for him, Ranold jumped in.

"I can't tell you how much it means to me to be invited here, Chancellor Dengler."

"Well, certainly, but I—"

"It's an honor to serve in this way, and while the NPO is a separate entity, of course all the service agencies—particularly the intelligence operations—function at the behest of the international government, and, thus, you. So thank you, sir. It's a pleasure."

Dengler folded his long-fingered hands in front of him on the leather desk blotter and leveled his gaze at Ranold. The general sat there, as if waiting for some formal words from the chancellor, but it quickly became clear that Dengler was on to him. And Ranold hated him for it.

"Is there something specific you wish to cover, General Decenti?" Dengler said, implying that otherwise he had a busy day.

"Yes, as a matter of fact there is, Chancellor. I need to know whether you are holding to your edict that the citizenry of the world must sign the oath of loyalty by March—"

"Pardon me for interrupting, General, but your jurisdiction does not extend past the borders of the United Seven States of America, does it?"

"Of course not. But naturally what applies to the world applies to my country."

"So, your question again?"

Ranold felt himself flush. "Are you or are you not going to hold citizens to their pledges of loyalty?"

"Have you heard otherwise?"

"I believe I heard equivocation from you."

The chancellor sat back and folded his arms. "In light of the worldwide mourning over—"

"It's a yes-or-no question, Mr. Chancellor."

Dengler lowered his voice and squinted. "You realize, I assume, General, to whom you are speaking."

"Yes, I do. To the man who is waffling on his own—"

"You're further aware, I assume, that I neither report to you nor am remotely obligated to answer to you."

Ranold scowled and shook his head, disgusted with Dengler beyond words.

Dengler glanced at Aikman. "Your boss is not a pleasant man, is he?"

Ranold swiveled to see if he could detect the slightest capitulation in Aikman, but to his credit the commander merely gazed at the chancellor, expressionless and silent.

Dengler pushed his chair back as if to rise, but Ranold stopped him. "Let me see if I can salvage this conversation, Chancellor Dengler, if you'll indulge me just another moment."

Dengler settled back. "I do have a pressing calendar."

"Surely you didn't expect this meeting to end so soon."

"Granted. But, please . . ."

"I wanted to show you our sidearms," Ranold said, pulling his left glove from his suit-coat pocket.

"Sir?"

"You didn't hear me, Chancellor?"

"Yes, but I . . . why would I—"

"Are you not fascinated with intelligence, espionage?" Ranold said, pulling on the glove.

"Of course, but—"

"Commander Aikman, show him your nine millimeter and

explain to him why we load them with fewer rounds than they are designed for."

It irritated Ranold that Aikman hesitated. As he feared, it gave Dengler time to protest.

"I'm intrigued by your area of expertise, but—"

"Show him your piece, Commander! Indulge me a moment, Chancellor."

Aikman unsnapped his holster and hefted the black gun slowly, apologetically, as if he could read Dengler's impatience and Decenti's impropriety. "We load the magazine with only ten bullets because the full complement has been known to threaten the integrity of the loading spring."

"It stretches it, in plain English," Ranold said, drawing his own weapon. For the first time he saw the alarm in Dengler's eyes. "See that we both carry the same model, being former military men."

"Yes, well, that's interesting. Now—"

Decenti reached for Aikman's gun with his left hand. The younger man hesitated, then offered it. Ranold fired two quick rounds at Dengler from Aikman's piece, one piercing his left eye and the other tearing through his cheekbone. The force of the shots drove Dengler's head back and made his chair roll. His remaining eye open, teeth bared, he was dead where he sat.

Aikman recoiled and tried to stand, but with his own gun Ranold shot him through the forehead, then through the heart as he fell.

The general heard screaming and footsteps, knowing no one would dare enter until they were sure the shooting had stopped. He dropped Aikman's weapon atop his body, slipped off his glove and pocketed it, then holstered his own gun.

"Help!" he yelled. "For the love of all things sacred! Help!"

# 30

**"HAVE YOU EVER PRAYED, BIA?"** Paul said.

"Not once, ever."

"Not even by accident, when your life was on the line, anything like that?"

"No. When I'm in trouble, I talk to me, to myself. I say, 'C'mon, Balaam, do what you need to do.' I never pray."

"But you believe in God now, right? Isn't that what you're telling me?"

"Of course."

"You can pray to Him."

"I gather that, but how? What does one say to God?"

"What do you want to say?"

"I'm getting another call, Paul. But quickly, I want to tell Him I'm sorry, and I want to tell Him I believe in Him."

"Then do it."

"I can't just talk to God like I'm talking to you, can I? I wouldn't know how to say it. Sorry, I've got to take this."

"Okay, call me back. But yes, talk to God the way you talk to me. He made you. He'll understand."

• • •

When Chancellor Dengler's executive assistant slowly opened the door, Ranold dropped to his knees with his hands to his head, swearing. "I had to shoot my own man! He murdered the chancellor! Call security!"

Before Ranold knew it, Dengler's office was swarming with security, aides, and onlookers. "I can't believe I could so misread my own man!" Ranold raged. "Who would have ever suspected? He was one of our top people!"

The woman who had tried to run them through security introduced herself and asked Ranold to step into an anteroom. "You know that man had a conniption when I tried to walk you two through the metal detector."

Ranold nodded miserably. "I didn't understand that myself, but it all makes sense now. I wasn't even thinking."

"Neither was I," she said. "I took him at face value. I thought he was just trying to make things easier for you."

"Me too, ma'am, and yet I, of all people, know the value of security. It would have been no bother even to be searched, and I often surrender my weapon in secure settings. I just didn't give it a thought this time."

"I understand. Now are you up to telling me what happened in there?"

"I'm pretty shaken, but I'll try."

"Take your time, sir."

"We were having a great meeting. I even offered to have Aikman wait for me, as he was just here to assist me and didn't really need to be involved. But the chancellor, kind and generous as always, insisted on inviting him in. Chancellor Dengler congratulated me on my promotion and said a few kind words about my background, that sort of thing. I commiserated with him because, as you may know, we both lost sons in The Incident."

"I'm sorry."

"Thank you. It's hard. My wife was murdered too, so—"

"Oh, my word!"

"I was doing okay. I'm surrounded by people who care, and they all thought this trip would be just the tonic for me. I must say, the chancellor was taking my mind off my troubles until Commander Aikman just stood, drew his weapon, and shot the man dead."

"Then what?"

"What could I do? Hardly thinking, because I have been trained a lifetime to react instinctively, I drew my own gun, and as Aikman turned toward me, I knew it was him or me, so I fired."

"I'm going to need your weapon, sir."

"Certainly."

"And I'm going to need you to remain in Bern a few days while we finish our investigation."

"Of course."

As they returned to the door of Dengler's office, an investigator emerged with three clear plastic bags. One contained Aikman's wallet and ID. One contained his nine millimeter. And the other contained the smooth, white stone.

"Oh no!" Ranold said. "Where did you get that?"

"Off the shooter's body, sir. Do you recognize it?"

"I sure do. It identifies him as a member of the Columbia Region zealot underground."

The investigator seemed to study Ranold. "Why would he be so stupid as to carry that if this shooting was premeditated? Did he know he'd never get out of here alive?"

Ranold shrugged. "How could we ever know?"

· · ·

Felicia wasn't reaching Cletus. Nothing she did or said seemed to make a difference. "What do you want?" she said. "Besides having Danny back."

"That's all I want," Cletus said. "Short of that, I don't know if I can go on."

"You're scaring me."

"I'm being honest, Felicia. If I can't be honest with you . . ."

"You can, but how do you think that makes me feel? I'm still here, you know, and I need you."

Cletus dropped into a kitchen chair and refused her offer of something to eat or drink. "I have nothing to give you, Fel. There's nothing left in me. I want what you've found. Of course I do. But even if I believe in God because I have no choice, I can't become friends with Him. Not while I'm hating Him."

· · ·

Twenty minutes later, while Paul was praying for Bia and hoping to get more sleep, she called him back. He hurried into the hallway.

"Paul," she said, "you're not going to believe this."

# 31

**THE ASSASSINATION** of International Government Chancellor Baldwin Dengler threw the world into yet more chaos. Paul didn't think it possible, the death of one man after the deaths of a billion seeming to knock the fragile door of society off its hinges.

The vice chancellor, the previously anonymous, almost invisible Asian woman few had ever heard of before, moved into the leadership role. But everyone knew that was temporary. She seemed powerless to stem the tide of unrest and protest around the world. The populace, even the hundreds of millions who still called themselves nonreligious, demanded that the government lift the ban on the practice of religion.

The tide was turning. Paul foresaw—for the first time in his life—the possibility that the oppressed, the distressed, the disenfranchised might actually emerge, squinting, from belowground and take their rightful place in society.

Three days later, Monday, February 4, Paul, Jack Pass, and Greenie Macintosh spent hours in a TV room, watching coverage of the investigation of the murder while planning the exodus from Washington to the Heartland salt mines. "With all the unrest," Greenie said, "maybe we won't be attacked after all."

Paul and Jack looked at each other, then at Greenie. "Dream on," Paul said. "How do you figure?"

"Your father-in-law is coming home a hero for killing the assassin. Is he going to want to spoil his image by massacring a thousand secret believers? The world is finally on our side, Paul."

Paul heard a tone in his mouth and turned away. "Stepola," he said.

"Bia. I need asylum." She sounded as he had never heard her. Terrified.

"Why? What?"

"Are you watching the news?"

Paul looked up to see a close-up of the talisman. "I'll call you back," he said.

"Don't wait. Decenti gets back this afternoon, and I have to have vanished by then."

"Why?"

"I gave him that talisman, Paul. I'm the only one who links Decenti to it. Aikman was not a turncoat. In fact he was anything but."

"What are you saying?"

"I gave that talisman to Decenti and it winds up on the body of the suspected assassin? This isn't brain surgery, Paul. The general wants me to pick him up at the airport. You think I'll ever see the light of day again? I'm coming your way. Can you leave my name at the entrance or something?"

"What good will it do you to come here? We're planning a mass exit."

"I don't know where else to go, Paul. Decenti's all but wearing a medal, and I'm nothing but a big target."

• • •

"Sorry to bother you at work, Mrs. Thompson," the principal at Lake-Cook Middle School said, "but we're worried about Cletus."

"Why? What do you mean?"

"Usually he or you call in if he's not going to be at work."

"He was getting ready when I left."

"He's not here, ma'am."

• • •

The men the Columbia undergrounders had taken to calling The Three Zealoteers stood watching the TV screen. "Aikman's not one of us," Greenie was saying. "I don't recognize him or even his name."

Paul filled in Greenie and Jack on what had to have gone down, also explaining his relationship with Bia Balaam.

Jack said, "Well, she's certainly welcome here if that's of any help and you're certain she's—"

"Whoa!" Greenie said. "Hey! Slow down. Is this not the very woman behind the attack on the Sunterra believers? You realize she and Decenti are pretty much solely responsible for bringing the drought upon Los Angeles?"

Paul held up a hand as the news showed the smooth white stone from all angles, and the scratch on the back was magnified. "There's the smoking gun," he said. "That positively links Decenti to the assassination."

"How did he pull this off?" Jack said. "Aikman's fingerprints are on his own gun. The only powder burns on Decenti's hand are from his own weapon. The talisman makes Aikman look like one of us. If this guy did it, he's awfully good."

"You have no idea."

The news channel ran a day-old tape of Ranold casting more aspersions on Aikman. "I'm ashamed of myself for not noticing signs earlier. Hindsight is twenty-twenty, of course, but only after the murder did it strike me that something might have been amiss. I couldn't put my finger on it, but Commander Aikman did seem distracted of late. I should have been able to read something in his demeanor, but I didn't."

The news also showed Mrs. Aikman with her two teenage daughters, all of them red-faced and puffy-eyed, glaring at the camera as they were being hustled away by NPO personnel. "There is no way my husband was zealot underground. He hated those people and spent his life trying to expose them."

"Of course," the anchorwoman said, "the rest of the family is under suspicion and will be detained and interrogated until USSA operatives are satisfied they were unaware of their husband's and father's clandestine activities."

An expert intoned that the only mystery remaining from the murder investigation was why Aikman suffered no powder burns. "On the other hand, with those types of weapons, that's possible and it happens, as apparently it did in this case."

• • •

"We are severely short staffed, as you know," Harriet Johns told an abjectly distressed Felicia Thompson. "We can't all be running home in the middle of the day because of marital problems."

"This is more than a marital problem, Chief Johns. Now I must go, and if it costs me my job, so be it."

"It's not going to cost you your job, Mrs. Thompson," Harriet said as Felicia rushed from her office. "But it will have to go on your record!"

As she sped up the Edens Expressway, Felicia called Cletus's friend and assistant coach. "Buddy, would you mind running to the house during your break and seeing if Cletus overslept? He hasn't been sleeping well and—"

"Way ahead of you, Felicia. I'm on my way there now."

"Thank you. Please call me."

But Buddy didn't call. And when she tried him again ten minutes later, he wasn't answering. She called the principal. "Have you heard from Buddy? He was running to my house to—"

"He'll see you there," the principal said.

• • •

"I'm not a big international espionage guy," Greenie said, "but I've sure got to argue on the side of caution. This woman is as highly placed at NPO as anybody but Decenti, and she knows where we are? You don't think allowing her in here is like letting the camel get his nose under the tent? For one thing, let's say she's legit, she's flipped, she can finger Decenti in the assassination. He figures she's hiding here, he's going to pull the trigger on us even faster."

• • •

Felicia pulled onto her street only to find her driveway and the front of her house crammed with two squad cars, an ambulance, what looked like an unmarked police car, and Buddy's station wagon. It was all she could do to steer to the curb and get her own car into park. She laid her forehead on the steering wheel and pounded her thighs with her fists. She looked up to a tap on her window.

Buddy opened the door and helped her out.

"Is he gone?" she said.

Buddy nodded, grim.

"How?"

"Car. Garage."

"Did he leave a note?"

He handed it to her.

*Fel, forgive me, please. I know you'll see this as my abandoning you, but you're strong. You'll make it. I tried everything, even praying. I'm sorry. I love you. Good-bye.*

*Clete*

# 32

**PAUL NEEDED A MINUTE.** In fact, he needed more than a minute. He needed Jae. He found her with Angela Pass Barger and the kids and stole her away. She followed him to their quarters, where he sat wearily and fought for composure. He knew she was seeing a new side of him, and while he didn't want to worry her, Paul felt at the end of himself.

"You know, I have to admit," he said, "I was thrilled with what God did in Los Angeles. He proved Himself, made me feel proud to be on the winning side, left me in awe of what He could do. I can't say I felt the same about the slaying of all the firstborns. I reacted the way most of the surviving victims did. Rocked. Devastated. That people are calling for an end to this religion-ban idiocy doesn't surprise me in light of all this. But look what's happening now."

He told Jae about the call from Felicia that had prompted

him to come and find her. "Look what's happening to my friends, my colleagues, even to new believers. Can I in good conscience point them to God when this is the kind of result they can expect?"

Jae reached to massage his shoulders. "Paul, think. We've all suffered. I'm a new believer too, remember. And look what happened to me. My brother. My mother. Our family living underground, afraid for our lives. Fugitives. My dad likely an assassin."

Paul nodded. "Felicia loses a son and now a husband, and she doesn't even have the comfort that he was a believer. And look at Bia. I wouldn't have given her a toddler's chance in the NBA to ever even consider God, and now she's trying to figure out how to talk with Him, to tell Him she's sorry, to come to Him. She's lost a son. And now she's running for her life. Where is this all going? Where will it end?"

Jae stood and moved to the window that looked out on the corridor. "I'm getting cabin fever," she said. "I know that sounds minor, compared with everything else, but—"

"Yeah, it does."

"But what do you always tell me, Paul? When I feel overwhelmed?"

"Something sage, I'm sure, babe. What? What do I tell you?"

"To refocus. To concentrate on some small thing I can handle. Isn't there something you can accomplish right now that will propel you, even a little? You can't save the world. You may not be able to save even this underground. You can't bring Cletus back. You can't change my dad. But maybe we *can* take in Bia Balaam. And maybe you can somehow come alongside Felicia."

Paul rubbed his eyes. "Bia is on her way. Let's hope she doesn't lead anyone else to us. As for Felicia, I'm at a loss. She's so brand-new, so fragile. What's going to keep her going?"

"Can she come here too?"

"Maybe, but that wouldn't be the best for us or for her."

"What are you saying, Paul?"

"Here she's even more vulnerable. Your dad gets back, finds that Bia has bolted, retaliates with an early strike, and here's where Felicia meets her end."

Paul realized what he had done even before Jae had flashed him a double take.

"An early strike? What are you saying?"

Had he deteriorated this quickly? That made twice that he had leaked something to Jae that he never would have before. He wished it said something about them, about their new relationship, their shared faith. But he had not planned to reveal first that he knew more about her father than she did—that he was only *interim* NPO chief and that he had been headed to Bern, and second, especially that he was planning a strike on the Columbia underground.

He set his teeth and shook his head.

"Paul. What? Are my children in danger even here?"

*Stupid, stupid, stupid!* It was all Paul could do to keep from smacking himself in the head. "We're all in danger," he said. "Yes, even here."

He saw Jae's eyes wander as he told her what was going on. He knew she had to be plotting how to get out of there, how to get the kids to safety. "Where can we go?" she said. "The salt mines?"

"Probably." He told her of the overwhelming logistics of a mass exodus of a thousand people. And then, for the first time in his life, Paul let his guard down and allowed himself to be vulnerable in front of his wife. He told Jae how worried he was that he—always lauded for his ability to maintain high-level confidentiality—had now told her two things he shouldn't have.

"I'm weak; I'm tired. All these people counting on me, and I don't feel half the man I was just weeks ago. I should be an asset here with my contacts and background and training. But I feel like a bumbler, like I'm going to mess it up for everyone. Rather than helping, I could be the cause of a disaster, a massacre."

Jae seemed to study him. She reached as if to touch him, then held back. "Focus, Paul. Get your mind off yourself and onto these women. Think of it. First me, then my mother, then Felicia, then Bia. They've all come to faith or are getting there. That's something. I mean, God did it, but you were involved."

"That's why I feel I owe something to both Felicia and Bia."

"You say Bia's on her way. We'll deal with her when she gets here. What can we do for Felicia?"

Paul shook his head. "She needs someone to talk to, and not by phone."

"What are we? Blind? Short of being there ourselves, we have the next best thing. Maybe better."

"What?" Paul said. "Who?"

"Straight."

•  •  •

Ranold B. Decenti's triumphal return to Washington was all over the news. Governor Haywood Hale of Columbia met him at the airport and presented him with a medal of honor for bravery in the midst of a deadly crisis.

Decenti took to the microphones and, with eyes cast down and his most humble look effected, expressed his deep sorrow over the loss of "our beloved world leader. Baldwin Dengler was a man of great vision, courage, and insight, and we are unlikely to see his ilk again in our lifetime."

• • •

Paul himself met Bia Balaam at one of the secret entrances to the underground but didn't even let her put her bag down. "We have no one else inside NPO USSA," he said.

"Good grief, Stepola, what are you saying? You want me to go back?"

"How good are you?"

"One of the best, but I'm not volunteering for martyrdom."

"We need to concoct a reason you stood up Ranold at the airport, and you need to convince him you're still a loyal soldier. We have to know his plans for the attack. It's four days from now, and we're out of options."

Bia closed her eyes and ran a hand through her silver hair. Paul could sense the wheels turning. "I knew the governor was meeting him," she said, "so I did some reconnaissance work with my underground contacts, taking over Aikman's role in planning the attack."

"Good, good."

"But, Paul, how do I get around Decenti's knowledge that I'm the only one who can tie him to the talisman?"

"Go right at him. Tell him you know what he did and that you consider it a stroke of genius. He knew something about Aikman that you had missed, so assassinating a weakling like Dengler and pinning it on Aikman—even implicating him as an underground zealot—merely solidifies him as your hero."

"Gag me."

"You can pull this off, Bia."

"I know."

• • •

Watching her husband's sheeted body loaded into an ambulance-cum-hearse was the hardest thing Felicia Thompson had ever endured. Hearing that her own son had died in The Incident had nearly destroyed her, yet to her knowledge he had not suffered. But Cletus. Cletus.

She considered riding with him to the overtaxed morgue, but there would be nothing more to do there. She had already identified him, and he would be slabbed in a human-sized re-frigerated file cabinet for who knew how long.

When the authorities finally pulled away, she thanked Buddy and assured him she would be all right, then took a con-dolence call from the principal. Still outside in the cold, dread-ing going inside the empty, echoing house, Felicia called Harriet Johns.

"I'm very sorry to hear that, Felicia," Chief Johns said, sounding more matter-of-fact than sympathetic. "Take a few days, if you must, and keep me posted about your return."

Felicia finally trudged inside and sat at the dining-room ta-ble, still bundled in her coat. She lowered her head and sobbed. She tried to pray, intending to blame this on God, to challenge Him, to question Him, but she didn't have the wherewithal. And besides, it didn't ring true. This wasn't God's fault. Cletus had made this decision. What worried Felicia most was that she could barely fault him for it. Oh, she was angry with Cletus. In fact, that wasn't a strong enough word for what she felt about what he had done. How dare he leave her alone now?

Her cell phone chirped, and she saw the call was from an un-known number in Chicago. What now?

• • •

Was Bia on to him? That was all Ranold B. Decenti wanted to know. Of course she was. Otherwise why would she have stranded him at the airport and made no attempt to contact him? He'd had to mention to Hale that he could use a ride to the office. "My people are all on assignment, as you can imagine. A significant underground strike is pending."

Hale asked his driver to slide shut the window separating the front seat from him and Decenti. "Forgive me, General, but are you mad? I mean, do your planning, but surely you're not going to attack an underground during the current popular climate."

Ranold wouldn't have minded putting a couple of rounds into Hale right then. "The current climate reeks of cowardice, Governor. Someone needs to step up. Are we going to turn tail and run because we lost a battle? It's time to win one."

Decenti's phone rang and he saw it was Commander Balaam. "Where are you?" he began.

"On my way to meet you at your office, sir. Terribly sorry about the disconnect, but I knew the governor was coming to greet you and hoped you might be able to arrange transport through him."

"Well, I did, but I should have heard from you."

"My apologies again, Chief, but I was in the middle of some clandestine arrangements, trying to stay on pace for the operation at the end of this week, in light of the loss of our colleague. By the way, that talisman plant was a stroke of genius. You never cease to amaze me."

Decenti cleared his throat. "Yes, well . . . then, it will be good to reconnect in a few minutes."

"You can't talk, I take it?"

"That's correct, Commander."

"Well, let me just say again, I was impressed anew. Not wholly surprised, because you have a long history of these kinds of things. Forgive me for gushing, but it's an honor to serve you, sir."

# 33

**"HE IS RISEN."**

Felicia was taken aback. Who was this on the phone?

"He is risen indeed," she said, her throat constricted.

A mature male voice introduced himself as a confidant of Paul Stepola's. "He asked that I see if I can be of any assistance during your time of grief. I'm so sorry to hear of your loss."

"Thank you. Needless to say, I will need to confirm—"

"With Paul, certainly. I understand. If I don't hear back from you, I'll assume he has vouched for me and that you are willing to meet with me. Do you know Ray Radigan's?"

"In Kenosha? Of course. It's just up the road. But I doubt I'll feel like eating."

"Well, I will. And it's a good place to meet and talk. If I don't hear back from you, I'll meet you there at six."

"How will I know you?"

"I will know you. Paul has described you. Let's just say both of us will be easy to recognize."

• • •

Bia Balaam had a snub-nosed .38-caliber pistol in a holster tucked into her belt under her blazer at the small of her back. She didn't expect that Ranold Decenti would kill her in his own office, but look what he had done to Baldwin Dengler. She simply wanted to be prepared, and she would certainly be on the lookout for any suggestion of meeting elsewhere alone.

To her utter amazement, when Decenti's secretary ushered her in, Ranold actually came from behind his desk and opened his arms to embrace her. She didn't recall his ever so much as touching her hand in all the years she had known him. She prayed his hands wouldn't stray to her waist, where he would be sure to notice her weapon.

Behind the closed door, he smiled as he sat at his desk. "So you figured it out, eh?" he said.

"As soon as I saw that talisman, it all came together. You are unbelievable."

"You're the only one who knows, Commander."

"That was my second thought. I sat there shaking my head at your cleverness; then I felt overwhelmed with pride and gratitude that you would entrust me that way. I'm honored to be your confidante, sir."

Unless he really was as good as she was implying, Bia believed she was getting to him. His ego knew no bounds, and while she wanted to rein herself in and not make him suspicious by too much flattery, he had enough self-love to go around.

"So," he said, still apparently trying to keep from grinning, "now that we have the pansy out of the way, where are we on the attack?"

Bia sat forward to keep the gun from gouging her back.

"Everything's come together well, despite the loss of the project leader."

"No real loss or I wouldn't have done it."

"I assume you knew things about Aikman that I didn't," she said.

"Of course, but I might have wished you would have given more credence to my suspicions. I knew something was up with him."

"Granted." If Ranold could feign remorse over misreading his own man, so could she. "I totally missed it, sir. It's made me reconfirm my commitment to try to be as meticulously observant as you."

"Well, don't beat yourself up over it. When you get to be my age, few things slip past you."

"I can only hope," she said. "I was wondering though, sir, how you're feeling now about the target date of the attack."

"Why?"

"The current climate of public opinion being what it is."

"You sound like you've been talking with Hale."

Bia shook her head and snorted. "Hardly. I've met the man once or twice to shake his hand."

"Well, he said the same thing. But tell me, how would a successful operation like this negatively affect the so-called current climate? Might we not turn the tide of public opinion back our way?"

"That's what I'm wondering. Curious whether even another week might make a difference." She handed him an envelope thick and heavy enough to contain a full notebook. "Bedtime reading," she said.

• • •

Felicia Thompson found herself amazed at how the prospect of a meeting with a secret believer could actually allow her to burrow her grief deep inside, even if only temporarily. When she allowed herself to think of the horror of how the love of her life had left her, she understood for the first time what depression was all about.

The future looked bleak, dark. Felicia couldn't imagine having the motivation to rise from her bed even once, let alone every morning for the rest of her life. All she had left was Paul and what she might do for him and her new brothers and sisters in the underground. And there was Hector Hernandez, whom she hardly knew. And Trudy Nabertowitz.

But to go back to work, back to the office where she was now a mole and her exposure meant capital punishment? What was the point anymore?

Radigan's, an ancient steak place just north of the Illinois-Wisconsin border, was busier than she expected. But when she spotted the tall, graying black man who stood as she entered the small foyer, she felt suddenly safe.

She noticed his slight limp as he used the handrail when they mounted the steps. As he had hinted, they were the only African-Americans in the place. By the time they reached their table, he had gushed his life story in a gravelly baritone. College prof, lost his whole family—and his foot—in a crash he caused while driving drunk. Lost his job. Got sober, came to Christ, now served the underground and worked as a greeter and encourager at PSL Hospital.

Felicia told him how she had found God after The Incident.

"Sad," he said, "that it took such devastation."

"Tell me about it," she said.

Straight ordered a generous meal. Felicia picked at a salad. Between bites, the big man spoke softly. "I know the timing is awful, Mrs. Thompson," he said. "And I can only imagine what you're going through. I do understand grief. I understand shame. And believe me, I understand what the future looks like when your world has collapsed. But as your brother in Christ, I am going to make a suggestion and challenge you to do the hardest thing you have ever done in your life."

• • •

Was it possible, Ranold wondered that evening at home, that he would not have to eliminate Bia Balaam? That would be nice, actually. Oh, he could do it. If he could take out the international chancellor and walk, he could certainly find a way to accomplish the same with another of his own people.

Ranold had considered her collateral damage right up until she recognized his brilliance. He was above being swayed by flattery; he really believed that. But Bia had always been one of his most trusted and best operatives. He put her in the same category as Paul.

Paul. Talk about a disappointment. And Jae standing right with him. Ranold had always had such high hopes for her. Bright girl. Or so he thought. Now she was little more than a female Berlitz, apparently a dim bulb under all that pretty hair.

Ranold changed into his robe and stretched out on his back on the bed, tearing open the package from Bia. She had really done her homework. Much of it was a rehash of Aikman's early work, but the plan had now been finalized, with implementation steps and all the rest.

It called for cooperation with the army, of course. No problem, with Ranold's history there. The documents showed the location of the Columbia underground—much bigger than Ranold expected—and reported on the population. He knew that included his son-in-law, which made him want to spit or rub his hands together; he didn't know which. It also included his daughter and grandchildren.

He looked away from the cold, bureaucratic pages and stared at the ceiling, remembering Jae's birth. How proud he was. What a wonderful child she had been. And the grandchildren. Should he be feeling something beyond nostalgia? Could he really arrange for air-to-underground missiles that would annihilate this place and all these people, even with his own blood down there?

He'd never gone soft before, and he wasn't about to now. He'd lost nearly an entire army once in a tsunami in the Hawaiian Islands. Life and death were the price of war. And despite the namby-pamby weaklings—one of whom had sat in the chancellor's chair and the other who now occupied the West Wing—war was still what this was all about.

War against God? Dare he admit it? Okay, fine, sure. So God did exist. This was a battle of wills, of ideologies. Ranold had never faced an enemy that gave him pause, let alone that produced in him fear or even hesitation. No question, this was his most formidable foe ever. That would make victory that much sweeter.

Ranold B. Decenti had tangled with the world chancellor and won. Now he was going to face God Himself and let the chips fall where they may.

• • •

Felicia sat shaking her head.

"Too much?" Straight said. "Too soon?"

"Too something," she said. "Too much to imagine, for one thing. I'm to stay inside, keep working the NPO to Paul's advantage?"

"Not just Paul's. The entire underground. We need you there. You're crucial. Besides, what else are you going to do? You sit in that empty house all day every day and you're going to be no good to anyone. Stay in the game and you could make a life-and-death difference to believers all over the world."

# 34

**TWO WEEKS TO THE DAY** after Bia Balaam lost her only son in The Incident, she sat on the couch in the living room of her Georgetown duplex, staring at the blank TV screen and wondering how she was supposed to feel.

She'd never had to consider it before, but now she wondered, *When does the sharp pain of grief give way to the dull ache of mourning?* Despite having to stay focused on kissing up to Ranold B. Decenti and searching her own soul for where she now stood on the subject of God and, yes, her own salvation, the deep bite of her loss was constantly with her.

At times Bia nearly collapsed under it. Did time really heal *all* wounds? This one had come so quickly and cut so deep that it seemed all she could do was try to survive until its piercing abated. Waiting and suffering gave her a new perspective on time. Surely she had never before considered two weeks a long period; she had recovered from minor surgeries in that time.

If this had happened to someone else, no, Bia would not have expected them to snap back within fourteen days, but she likely would have thought they would start to see light on the horizon.

No such luck for her. It still felt as if Bia's son had been there one instant and was gone the next. If someone had told her it had happened the day before, she would have wondered, *That long ago?* She finally understood the cliché that time can seem to stand still.

*Oh, God,* she found herself praying silently, *let me up, let me breathe, let me know this is something that one day I will be able to live with.* That was all she wanted. Not instant relief, though that would have been nice, but just to know that some passage of time would make a difference. That her pain had not abated an iota in fourteen days scared her. For how many more days, weeks, months could she bear such an aching hollowness in her heart? She could not remember crying since elementary school, and she didn't cry now. What was wrong with her?

Strangely, part of Bia didn't want the injury to lessen, for wouldn't that be an insult to her son? She would never forget him, never get used to his absence, and it would never become okay. She just had to know that life would be worth living again one day.

She had prayed. That gave her pause. Paul Stepola had urged her to try to talk to God the way she talked to him. That seemed bizarre. What little exposure she had to ancient religious rites made them all seem formal, rigid, ceremonial. She knew international protocol. Could she really chat with the God of the universe when she wouldn't dare speak informally to a head of state or even a midlevel bureaucrat?

And yet she just had. Bia had acknowledged that God had the power to give her some relief or at least some knowledge. She was long past wondering if He existed. The very idea of atheism seemed silly now, and she wondered if her boss was the only man left on the planet who lived in such denial.

When first confronted with the idea of a God who was there and active and, apparently, vengeful and out of patience, Bia had been overwhelmed with fear. In an instant, she had become a believer. It was like discovering that the great face and voice in the flames of *The Wizard of Oz* turned out not to be a ruse but real and great and powerful and terrible.

But to now consider Paul Stepola's notes on how to connect with that fearsome Being left her confused and restless. It was a short trip from where she was to admitting that she was nothing compared to a cosmic force like Him. But did that make her a sinner, one separated from Him, one who needed to acknowledge her evil and receive the gift of a bridge to God?

Bia could hardly fathom it. And yet, in some disconcerting way, she felt pursued. Was she feeling pressure from Paul or from God Himself? Was fear a legitimate reason to humble herself? Paul's notes seemed to point to a God of love and forgiveness and reconciliation, and yet she simply feared Him. "God, show me," she whispered.

• • •

Ranold Decenti had an appointment with the General of the Army, Chester "C.C." Creighton, whom he had known since World War III. Though they had had little contact during the last decade, C.C. had been one who showed true compassion for Ranold when he lost most of the charges under his command to the tsunami that obliterated the Hawaiian Islands more than thirty years ago. "You don't need me telling you,

Dece, that there was no way for you to foresee or forestall such an eventuality."

That hadn't made Decenti feel any better, but he never forgot the effort.

Legend had it that General Creighton, even in his late sixties, still worked out every day and weighed virtually the same as he had three decades before. Ranold decided C.C. would be impressed if he showed up in his army uniform, displaying the same achievement.

Ranold was shocked to discover that he had been lying to himself for years. The mirror did not lie. Neither did the old uniform. He had told himself that just because he had gone up a couple of suit sizes, that was merely a sign of age and that—while he would not be as comfortable—he could still squeeze into his old uniform.

Wrong. He could barely yank the trousers up over his thighs, and there was no room for his expanded derriere. The clasps at the front were nearly three inches apart, even when he bent and twisted and tugged. The jacket was binding at his shoulders and chest, and there was no buttoning that either.

Ranold was angry at himself as he returned the uniform to its hangers and entombed it again in the thick, transparent plastic. He would just have to wear his finest suit.

Half an hour later his driver dropped him at the steps of army headquarters, an ornate, grand building that had largely been ignored and forgotten since the end of the war, when the attempted eradication of religion had succeeded in eliminating conflict. The U.S. military was a shell of its former self and had been engaged in merely minor skirmishes in third-world countries and attacks on its own citizens—the zealot underground. There had not occurred what anyone could refer to as a real war in all that time.

Ironically, weapons of any kind were verboten at army headquarters—no exceptions. Ranold had known enough to leave
his nine millimeter at home, though it would have been fun to
reminisce with C.C. about their training with it.

Ranold liked the décor and quaint formality of the headquarters even more than the ostentation and opulence at the international government building in Bern. While many
considered the vastly deflated U.S. Army a relic, it was Ranold's
proud heritage, and he loved every inch of this facility.

Chester Creighton and Ranold Decenti were a study in con-
trasts. In fact, Ranold took pride in that if the uninitiated were to
see them side by side, nine of ten would guess Ranold as General
of the Army. Creighton was short and muscled to Ranold's tall
and broad beefiness. They saluted each other and shook hands
warmly.

General Creighton ushered him into his office, and again,
Ranold preferred it over the chancellor's in Bern. Here
everything seemed to be purposeful, functional, with little
thought to glitz and glamour. It was pristine, and everything
was centered. Every plaque and photograph gracing the walls
appeared to have been secured so as not to angle out of square,
ever.

C.C. pointed to a chair at a side table and sat directly across
from Ranold. A strange emotion and temptation came over the
visitor. Ranold found himself having to bite his tongue to keep
from saying something cheeky about C.C.'s holding down the
top job in an organization that had become a sham. There was
no war. Why did anyone need an army?

And yet Ranold believed that very issue would excite an old
warhorse like C.C. After they had teased each other and brought
each other up to date on their families, Creighton, as was his nature, cut to the chase. "So you want to drop a bomb on the

Columbia zealot underground. You sure it's not revenge over the loss of half your family?"

That had not even crossed Ranold's mind, and it must have showed.

"You must know that I am aware who's down there, Dece," Creighton said. "What're you going to do, get your daughter and her family out somehow?"

Decenti looked away. "Not on your life," he said. "They've chosen sides. They're the enemy."

Creighton seemed to freeze. His stare made Ranold uncomfortable. He looked at his old friend, then looked away again.

"What?" Ranold said.

"You take me for a nincompoop, Dece? This army may not be what you remember, but don't even suggest that we're not still one of the finest intelligence agencies in the world, and that includes your shop."

What was C.C. saying? Was he casting aspersion on the NPO? Ranold wanted to give him the benefit of the doubt. "I didn't intend to insult—"

"Well, you did, Dece! You implied that the General of the Army wouldn't know that you have two grandkids under the age of ten in that underground."

"What do you mean? I didn't say that."

Creighton cocked his head. "You've become an old fool."

"What're you, serious?" Decenti said.

"First you deny any revenge motive when your son and your wife were lost two weeks ago, and—"

"You must know my own daughter murdered my wife."

"I'd heard that, but frankly I find it hard to believe. Her autopsy showed no neck trauma consistent with—"

"Autopsy?" Ranold thundered. "There was no autopsy! I would have had to have been consulted."

"Dece! It's me you're talking to. You dump the body in a mass morgue, then—"

"They were *all* mass morgues, C.C.!"

"—then you tell them there'll be no service, to just cremate her and let you know when it happens."

"Where are you getting all this?"

Creighton shook his head. "You're coming off pretty naive for a man in your position, Dece. You think I'm not as well-placed in this government as you are? You went public with this charge that your son-in-law brainwashed your daughter into murdering your wife. Did you think that would go unchallenged or at least not investigated?"

Ranold had never had a fleeing instinct in his life. But this was going badly. His old friend—his old, trusted friend, the man he assumed would thrill at the chance to launch a real military attack on an enemy—had somehow turned on him.

"I was doubted?" Ranold said. "Promoted to head of the NPO while being invest—"

"Interim head," Creighton said with a disdain so obvious that Ranold wanted to stand and accuse him of holding down a paper-tiger job. "C'mon, old buddy. Your wife exhibited cranial trauma consistent with a blow to the head or striking something while falling, but a heart attack killed her."

"You're telling me I didn't walk in on my own daughter strangling her mother to death, arms around her throat and thrashing her side to side, bashing her head in the process?"

"I'm not telling you anything but what the autopsy showed."

"An illegal autopsy! An autopsy not sanctioned by the next of kin let alone even revealed to the next of kin."

"Cool your jets, Dece. The only thing that surprised me was that there was enough personnel to get to it with all the other deaths. But you know an autopsy is standard operating procedure in a suspected homicide. Did it never strike you odd that your daughter was not immediately put on a wanted list?"

"My son-in-law was."

"Dr. Paul Stepola disappeared after The Incident, and from what we can determine from your own testimony, he's a first-born son still alive. That pretty much establishes his status."

"Turncoat."

"Granted. But there's no evidence his wife is also—"

"She's with him, C.C.!"

"And you're so bound and determined to win this family squabble that you're willing to bomb your own grandchildren?"

# 35

**"WE'RE LESS THAN SEVENTY-TWO HOURS** from D-day," Greenie Macintosh said, "and I say it's time to get everybody on board."

That was hard for Paul to argue with, but he looked to Jack Pass, frankly hoping for some reason to delay. "What if we spark a panic?" he said.

"C'mon, Paul," Jack said. "The time has come. I can't believe the NPO would go through with this, given how the public is responding to The Incident. But if your father-in-law starts thinking he's in the minority, might he even move ahead of schedule?"

Paul nodded. "Unfortunately, I do know how the old man thinks. I believe he sees himself as the last defender of the atheistic regime."

"Oh, he's not alone," Greenie said. "I agree most people are turning, but there are still angry pockets here and there in Decenti's camp."

"He's got access to vigilantes, mercenaries, and revolutionaries," Paul said. "For one thing, he's prosecuted them in the past, but he always spoke glowingly of them as patriots. I never understood that. I fear the general if he comes to the realization that his own government is loath to eradicate us zealots."

Greenie was pacing. "We've got to quit talking and start acting. We can do this logistically. It won't be easy, but the salt miners are expecting us, we have transportation in place, and it's a matter of starting to move out. We don't intend to draw attention to ourselves by doing it all at once, so we ought to start moving by tonight."

"Who goes first?" Paul said.

He caught Greenie and Jack glancing at each other.

"What?"

"Seniority," Jack said. "I know this affects you and your family, Paul, but—"

"Hey, that's fair," Paul said. "The ones who were here first ought to leave first, and vice versa. I understand."

"Leadership would stay to the end anyway," Jack said. "Someone has to turn out the lights."

•   •   •

"My grandchildren are not your concern, C.C.," Ranold said.

"They are if they're not your concern, Ranold. They're innocent civilians, and I for one want nothing to do with attacking a nonmilitary site."

"What're you saying, C.C.? You're not going to give me the firepower I need, after all the planning we've done? You can see the tide of public opinion turning on this. If we don't strike on schedule, we'll lose all kinds of momentum and popular support."

"You have no public support, Dece. Don't you read the papers? watch the news?"

"Don't insult me."

"I could say the same. You sit here and tell me you have popular support for retaliating against The Incident by wiping out a thousand or more underground zealots? You'll be the most hated man in America."

"I'll be a hero!"

It was out before Decenti could take it back. The fact was, he really believed it. Sure, people were scared. They didn't want to further agitate the monster they had awakened. But if he won this small battle, they'd have to see that God couldn't or didn't choose to control everything.

Ranold could tell he had alarmed C.C. even more. He had to salvage this meeting. "C.C., listen, let's grab a jet to Georgia and talk to the Third—"

"Talk to Central Command? About what?"

"Say I concede you're right and that this is a nonwar situation. Fort McPherson can provide land forces."

"What for?"

"To follow up the air attack. Make sure we round up survivors."

Chester Creighton stood and leaned on the table. "Old buddy, let me tell you something. You have lost your mind. For one thing, if I was crazy enough to give you the firepower you're asking for, there would not only be no survivors, but there would also probably be further widespread casualties. Is that what you want? Because I want none of it."

"You're as yellow as Dengler was."

Creighton straightened and stomped to his desk, dropping into his chair. "Those are fighting words, Ranold, and you know better. You would call the General of the Army a coward? I ought to have you written up."

Ranold sat back and folded his arms. "You have no jurisdiction over me."

"We both report to the governor, and he would bring charges."

"He's no better than Dengler was."

"What's your beef with Dengler, Ranold? I saw you on the news praising him to high heaven."

"What else was I going to do?"

"Did you go over there to assassinate him, Dece?"

"What? No! But I'll admit it didn't break my heart. What's come over you, C.C.? Where's the soldier I knew? The zealot underground is the enemy and has been for years. We take one setback and now you want to go soft on 'em?"

"Setback? That's like saying Hiroshima and Nagasaki suffered setbacks a hundred years ago."

"So that's it," Ranold said, moving to a chair across from Creighton. "You want to do like the Japanese did. You want to unconditionally surrender. Shall we do it on a battleship and ask God to attend?"

Creighton looked at his watch. "Your time is up, Dece."

"No it isn't, C.C. Now come on. Let's go to Space and Missile Defense. It's just a short drive."

"You don't get it, Ranold. I don't want you to have that kind of access or support."

"You don't believe the lawbreakers are the enemy."

"They may be, but who knows if or when that might change, based on public opinion?"

"Since when have we allowed public opinion to shape the law?"

"Since we were founded as a democratic republic, Dece."

Decenti sighed and looked away. "You're not going to let me even visit Materiel Command, are you?"

"I might."

"You might?"

"If you would change your approach. These are likely un-armed people—"

"Now see, that's where you're wrong, C.C. They found two of our plants and murdered them, one of them while he was reporting in."

"Why do you lie to me, Dece?"

Ranold squinted at him. "What are you talking about?"

"You don't realize yet that I know as much as you do? If you believe both your men were killed in there, you're out of touch. Your younger man—the one playing the son—died in The Incident because he was a firstborn. But don't be so sure your main mole is gone."

Ranold fought for composure. If there was an ounce of truth to what C.C. was saying, that was strike two against Bia Balaam. And there was no strike three in this game. She told him Roscoe Wipers was dead, and if it wasn't true, she had to go.

The question, of course, if she had misled him on that, was whether she had already incriminated him by his connection to the talisman found on Dick Aikman.

"Now hear me," Creighton was saying. "If you're looking for military support for a standard roundup of dissidents, I could get behind that."

"What?"

"The Columbia chapter of the underground zealots clearly consists of lawbreakers, based on how the law reads now. Why not take your intelligence, if you have the location pinpointed, and commandeer the entrances? Inform the people inside that they are surrounded and without recourse and that if they surrender peaceably, no one will be harmed?"

"That's disgusting, C.C., and you know it. We retaliate for a billion dead men by arresting a thousand men, women, and children?"

"Better to slaughter them?"

"Yes!"

C.C. shook his head and looked sad. "The suppression of the practice of religion was intended to eradicate war. What you're suggesting *is* a holy war. If you really believe it's better to slaughter these people than arrest and try them, Dece, you're guilty of egregious incompetence to lead."

# 36

**BIA BALAAM HAD NEVER BEEN** the kind of a woman who took a break at work. She held nothing against people who did. It simply wasn't her way. And yet today she was so distracted she needed time to herself. Where did one go for that? There weren't many private nooks or crannies at NPO headquarters.

She grabbed her leather portfolio containing the Stepola notes and asked her secretary where she went when she just wanted to be alone.

The young woman flushed and spoke softly. "That's easy. My car."

"I don't want to leave the premises. I just want—"

"No, I never leave either, ma'am. I just go sit in my car."

"In the parking garage?"

It was a concept.

Bia's car sat in the shadows, backed against the wall. Would she feel conspicuous? No one was around, and unless someone parked next to her, they would not likely see her. Sitting there in the silent darkness was like having a delicious secret. Even more intriguing was the idea of talking to God in a concrete structure that interfered with cell-phone communications. It would be a true test.

Paul made a lot of sense. If God was who He was supposed to be, she ought to be able to talk to Him in any manner she felt comfortable, and He ought to be able to hear and understand her. For some reason it seemed appropriate to whisper.

"God, I feel so strange," she began. "I don't know where to start. I believe in You; I know that, and I suppose You know it too, because You know everything. I don't understand You. I don't know why You had to do what You did, but I'm smart enough to see that it was You and only You. It couldn't have been a trick or some human effort. Your followers said there was a record of Your doing the same thing thousands of years ago, but most people—me included—thought that was a fairy tale. When they said they were praying You'd do it again, nobody believed them.

"Well, maybe some did because of what happened in Los Angeles. Now, see, that I thought was something else. I didn't know what, and it sure was coincidental that what happened was what the zealot underground warned would happen. But You know what I made of that? Of course You do. I thought some of their very bright scientific minds knew some freak of nature was coming and then predicted it and gave You the credit. It had its desired effect; I gave them that. But divine intervention? No, I wasn't falling for it."

Bia stopped and looked around every time she heard a noise. All she needed was someone seeing her alone in her car talking to herself.

"God, I miss my son, and I hurt so bad I can hardly stand it. I don't know why I'm telling You. You're the one who took him, so am I supposed to ask You to make it better, to give him back, or to promise me he somehow made it to heaven?

"Okay, here's where I am. I'm hurt. I'm mad. I'm ashamed. I blame myself for his death because it seems I should have been able to recognize You long before something this awful had to happen. But I know myself, and I doubt anything short of that would have gotten my attention. I'm sorry. I'm unworthy. I believe. I don't know what else to say or do."

Bia found herself suddenly emotional. What was this? She had not even wept at the loss of her son. And now, making a decision like this brought out feelings in her she had fought since childhood. The monumental significance of the about-face in her life overwhelmed her. She cradled her face in her hands and felt the tears cascading through her fingers. It was as if she had come home to a place she didn't even realize was there.

Strangely, she felt different physically too. It was as if tension poured from her body. Bia felt she could dissolve into a puddle. Her limbs felt heavy, logy, without definition. Had she been ordered out of her car right then, she wasn't sure she had the legs to stand.

What was this slow blinking, this head bobbing? Was it possible she could actually fall asleep, after having seemed to be on autopilot for two weeks? She didn't recall sleeping during that time, though she knew she must have. That had been more like passing out, and even then she had never been far from consciousness.

If God's response to her awkward prayer was even just this, an ability to shut her eyes and finally drift off, it struck her as a gift so sublime she could hardly frame it in words. Did this mean she was in, part of His family after all she had done, after the person she had been her whole life? What sweet mercy this represented!

She let her chin rest on her chest and felt her breathing even out and grow rhythmic. "Thank You, God," she said as she fell limp. "Thank You. Thank You."

• • •

Ranold B. Decenti wasn't sure why, but before he left Chester Creighton's office—under much different circumstances than when he had been invited in—he was compelled to somehow try to right the ship. He and his buddy had gotten off on the wrong foot. That part was okay; it wasn't unusual for Ranold to disagree with people. But the terminology C.C. had used seemed to have a legal bent to it. Would the General of the Army undermine Ranold by going to the governor?

As C.C. had said, they both reported to Haywood Hale, and nothing of the nature of what Ranold had in mind could be initiated without Hale's blessing anyway. He would never get that if Creighton got to Hale and used words like *innocent civilians, non-military site, widespread casualties, have you written up, incompetence.* For that matter, Creighton could tell Hale Ranold said he would be a hero, that he called Creighton and Chancellor Dengler yellow, and that he said Hale was no better than Dengler.

Decenti rose and thrust out his hand, and he was wounded when Creighton was slow and clearly reluctant to reach for it. They shook hands, and Ranold said, "C.C., we go back a long way, and you know I'm a son of a gun when it comes to apologizing. 'Fact, you've probably never heard me do it. Well, let me just say that I hope you know me well enough by now to know that I did a lot of barkin' here just because I was upset. You know I'm hurting over the loss of my son and my wife, and of course I don't want any harm to come to my daughter and her kids. I admit I don't feel the same about that husband of hers.

"But what I'm tryin' to say is, take what I said with a grain of salt. Give me the benefit of the doubt that I was just gassing. Nothing personal, no hard feelings. Okay, pal?"

When Decenti got to the door, he spun sharply a hundred and eighty degrees and snapped off a crisp salute. That should have said everything. It should have clarified to C.C. that Ranold meant every word of his so-called apology and that in the end he respected the General of the Army.

But C.C. just looked pitifully at him, lifted a hand in a weak wave, and said, "I'll see you, Dece."

It was the ultimate insult. Ranold strode to his waiting ride wounded, worried, and determined to deal with at least one thing he could manage before calling it a day. He had to do something about Bia Balaam.

• • •

Bia was as sound asleep as she'd been in two weeks when her phone awakened her. She tried to speak through a cottony throat. "This is Balaam," she said.

"Decenti. Where are you that I'm getting such a bad connection?"

"Parking garage, sir. Sorry."

"Where you going?"

She leaped out of the car. "Not going, sir. Coming. On my way to my office. You want me to find a better cell?"

"I can hear you, but if you find a spot that's better, stay there."

"You want me to come to your office?"

"No, I want to deal with this right here and right now. I want to know the status of Agent Roscoe Wipers."

"I thought we were clear on that, Chief."

"So did I. Now what is his status?"

Bia's pulse seemed to double, and as she heard heavy static, she stopped, hoping the bad connection would buy her time. "I'm not able to report anything different than what I reported several days ago, sir."

"I missed some of that, Balaam. Find a clear spot."

"Sorry, sir."

"Now what's the skinny? That man dead or alive?"

"Would it help for me to rehearse for you what happened when I was on the phone with him the night I heard the gunshots?"

"It would help if you would get to a clear area and call me back as soon as possible. And be ready to tell me the truth. Then we'll meet in my office in half an hour. Are we clear?"

"Sorry?"

"Are we clear?"

"Bad connection. I'll call you from a better cell, sir."

# 37

**FELICIA THOMPSON** could tell something was up the minute she reached the Chicago bureau office. First she assumed people looked and acted differently because they didn't expect her back so soon and didn't know what to say about her husband's suicide. But soon she learned it had nothing to do with her. More likely it had to do with what she had heard on the radio during her drive.

Felicia was still living in a haze, stunned and numb and frequently wondering what was the point. But getting up and out and back into the game—as Straight, her new mentor, had suggested—proved a tonic for her. She couldn't say she was excited or enthusiastic. But having something to do—even if it meant only getting out of bed, eating, showering, dressing, driving in—well, that was better than nothing.

It wasn't that anything could take her mind off her losses.

The best that busying herself had to offer was, unlike sitting home alone with her depression, it made the clock move.

Felicia had turned on an all-news station for the drive and was barely listening until one piece caught her attention. Rumors were flying around Washington that a high-level meeting had been called by interim international chancellor Madame Hoshi Tamika. Heads of state from all over the world were expected in Switzerland within twenty-four hours.

People noticed Felicia in the elevator but looked away—all but Trudy Nabertowitz, who squeezed her shoulder, saying nothing. Otherwise, it seemed that Felicia was able to get all the way to her office without being seen.

Strange. In her in-box, along with the normal buildup of busywork, were more than a dozen sealed plain white envelopes. Each contained a folded sheet depicting a simple ichthyic symbol, the sketch of a fish made by two intersecting curved lines. Could there be that many secret believers here?

Hector Hernandez called. "Mrs. Thompson, I wonder if you have time to help me with something?"

"Be right there."

So she hadn't been invisible. How could Hector, being on a different floor, know she was even there? Trudy.

On her way down to his cubicle, carrying a stack of files and folders as a cover, Felicia became aware that the brass were all away from their offices. Every conference room, large and small, was full, and people milled about, engaged in conference calls.

Hector stood and formally shook her hand, otherwise keeping his distance, apparently to mislead the curious. "Just fan out some papers on my table," he whispered.

As they sat across from one another, ostensibly studying printouts, Hector spoke under his breath. "You doing all right?"

"Under the circumstances."

"I was so sorry to hear—"

"Thank you."

"Did you get some notes of encouragement?"

She pointed to a row of numbers and he leaned forward as if to read them. "Let's just say my office is swimming with fish," she said. "Were those all from different people?"

He nodded. "You'd be amazed at how many there are here. You know tonight is the monthly meeting."

"I didn't know. At Wilson's?"

"In Joliet, right. Need directions?"

"No, I know the place."

"Six o'clock for dinner. We have a private room."

"How many will be there?"

"Nearly thirty."

"Not all from this office."

"Oh yes."

"You're right, Hector; I *am* amazed."

He turned to a file cabinet and rummaged through it, she guessed just for effect. When he turned back he said, "I suppose you know what's going on."

"Just what I heard on the news. The new chancellor has summoned the heads of state."

"More than that. She's including each of the seven USSA governors."

"For?"

"No one knows," Hector said, "but we can guess."

"So guess."

"Has to be something to do with the looming oath-of-loyalty deadline."

"Is she going to accelerate it?" Felicia said. "Find out who's with her and who's not?"

"That's one theory."

"There's another?"

Hector leaned back and sucked air through his teeth. "Some think she might call for a vote on lifting the ban against the practice of religion."

• • •

"We have to hold," Paul said, and that Jack and Greenie flinched was no surprise. They huddled around an institutional table in a room not far from where Roscoe Wipers was incarcerated.

"Hold nothing!" Greenie said. "We should have started moving people out of here last night. We're talking seventy hours max now, and who knows if your contact's information is good?"

"She was my secretary for years," Paul said. "She has access to everything in Chicago."

"The international confab," Jack said, "if there really is one, ought to be easy enough to confirm. But how can we be sure what they're talking about? What if it's the opposite of what you're hoping, Paul? What if they decide to move up the deadline on the loyalty oaths?"

Paul slid his chair back. "Don't assume I'm unaware of the risks here, Jack. But nothing is riskier than exposing a thousand zealots to the light of day, or even the darkness of night."

"Nothing?" Greenie said. "Nothing is riskier than getting out of here? That's lunacy. Riskiest is sitting here like so many targets for that crazy father-in-law of yours. Who knows what he might do, especially if the vote went our way."

"How do you figure?" Jack said.

Greenie stood and paced. "Okay, best-case scenario: the international government lifts the ban. All of a sudden we're free. Decenti is bound to know that before we do. He still wants us dead, so he triggers. Regardless of what happens in Bern, we've got to get out of here."

If Paul knew anything, it was that *he* needed to get out. He'd never felt so restless, so confined, so powerless. He wanted to be topside, and in his heart of hearts, he wanted to confront Ranold face-to-face.

"I'm going to make an executive decision here," Jack said.

"You're not going to consult the elders?" Greenie said.

"No, but don't worry about it. This is going your way anyway. If everything is in order, let's start the exodus at sundown tonight. Begin with the original families. Follow with the rest of the women and children. By Thursday night we'll be down to the men, and then the elders, and then us."

• • •

Ranold returned to his office, his mind full of options—few of them good. He had hoped his ascension to head of the NPO would return him to the status of a real mover and shaker in Washington. He hadn't enjoyed the deference and respect commensurate with his history and accomplishments since shortly after the war, when he had been in on the ground floor of the founding of the organization.

Now he was not only reminded frequently of his interim status, but he was also challenged, argued with, disagreed with, even by old friends. Was he the man he used to be? He wanted to think so. Sure, the years had cost him some of his reflexes and acuity, but for an old man, he believed he still had his chops.

But could he trust his staff? He'd been right about Aikman, hadn't he? How could he know? He was sure right about Dengler. That had to be the highlight of his career. But without Governor Hale's approval of and Chester Creighton's cooperation in the attack on the Columbia zealot underground, eliminating Dengler may have all been for nothing.

Was Ranold supposed to feel some guilt, some twinge, some

something about having murdered two men? He had come to acknowledge that he, along with most of the rest of the known world, had been wrong about the existence of God. But did that mean he had to find God's law and live by it? Everybody knew murder was wrong. You didn't have to be religious to understand that. But he was a soldier, in combat. Not all killing was the same.

God must not have wanted Ranold B. Decenti dead or He'd have slain him by now, right?

His secretary slowed him as he strode toward his office. "Governor Hale will be back in town Monday and would like to visit you at your convenience."

"He'd like to visit me? I'm not going over there?"

"No, sir. That's the message. I asked the same question."

"Well, book it for the morning then, I guess."

He hurried into his office suite and into the bathroom, where he studied himself in the mirror. He was going to be fired. That was it. Why else would Hale want a meeting here? It made no sense otherwise. Unless . . . unless Hale was going to personally report to him on the big confab in Bern. And why had Ranold not been invited? He had been cleared in the assassination probe, but did they still suspect him?

Decenti planted himself behind his desk and informed his secretary to have Commander Balaam wait ten minutes from when she arrived and then to announce her. He got on the phone.

• • •

Bia hesitated in an alcove down the hall from Ranold's office and dialed Paul. "He's going to push me to the wall," she said. "Do I just flat out lie to him?"

"Why not?" Paul said, hoping her answer would tell him more than he asked.

"Because I'm one of you now. I'm not supposed to do that, right?"

"That's the question of the ages, Bia. But let me be the first to welcome you to the family."

"Thank you, but do all the rules change now?"

"Do you have to be good, you mean?"

"That's what I mean. I know how to dodge, to bob and weave, but what if he asks me straight-out whether I know Agent Wipers is dead?"

"Do you know?"

"Don't I? You told me he was fine, that the shooting was a setup for my benefit."

"It was, but he has since died."

"Oh, he has, has he?" she said. "Of what? Natural causes?"

"How'd you guess?"

"You're lying to me, Paul. Is that okay, as long as it's between believers?"

"Let me take the heat for this one, Bia. You won't be lying. I will be. I'm telling you the man's dead, so what can you tell your boss when he asks?"

"That I called to reconfirm and was told that Wipers is dead."

"There you go."

"You're going to get me shot, Paul."

"Oh, I doubt it. You're good and Ranold trusts you. Plus he needs you."

"Don't forget I'm the one person who can pin the assassination on him. Hey, listen, when he asks who I confirmed Wipers's well-being with, what am I supposed to say?"

"Tell the truth."

"That I talked with you? Are you serious?"

"I'm trying to draw the man out, Bia. I want a face-to-face."

"He's been waiting for your call for ages, Paul."

"That's different. Maybe I'll call him later, but only if he agrees to meet me somewhere."

"You want me to set that up?"

"Not formally. Just tell him you confirmed Roscoe Wipers was dead and tell him I told you so, and the rest should take care of itself."

# 38

**BIA BALAAM WONDERED** if this would be the end of it then. When Decenti's secretary told her the director would be a few minutes, she was glad she had brought her briefcase and had something to read.

But she couldn't concentrate. All she could think of was how to phrase her answers to keep the old fox at bay. But that was the problem. He was old, but he was still a fox. His ego had always clouded his judgment, and he was nowhere near the man he had been when he hired her years before. But could she keep playing him as she had the last several days? He sounded mad now, as if he was really on to something. When he suspected a person, especially if he was right, he didn't let up until he knew all.

Would this new chapter in her own life make Bia less of a professional? It shouldn't, she thought. It had better not. Her life was at stake. She had, however, always viewed believers as weak.

They hid, after all. Lived underground. Did everything surreptitiously. On the other hand, what were they supposed to do against a powerful government and world opinion? It would have been foolhardy to mount a frontal attack.

Her view was already changing, of course. Paul Stepola was no wimp. She wouldn't be either. She couldn't afford to be.

When finally Bia was summoned into Ranold's office, the tenor was different right from the start. Not only did the boss not rise or attempt to embrace her, but he also didn't so much as move, let alone smile. His head was cocked, his elbows on the desk, fingers interlaced before him. He was clearly not trying to hide his suspicion, mistrust, and cynicism.

Bia nodded to him. "Chief Decenti," she said, moving to a side chair and standing before it.

"If you're waiting to be asked to sit, you'll wait a long time, Commander."

She sat.

"I asked you a direct question, and I'll ask it again right here, right now, with you not eight feet from me, no bad cells, no weak connections. Is Roscoe Wipers dead or alive?"

"Are you asking me what I believe or what I know?"

Decenti slapped both palms on the desk. "Stop making a game of this! Is the man dead or alive?"

"I don't know."

"You told me he was dead!"

"That's what I believed at the time."

"Have you changed your mind?"

"I can tell you only what I heard. I was on the phone with him when I heard voices call him by his alias. He gave me the signal that he had been made; I heard the phone drop. I heard two shots. And I have not heard from Agent Wipers since. You can see why I believed him dead."

"So why do you now say you don't know?"

Bia shifted in her chair. "Frankly, sir, your questions have made me wonder. It appears you have information to which I have not been privy."

Decenti swore. "You're right. I have. And from none other than the General of the Army."

"I have not spoken to General Creighton in more than a year, sir. If he has any conflicting information, he did not get it from me."

"You know he and I go back to before the war?"

"Yes, sir."

"I could get him on the phone in sixty seconds. Would you have any problem whatever in my asking him to corroborate that you have not talked with him in over a year? You want to think that through, change your claim, anything?"

"No, sir. I have no recollection of any interaction with the general by phone or in person. In fact, I believe the last time I saw him was at a Wintermas party a year ago December."

"Why is he implying that Wipers may still be alive?" Decenti said.

"I have no idea."

"And have you followed up to confirm what you believe you heard?"

"I have tried calling Wipers's secure line, yes. No luck."

"You know who would know for sure, don't you, Commander?"

"I do, sir, but I assume you would not want me communicating with your son-in-law."

She expected Ranold to immediately agree and didn't know what to think when he did not respond. He stood and moved to a window, parting the horizontal blinds and looking out over the capital. "When was the last time you spoke with him?"

"Excuse me?"

"Did you not hear me, Commander," he said, turning to face her, "or are you stalling?"

"I thought I heard you ask when was the last time I spoke with former agent Stepola."

"At least you call him *former*."

"Well, that goes without saying."

Decenti returned and sat on the corner of his desk, peering down at her. "What makes you think Paul would know the status of Roscoe Wipers?"

Bia froze. Didn't Ranold know Paul was in the Columbia underground? Was that not common knowledge or at least a common assumption within the NPO? She wasn't so sure.

"Well," she began slowly, "as it's clear, ah, that he is AWOL from the NPO and was spared from The Incident, he's obviously a person of faith. I guess I'm assuming they're a close-knit group that keeps its members informed. I could be wrong, of course."

"You're really nervous, aren't you, Commander Balaam?"

"No, sir, it's just that you are clearly agitated with me. You seem accusatory, and I am frankly in the dark."

"You've forgotten that we had not one but two moles in the Columbia underground and that they reported—specifically to you—that Paul Stepola was a legend there even before he showed up the night of my son's death and my wife's murder?"

"Well, sure, I remember."

"Then why all the hemming and hawing about his being a member of a small, close-knit group and—"

"I wasn't thinking, sir. I haven't been sleeping. I'm still grieving my son. I'm sorry."

"Aren't we all? Now I asked you a question, which you have again deflected. When was the last time you spoke with Paul Stepola?"

"I don't recall, sir." It was true. She had not looked at her watch. It had been within the last hour, in fact the last few minutes, but the time? She was relieved to be able to say she didn't know.

"Since The Incident?"

So there it was, the mother of all questions. Was a lie permissible now? It would save not only her life but probably also Paul's, his family's, and a thousand others. She was too new to this, didn't know the rules.

"Yes, I have. I urged him to return your calls."

"You've talked with Stepola and have not informed me?"

She nodded. "I'm sorry, sir. I probably should have. But I didn't want—"

"Probably? *Probably?* Where is he?"

"I spoke to him on his cell phone."

"He answers your calls and not mine? Why?"

"Well, I could think of a few reasons, sir. I didn't want to make it so plain to you that he was talking with me and not with you. Perhaps I was being too sentimental."

Ranold returned to the chair behind his desk, leaned back, and clasped his hands behind his head. "Have I ever struck you as sentimental, Commander?"

"No, sir."

"Ever?"

"Not in the least."

"My feelings would have survived. What rankles me is when subordinates keep information from me."

"Acknowledged, sir."

"I left messages on his machine! I told him I had flipped, had become a believer, that he was right, I was wrong, I wanted to repent, get right, come to Jesus—whatever they call it. I was good, Commander. I would have fooled the devil. But I didn't get so much as a callback."

"Trust me, sir; I have encouraged him to make contact with you. I have urged him to call you."

"Then why hasn't he?"

"Only he could answer that, Chief. But I would recommend that you not give up."

"Not give up? How many times am I supposed to leave messages on his system? After a while, a man gets the point."

"Maybe he wants to meet face-to-face."

"I'd do that in a second," Ranold said. "You find out when and where, and I'll make it happen."

"I'll try."

"When was the last time you spoke to him?"

"As I said, I don't—"

"You don't recall, but it's been since The Incident. Has it been a week?"

"I spoke with him about a week ago, yes."

"Since then?"

"Sir!"

"What? I don't have the right to ask?"

"Of course, but—"

"Just answer the question! How recently did you speak with Stepola?"

"Recently." She saw him flush.

"Today?"

"Yes, sir."

"Get him on the phone."

"Now?"

"Right now. In fact, use my phone."

"But he has caller ID and—"

"That's the point, Commander. Try my phone first."

# 39

**PAUL WAS IN THE MAIN ASSEMBLY ROOM** with more than seven hundred of the residents, waiting to hear Jack Pass address them, when he got the call from Ranold's phone. Wasn't Decenti supposed to be meeting with Bia right now? Paul resisted the temptation to step out and take it. Maybe she had talked Ranold into meeting with Paul, but he could always call the old man back.

Soon another call came, this time from Bia. That one he knew he had better take. Something sounded strange when he picked up, however. "Am I on speaker, Bia?" he said.

A pause. Then Ranold. "Yes, you're on speaker, you coward. Why do you answer her phone and not mine?"

"Because I want to talk to her."

"And you don't want to talk to me."

"You're a quick study, Dad."

"What if I wanted to make peace?"

"You've already tried that ploy, how you'd seen the light, all that. But refresh me: was that before or after you accused me of brainwashing your own daughter into murdering your wife? Jae was there, Ranold, remember? I trust her. I know what happened."

"Oh, you do, eh? Well, good for you. Where are you, anyway?"

"You know where I am. You know, the crazy thing is, I do want to talk to you, but in person."

"What's wrong with the phone?"

"Well, the phone would be safer, that's true, judging by the experiences of Dick Aikman and Baldwin Dengler."

"I was cleared in that, you know. Well, of course you know. You know everything. How long was Aikman a member of your underground?"

"Don't insult my intelligence, Ranold. I knew Dick, and he was as true to the NPO as you are. Somebody framed him."

"Maybe we do need to talk, Paul."

"Where? When?"

"When is your call. Where? How about the site of my first brilliant operation with the NPO, back when you were a baby?"

"I may have been a baby when it happened, but I studied it in grad school."

"Arrested more than four hundred supplicants right out of their Eucharist service," Ranold said. "It was a stroke, Paul, a thing of beauty. Those Episcopalians didn't know what hit 'em."

"I was taught that they were still being grandfathered in and were allowed to celebrate Communion for another couple of weeks."

"Who can remember after all this time? All I know is, I was on the front page of the *Post*, along with a bunch of religious nuts being herded like cattle out of the National Cathedral."

"Real proud of you, Dad."

"Thanks, I can tell."

"And that's where you want to meet? Of course, it's not a church anymore."

Ranold laughed. "Hardly. Most of it is unused. They lease out the downstairs for art fairs and bazaars, stuff like that."

"How about Friday night?" Paul said. "Seven o'clock."

Another pause. What could Ranold say? Paul wondered. Surely he wanted Paul in the underground when the attack came.

"Friday night's bad for me," Ranold said. "How about earlier?"

"No can do," Paul said. "Sorry. Let's keep working on it and keep in touch."

"You'll answer my calls?" Ranold said.

"If you promise you'll call when we have an appropriate time."

• • •

Suddenly Bia wasn't all that sure about this faith thing. She walked unsteadily back to her office, feeling vulnerable and weak. Where had her trademark toughness gone? Could the depletion be attributed to her having flipped to the other team? That was not good. It wasn't as if she was going to flip back, but as of this instant she didn't feel she was bringing much to the table. Maybe that was the point.

She had not been behind her desk two minutes when her secretary told her Chief Decenti was on the line.

"Yes, sir," she said.

"You mind a little overtime tonight?"

"Sir?"

"I want you to review the attack plans. I've done a little tweaking."

"Sure. Any problem with my doing this at home?"

"You're joking, right, Commander? When have we ever let this level of classified document out of the building?"

"Of course. I'll review it here."

"I'll just leave them with you, and we can debrief in the morning."

Now how did that compute? He wanted *her* to review the battle plan when it was clear he had lost all trust in her? It had to be a test. Had he changed the date? Had he made obvious changes that, if showed to Paul or anyone in the underground, would give NPO the advantage? Or would expose her as a traitor?

The date had indeed changed. The attack was scheduled for the last hour before dawn, Monday, February 11, 38 P.3. The dignitaries would not even be back from the Bern summit yet. More likely, however, except that it seemed such an amateurish, transparent ruse, Decenti may have wanted Bia to spill this to Paul. That would make the underground think they had most of the weekend, only to face the attack at the original coordinates just after dark on Friday. Paul would hear about this, all right, but he certainly wouldn't need to be reminded how misleading it likely was.

For the life of her, Bia could find not another detail that was changed in the entire plan, not even a comma. She said good-bye when her secretary left and was aware that almost everyone else was also leaving the building, but she fought to stay awake and alert as she pored over the document.

If the timing was the only change, why didn't Chief Decenti merely inform her of that and ask her opinion? He knew she was lobbying for a later attack deadline, but this one didn't go nearly far enough. The fact was, she was pushing for a full two-week delay, representing that she simply worried about public opinion in light of the assassination of the chancellor following global grief over the deaths of a billion men. In truth, naturally, she hoped the ban on religion would lift in the meantime and make all this moot.

At eight o'clock, Bia checked the thermometer outside her window and saw the needle buried near ten below zero. She locked the file away, then pulled on her fur coat, hat, and gloves, and slipped her flats into her bag, replacing them with tall boots.

Few stragglers moved through the building, and fewer still acknowledged her with so much as a nod. She had grown used to that over the years. Her bearing, her apparel, her reputation preceded her. Maybe that was something she could work on.

Her floor of the parking facility had been jammed when last she sat in the car, but now hers was one of only three in that section. How long would it take to warm? She had learned not to venture out until the interior temp had risen. Otherwise the windshield developed condensation, and she would have to pull over to manage that.

When the interior light did not come on when she opened the door, she sighed and assumed the cold had affected the battery. On the other hand, she knew little enough about mechanics to assume the hybrid car wouldn't start, so she slid in behind the wheel and inserted the key.

Bia had not even begun turning it when she felt cold steel at the base of her neck. *Unbelievable,* she thought. She had not seen it coming. The strange request to stay late. The report with only one minor change in it. The interior light.

She began to turn and plead her case, but she knew it was too late. They say you don't hear the shot that kills you, so the first two must not have been deathblows. Bia heard them both and saw her own blood on the windshield and dashboard. She felt the barrel rise to the middle of the back of her head, and then she heard no more.

# 40

**THE MORE THAN THIRTY MILES** south from the Loop to Joliet could take well over an hour during rush hour, and Felicia certainly didn't want to go north to Deerfield first. That would have made Joliet a brutal round-trip. So she hung around the office after most others had left.

Harriet Johns stopped by Felicia's office on her way out. "I commend you on your ability to put personal issues aside for the sake of the organization," she said, standing in the doorway, dressed for the weather.

"I appreciate that," Felicia said. "But it's not easy."

"No one said this would be easy," the bureau chief said. "But it should be easier for you next week. An old friend of mine is coming to replace your former boss. She was my deputy in L.A. and then San Francisco. You'll like her. She's no-nonsense."

Felicia nodded and managed, "I'll look forward to getting acquainted."

The truth was, if the woman was anything like Ms. Johns, Felicia wasn't so sure. She had wondered, naturally, who could ever replace Paul, and she had to admit, to her own chagrin, that she had not even considered it would be a woman. She had speculated on whom among the men it might be, and she could tell several were angling for the position. She should have known Harriet would bring in a known quantity. Well, next week would be interesting.

Felicia slipped down to Hector Hernandez's cubicle as he was getting ready to leave. He looked taken aback to see her. "We try to be pretty careful on meeting days," he said. "Lots of curious eyes, you know."

"Sure. Okay."

"And we don't caravan to Joliet. I'm sure you understand."

"Of course. I assume we go individually. And then how do we find the party?"

He smiled. "We call ourselves the South Side Mix 'n' Match Bowling League. The host or hostess will point you to our private room."

"Bowling?"

"We've even been known to pass out phony trophies if we fear there's an interloper."

"Seems you'd know if a stranger showed up."

"Well, sure, but though we shut the door, Wilson's is hardly a secure environment. Who knows who might be on the waitstaff?"

"Risky meetings."

He nodded. "But a breath of fresh air. It's like going to church."

"I wouldn't know."

"Me either, before. But you'll get a taste of it tonight. You can't imagine the feeling of being with so many others of like faith. It's dangerous, yes, but we need each other so badly. The public stuff, from the platform with a microphone, is phony bowling results. It's around the tables, drowned out by someone jabbering away over the loudspeaker, that we trade prayer requests, pray, tell our stories, pass along plans."

"I can't wait."

Felicia noticed Trudy bustling their way. "Uh-oh, we've been seen again."

"Boss is still suspicious," Trudy said. "And watching. Let me go through the motions of checking your after-hours passes; then I'll tip my hat and be on my way. You might act a little offended so it looks realistic."

Felicia and Hector immediately went into playacting. Felicia put her hands on her hips. "Haven't we already been through this?" she said. "Didn't I show you my pass days ago? You think my status has changed?"

"Excellent," Trudy said, extending a palm. "Now let's see it."

Hector shook his head and seemed to be reluctantly pulling out his wallet.

Trudy made a show of copying down the numbers off each pass. "See you tonight at school," she said, tipping her cap. "Little fish joke there."

• • •

The first wave of evacuees left the Columbia zealot underground fortress that night under the supervision of Greenie Macintosh. About two hundred original members loaded what they could in the trunks of cars and the storage areas of mini- and regular-sized vans, pulling out of the exits randomly and taking varied routes that would eventually point them north toward the Heartland salt mines.

Paul still wished they could wait, hoping for some eventuality in Bern that would change the course of history and bring amnesty to all these people—himself included. But he knew the latter was not in the cards. Regardless the status of secret believers after Bern did whatever it was going to do, he would have to face justice for his crimes.

Because they were crimes. Even if he was exonerated as a private citizen wanting to practice his faith, Paul still had to take responsibility for breaking the law, for posing as a loyal member of the USSA government and thwarting its policies by living as a double agent—encouraging the opposition while sworn to help expose it.

Jae didn't seem to want to discuss the ramifications if Paul was sentenced. She made her case about how much she needed him and his maturity in the faith—limited as it was, he was light-years ahead of her—and said she would feel lost without him.

"And what of Brie and Connor?" she said. "How long are they expected to go without a dad?"

The conversation didn't go much longer, because the kids were in and out of the room, as excited as Paul had seen them in days. They had been assigned to choose only those things each could fit into one suitcase. Brie was carefully selecting her favorite clothes, leaving room for just one doll. Connor had stuffed his suitcase with toys, initially leaving no room for even underwear.

Angela Pass Barger had had what Paul considered a brilliant idea. She suggested that the kids, who would go in the next wave, get packed and then join her for a party and movies. That would get the kids' minds on something else and give their parents time to pack.

• • •

Straight Rathe took a call on his cell from Dr. Graybill. "Glad I caught you," the surgeon said. "Interesting patient I thought you might want to know of. Name's Stephenson Davis, goes by Scooter. He's a cameraman based here in Chicago but working for the USSA Television Network."

"He get caught in that accident this morning?"

"Yep. Drunk driver somehow got into the northbound lanes on Lake Shore Drive heading south. Hit the USSATN van head-on. Davis was the only survivor."

"The Drive can be dangerous," Straight said. "So, you're going to slow him a little, keep him sedated here so he can't be helping broadcast propaganda over the state network?"

"That's the thing, Mr. Rathe. He's not hurt as bad as he looks. He was in the front passenger seat, belted in. His forehead apparently hit the visor, and that gave him a couple of colorful black eyes. They called me in to release liquid pressure in his skull. I was doing my customary inventory of his body first, just in case Emergency missed anything, and what do I find between his big toe and the next? A tattoo. The ichthus."

"You don't say."

"And get this. I determined he had no unusual cranial pressure, so I didn't have to operate. I did, however, mark in his chart that he needs to stay in ICU for a few days of observation. Didn't want Scooter to scoot away before I found out whether he might be of any use to you."

"He's conscious?"

"And lucid. He looks like he's been through it, but he wants out, and I can't blame him. But I put enough in his chart to make his superiors agree he should stay under my care awhile longer."

"I'll try to get over and see him yet tonight."

"That won't draw any suspicion? You could see him in the morning on your regular rounds."

"Nah," Straight said. "I do this all the time. People see me there all hours. I set my own schedule."

• • •

Hector had advised Felicia to be careful of anyone following her, but how would she know? Paul had been one of the best at espionage and counterespionage, but that sure wasn't her game. How was one supposed to know if any of the thousands of cars also heading south on I-294 were following her specifically? It seemed they all were.

She couldn't determine one car from another anyway. The sun sank early during Chicago winters, so everything behind Felicia was just pairs of headlights. One set that had stayed consistently about a dozen cars behind her exited toward Joliet when she did, but so did a score of others. Felicia decided she simply couldn't concern herself with tails unless one became obvious. And what had Paul told her? That professionals were never obvious. Only someone from the NPO would be following her, and they were the best in the business.

• • •

Ranold B. Decenti sat at his kitchen table eating delivered Chinese, his leg bouncing. He kept glancing at his watch and was tempted to call for a status report. But she had promised to let him know when the deed was done.

His eagerness made him eat too fast, and the food stuck in his throat. Was he off base to wonder if someone had poisoned him? Maybe delivery was not the way to go anymore. He had been a pursuer for decades. Was he now the pursued? Well, people were going to pay.

His home phone rang. Surely that would not be her. He hadn't even given her that number. On the other hand, she was well-placed and could probably procure any information she wanted. He certainly hoped she was trustworthy. She had to be. She owed him.

"Decenti residence," he said.

"Chief, this is security at headquarters, and I'm afraid I have bad news for you."

"I'm listening, son. What've you got?"

"Commander Bia Balaam works for you, does she not?"

"Yes, now what's happened?"

"We found her dead in her car, sir."

"Dead? What happened?"

"Looks like a professional hit, sir. Three small-caliber rounds to the back of the head."

Ranold affected his most grave tone. "I can't believe it. Would you mind calling the motor pool and sending a car for me?"

"I'd be happy to, sir, but the body has been removed, and there's really nothing you can do here."

"Has someone informed her daughter?"

"I'm not aware of any of that, sir."

"I'll see to it someone does."

"Thank you, Director Decenti. I'm sorry to have had to—"

"That's all right, son. I appreciate it."

Ranold rang off and threw his food box across the kitchen. Could he trust no one anymore? This news should have come from Chicago before the body was even discovered.

# 41

**STRAIGHT STARTED** in the locker room, where he changed into his greeter's uniform, the adult clown version slightly different from the children's. For kids he wore the big shoes and the bulbous red nose and made up his face. For adults he just wore an ancient zoot suit and pushed a cart with reading materials on it.

The nurse in ICU greeted him by name. "Who you seeing to-night?" she said.

"A Mr. Davis. Stephenson Davis."

She pointed to the room and said, "Word to the wise. He hates that first name."

Straight stopped and leaned back conspiratorially. "He's got a nickname?"

"Scooter."

He winked at her and pushed his cart down the hall, singing quietly: "Nobody knows the trouble I seen. Got me a first name that's not too keen. Name's Stephenson but I go by Scooter. . . ."

Straight pushed the door open to find a patient with the raccoon look of two purple eyes and a discolored forehead. "If you don't like my singin', I can dance."

Scooter Davis seemed to force a smile, and Straight shut the door. "I'm the official greeter," Straight said. "If you're hurting, I can come back."

"No, I'm fine. Could use the company. Truth is, I want out of here."

"That's out of my jurisdiction," Straight said. "Reading material?"

He shoved the cart next to the bed, and as soon as Davis looked at it, Straight tugged at the tucked sheet, exposing the man's feet.

"Hey! What're you doin'?"

"Just checking," Straight said, reaching for the man's toes.

Davis wrenched away. "You want trouble, old-timer? Do I need to call someone?"

"What's that between your toes, young man?"

"I don't know what you're talking about."

"I heard you've got a tiny tattoo."

"That's just something I did as a fool kid. So much for protecting the privacy of patients, hey? What're you going to do, turn me in? I work for the government TV network, you know."

"I know," Straight said. "He is risen."

Scooter Davis stared at him, and Straight went cold. If he didn't get the proper response, he had exposed himself to the wrong person—big time. Was it possible this guy *had* gotten a tattoo as a kid, just to be rebellious? to bug his parents?

"He is risen indeed," Davis whispered.

. . .

"I already got the word, Harriet," Ranold said. "No thanks to you."

"It's not as if I don't have other things on my mind, General."

"You should have called me."

"I'm calling you now."

"You use local muscle?"

"Of course. You certainly didn't give me enough time to send someone from here."

"How's the other thing going?"

"On schedule. I'm on my way there now."

"Who you using for that?"

"Mostly Chicago-based personnel. I don't know anyone here outside the bureau."

"You sure everybody's true?"

"Are you kidding? After finding out how many cohorts Stepola had here, what could I do but run them through lie detectors and sodium pentothal? Caught one in that net. The rest are mobilized."

"The one you caught. Anyone I know?"

"Doubt it. Security guard. Sang like a canary when I promised his life in exchange for the truth."

"You promised him his *life*?"

"So I lied."

. . .

Once behind closed doors in a private room at Wilson's in Joliet, Felicia found Hector and embraced him. "Does everybody always look this petrified at these things?" she said.

"Actually, no. We're all spooked right now. Hopeful about what's happening in Bern, probably within the next few hours. I mean, if it doesn't go our way . . ."

"You've got to think positive."

Hector recoiled. "You're kidding, right?"

Felicia studied him. "Yeah, I guess. Not too much to be optimistic about, is there?"

"Not this side of eternity."

Felicia scanned the room as others arrived; many were as shocked to see her as she was to see them. They all began their greeting the same way. Rather than "He is risen," they said, "What are you doing here?" leaving her to start the proper greeting and put them at ease.

Once everyone was assembled, Hector shut the door and a woman Felicia recognized from data processing took the microphone. "Welcome to the monthly meeting of the South Side Bowlers," she said, and people chuckled and clapped. "Let me read off the top scores from last week."

The names associated with the high scores bore no resemblance to any real names here, Felicia decided, unless there were that many people she didn't know at the bureau. And she thought she recognized everyone.

Trudy showed up a little late and sat next to Felicia. She leaned over and whispered, "I was afraid I was being followed, so I drove around a little once I got in the neighborhood."

"Be sure to greet the newcomers," the emcee said. "And enjoy your fish dinner."

There was no menu. The waitstaff entered in a neat row, trays held over their heads, and quickly distributed combination seafood platters and took drink orders. When they left and shut the door, people began picking at their food. Felicia saw some holding hands and praying, others talking softly.

The place went dead silent when the door opened and Harriet Johns stepped to the dais. "Well, good evening," she said. No one responded. "I said good evening!"

A few mumbled a response.

"Isn't this nice? I so love that bureau employees get together informally. It makes them work better together, don't you think? Oh, say, do you want to hear something? Listen to this."

She produced a tiny tape player and held it to the microphone. The raspy, staticky voice of Trudy Nabertowitz filled the room. *"Boss is still suspicious. And watching. Let me go through the motions of checking your after-hours passes; then I'll tip my hat and be on my way. You might act a little offended so it looks realistic."*

Felicia felt Trudy shuddering and turned to see her red-faced, tears rolling. "Oh no," she squealed. "Oh, God, please. No."

Felicia reached to touch her, and Trudy lowered her head to the table.

The tape continued. Felicia's voice: *"Haven't we already been through this? Didn't I show you my pass days ago? You think my status has changed?"*

Trudy: *"Excellent. Now let's see it. . . . See you tonight at school. Little fish joke there."*

"'Little fish joke there,'" Harriet echoed. "Hey, know what? He is risen!"

People looked at each other.

Felicia knew her life was over.

"Did I say it wrong?" Harriet said. "Yes? No? I guess I'm not welcome here. Well, enjoy your meals *and* your drinks."

She left and the waitstaff reentered, delivering the drinks. As soon as they were gone, Hector rose. "Don't anyone be foolish enough to eat another bite or take a drink. Does anyone happen to be armed?"

The door locked with a loud click, and Felicia heard something being forced up against it. From beneath it came a cloud of white smoke, and as soon as some tried to block it with cloth napkins, they fell, convulsing. Felicia grabbed the tablecloth and yanked, sending eight settings flying, but the cloud was already reaching her, burning her eyes and throat.

"The window!" Hector shouted, and a dozen people streamed toward it.

Felicia fell to her knees, then rose and followed the crowd. But when Hector removed a shoe and threw it through the glass, a shot erupted from outside and his head seemed to explode as he hit the floor. The others dove away from the door and the window, filling the opposite corners of the room, dropping one by one.

· · ·

With the kids at their group activity, Paul and Jae were discussing the vagaries of their future, as if he or she had a clue what was in store. At the tone in his mouth, Paul checked his caller ID and answered.

"Hello, Ranold."

"Paul. I can meet you on your timetable if you can meet me at my suggested location."

"Friday night at seven at the former National Cathedral."

"I'll be there," Ranold said.

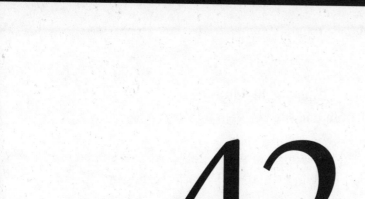

# 42

**STRAIGHT HAD NEVER HEARD PAUL SO LOW.** "Have you been watching the news?"

"No," Straight said. "Why?"

Paul's voice shook. "Word out of Washington is that Bia Balaam was assassinated in her car in the parking garage at NPO."

"Oh no."

"I'm convinced she was a believer, Straight, but it's just . . . I can't—"

"I know, Paul. This is no game. This is real life-and-death stuff. We have to realize we may not be long for this world ourselves."

"That's not all, Straight. Did Felicia tell you about her meeting tonight?"

"The one in Joliet, sure. What?"

"They were made, and Harriet Johns personally supervised the gassing of the place. Nitric oxide. No survivors."

"Felicia—"

"No survivors, Straight."

•  •  •

Jae had never seen Paul like this either.

"This is all your dad's work," he said.

"Now, Paul . . ."

"Nothing that big within the NPO would go down without his blessing, or likely without his planning. He's just eating this up, Jae. He can't wait to hear how I respond. It's a good thing we're not meeting until Friday night, because right now I'm murderous."

She let him stew, not knowing what to say. Finally, after several minutes of silence, she said, "I know you won't take the law into your own hands, Paul."

"I won't? Why won't I? That's what I've been doing since I became a believer, isn't it? We're at war, Jae. You don't think your dad already knew what had happened when he called to arrange our meeting? He can't wait to see the look on my face."

"What are you going to do, Paul?"

"I don't know yet. Straight has an interesting possibility though. He's found a secret believer who works for the state television network. He's supposed to be in the hospital over the weekend, but Straight's doctor contact assures him he's all right. Maybe we can make use of him somehow."

Jae opened the door to vigorous knocking. Jack Pass and Greenie Macintosh entered with apologies. "Can we steal Paul for a few minutes?" Jack said.

"Let's talk here," Paul said. "There's nothing Jae can't hear."

Pass and Macintosh glanced at each other, and Jae offered to make herself scarce.

"Don't worry about it, Mrs. Stepola. No need for secrets anymore."

They sat, and Greenie jumped in. "These NPO executions have hit the news, and people are outraged. It's fixing to be a true backlash, Paul, and it could affect the Bern meetings. This is the very kind of thing people wanted to avoid, and now, with peace and—who knows—maybe amnesty on the horizon, it's like the NPO is getting in its last shots."

"That's why I want to do something drastic," Jack said. "I know how y'all feel about praying down a flood from heaven—"

"Don't be so sure you know how I feel about it anymore," Paul said. "I thought you were nuts at first, but now—"

"Same here," Greenie said. "If your father-in-law is worried about what's happening in Bern, he could do anything anytime."

"May I say something?" Jae said. "I don't care what you do. Call down rain. Call down fire, whatever. But we've got to keep getting people out of here. We've got children, babies, and you think anyone topside gives a hamster's hide whether they're safe?"

"I know you're right," Jack said. "Greenie, let's tell the guys that we'll stay in the same order, but no breaks between shifts. Everybody just gets in line to get out of here."

"You still gonna call down the rain?" Greenie said.

"I don't know," Jack said.

"I'm going to the other end to see Angela first."

"Fine!" Jack said. "Just go!" As Greenie left, Jack turned to Paul. "I'm curious about your meeting with Decenti. If his attack is planned for then, why would he want you safe?"

"I wouldn't be safe," Paul said. "At least not in his mind. Maybe he doesn't know I know when the attack is planned."

"Then why'd he kill this Balaam woman?"

"Lots of reasons, not the least of which is that she's the one who gave him the talisman found on Aikman. But even if he knows I know the attack is coming at dark on Friday, our meeting is a couple of hours later. If I'm there, he'll know I was out of here when the missiles came."

The explosion that broke windows and sent Jae flying to the floor knocked out the lights too. She screamed and leaped to her feet. "The children!"

"You all right, Jae?" Paul said.

"Yes! You? Jack?"

"I'm okay," Paul said, and she could tell from his voice that he was standing.

"Nothing serious here," Jack said, "but that won't be the last of it. Emergency lights ought to be burning in the hallways."

Jae felt for Paul in the dark, and the three of them edged through the damaged door. Jack was right. Lights dimly illuminated the corridor for as far as she could see to the left and to the exits people had been using.

But the kids were to the right. And that's where she was headed.

•  •  •

If Ranold Decenti had killed Paul's kids, Paul would find him and exact revenge and seek forgiveness later. He grabbed Jae's arm and turned to Jack. "Keep in touch with me by cell. Assess the damage and casualties and see if we can keep people moving out. If you hear anything more, hit the deck."

He and Jae ran the other way, and Paul felt as if he could trip or run into something any second.

Jae pulled away from Paul and said, "I've got to call Angela." To Paul's enormous relief, it quickly became clear Angela had answered.

Jae stopped and began parroting Angela to Paul. "The noise scared the children. She told them she thought it was thunder, but she knows better. Wants to know if we've been attacked."

Paul took the phone. "Do you have lights, Angela? electricity?"

"Yes. The movie's still running."

"We took a direct hit, probably right in the middle of the compound."

"There is a God," Angela said.

"Say again?"

"It was providential! The kids are all here. The adults should be at the other end, ready to leave."

"You're assuming we won't be hit again."

"I'm not assuming anything, Paul."

"We're heading your way," he said, as he and Jae set out again.

Soon they came to a pile of rubble that extended floor to ceiling and wall to wall. Jae immediately tried picking at the bricks and chunks of concrete, but there would be no getting through it.

"This is hopeless, babe," Paul said.

"Don't tell me that. I'm going to get to the kids if it takes all night. Is there another route?"

He shook his head. "I'll see if I can get a piece of equipment sent down here."

"I'm going to keep working at it anyway, Paul. Then you go do what you have to do. I'm not leaving here without Brie and Connor."

"Well, neither am I, Jae, but it will take a team of people to break through this."

"I have to try. You go. I'm serious."

"I'm not leaving without you either, Jae."

"Keep your phone handy, Paul. You know where I am."

"I'll be back."

• • •

Paul caught up with Jack and ran into frantic parents demanding to know how to get to their kids. Paul reported what Angela had told him. "We may have not yet suffered any casualties," he said.

"Don't be naive," a man called out. "We had six security personnel at the middle entrance. Anyone heard from them?"

Jack began dialing. Paul said, "Anyone heard from Greenie?" The others shook their heads. "He was supposed to come back here and accelerate the exodus."

"If you didn't see him on the way, Paul, that means he had to go the other way."

*That's right.* He had been going to see Angela. But she had said nothing about seeing him. He had to have been lost under the collapse of the tunnel.

The major exits used by cars full of refugees were still intact. Paul urged Jack to keep people moving out. Those who wanted to could help Jae try to get to the children, but the rest had to go, and right now. More than a dozen ran toward Jae and the rubble. At Paul's urging, Jack called for a small front-end loader. Maybe with lots of help, it could break through the pile.

Jae called. "I just found Mr. Macintosh," she said. "No way he should be alive, but he is. His head should have been crushed. If I ever wondered whether God was real and cared . . ."

"I'll be right there."

"No, Paul. We're all right. I'll let you know when we get through."

"Jae, people and equipment are on their way to help."

# 43

**THE SECOND MISSILE HIT** as Jae and Greenie and more than a dozen other parents were trying to stay out of the front-end loader's way while still helping to dig their way through to the children. The concussion shook the corridor and sent clouds of dust rushing at them. The emergency lights went out.

"They're going to kill us all!" a woman shouted.

"We'll suffocate!" a man yelled.

"Cover your mouths and keep working!"

"I can't see anything!"

Jae called Angela.

"We felt it," Angela said. "But we're okay."

"You still have electricity?" Jae said.

"Yes, but the kids are scared and many are crying."

"We're trying to get to you."

• • •

Paul wanted Ranold. It was as simple as that. He called Straight and told him to pull out every stop, spend whatever he had to, and get the USSATN cameraman to Washington. Paul gave him an intersection three blocks north of the National Cathedral. "Have him call me when he gets there, and I'll meet him."

A few minutes later, Straight called back. "This is going to cost you. A limo is on its way to PSL to pick us up."

"*Us?* You're not coming."

"Oh yes I am, and don't waste your breath trying to talk me out of it. Graybill is signing the guy out, and we'll be at Midway in fifteen. We're chartering a fast one, Paul. I assume you meant what you said."

"About doing whatever you had to do? Yes."

"We'll be there within an hour."

Jack and Paul were supervising the exodus when Paul got a call from Abraham at the salt mines. "Paul, you must not make this personal between you and the head of the NPO."

Straight always had made a practice of pulling other elders into Paul's business. "I don't have time to discuss this, Abraham. It's been personal for a long time. The man is my father-in-law, and he cares for no one but himself. Not for his own son or wife or daughter or grandchildren, and certainly not for me. Now he's bombing our underground, and we already should have at least seven casualties. God miraculously spared one of our men, and somebody's signaling me now with a thumbs-up about six others who were guarding the entrance where we took a direct hit."

"So God *is* protecting you, Paul. Let Him deal with your father-in-law."

"He can deal with Ranold through me, Abraham. Just because these seven were spared doesn't mean the man didn't want

to massacre us all. Who knows how many dead we might find? If
he keeps attacking, our losses could be monumental."

"Vengeance is the Lord's."

"You're suggesting I sit on my hands?"

"I'm suggesting you count on cooler heads."

"There are no cool heads here anymore, Abraham."

"We're praying for you."

"Thanks."

"Praying you'll do what Jesus would do."

*Save your breath,* Paul thought, but he held his tongue.

• • •

Ranold sat in the passenger seat of a Jeep next to the head of a
militia group he had once attempted to prosecute. A sketch of
the zealot underground layout was spread across their knees.
"That's one there and one there," the man in fatigues said. "And
that's all we've got."

"What if I paid you more?"

"I told you, that's all we've got and all we care to risk. You
should have a 50 percent kill rate with those. If we could have
launched them from the air, we could have been even more
accurate."

"You don't know the kill rate, man. You'd have to know
where everyone is down there to know that."

"We hit as centrally as we could, General. Hang on." He
looked at his cell phone. "It's one of my guys." He turned away.
"Go ahead, Jimmy. Which end? No, let 'em go. We've done all
we can do."

He clapped his phone shut, and Decenti demanded to know
what was going on.

"A mass exodus," Fatigues said. "Guess we sent 'em pouring
out of the south exit."

"You should have troops there to mow 'em down," Ranold said.

"I'm gettin' my people out of the area. You couldn't afford it anyway. This can't be from your budget, can it? You have to do this off the books."

"I can juggle some things. What would it cost me to—?"

"Listen, we're done here. I'll drop you somewhere, but this was a mercenary mission for us. We're as exposed as we want to be, and I don't need to be seen with you."

"Drop me at NPO headquarters so I can get a car."

"Yeah, right. The night the zealot underground gets bombed, I'm seen dropping you off. Get serious."

"Well, at least take me to where I can get a cab."

• • •

Jack pulled Paul aside and pressed him against the wall. "We've got to do something," he said. "We can't sustain another hit. This whole place is going to go. People are stampeding as it is, frantic to get out of here. How do we know we're not sending them into an ambush?"

"I'll do anything you suggest, Jack. I brought this on just by being here."

"Get to Decenti and do whatever you have to do to stop this."

"I might have to kill him."

"It's kill or be killed, Paul."

"I'll call him, but I'll need a vehicle."

"We're fast running out, but maybe you can take some people with you? drop them on the way?"

"Drop them where, Jack? I can't leave them on the streets."

"Oh, man!" Jack said. "Do you know who we have to get out of here? Marmet!"

"You mean Wipers. He still chained to the wall?"

"Yeah, probably screaming his head off and scared to death."

"I wouldn't mind leaving *him* on the street."

Jack handed him keys. "Go get him. I'll have a car and a weapon waiting for you at the southeast ramp."

• • •

Still in pitch-darkness, Jae continued to work, her nails torn and her fingers bleeding. How thick was this pile of rubble? She didn't care. She would dig until she saw light, and then she would make a hole big enough to get through or die trying. She was sickened by the propane exhaust of the loader and was likely going to die tonight anyway, but she would not go to her grave without knowing she had done everything she could to get to Brie and Connor.

"God, help us," she said. All around her people gasped, grunted, dug, and tossed bricks and chunks of concrete.

"It's no use!" someone said.

Jae kept working.

• • •

As Paul sprinted toward where Roscoe Wipers was detained, he wondered if he would ever forgive himself for leaving the compound without his kids. He was desperate for news, frantic to know whether Jae had gotten through and that they were all right. But he also knew there was nothing more he could do, short of digging through the rubble himself. And there were enough doing that. Probably too many. They were likely in each other's way.

He called Ranold.

"Surprised to hear from you," Decenti said. "Rumor has it there's fireworks in your neighborhood."

"Nice try, but you missed everybody, Dad."

"That can't be."

"National Cathedral in ninety minutes."

"I'll be there, Paul."

Paul felt his way into the dark room.

"Who is it?" Roscoe called out, whining. "Shoot me, please! Don't let me die like this! I don't want to be crushed! Or starve to death!"

"Calm down, Roscoe," Paul said. "You're coming with me."

"What?"

Paul took off Roscoe's handcuff that had tethered him to the wall. "You're not going to hurt me now, are you, Wipers?"

"Hurt you? I should kiss you! Where we going?"

"I'm trying to get to your big boss, and meanwhile I'm turning you loose."

"You're kidding."

"If I was kidding, I'd have left you here."

# 44

**JAE HAD NEVER WORKED** so hard in her life, and from the sounds of the others wheezing, she assumed the same of them. There was nothing like the motivation of trying to get to your kids.

At one point one of the men shushed everybody. "Listen!" he said. "If we can hear through the rest of this, we'll soon be able to see light peeking through."

They listened. Jae heard nothing. Others said they heard voices, maybe the movie. Jae believed they were imagining it and was eager to get back to work. Half the time she didn't know if her eyes were open or closed, it was that dark. She tasted grit and blinked away dust.

• • •

Paul and Roscoe felt their way to the southeast ramp, where cars waited, headlamps illuminated. Jack was there with others who had found flashlights. He gave Paul an ancient Uzi. "Fully loaded and like new," Jack said.

Roscoe was jabbering away, apparently intoxicated with having gone from certain death to what appeared to be freedom. But Paul wasn't listening. He was examining his own motives. How could he leave his wife and kids in harm's way while he escaped?

Well, it was hardly an escape. Who knew what his father-in-law had in store? But Paul would never forgive himself if he survived this and his family didn't. He called Jae as he and Roscoe slid into the car.

"Don't be silly, Paul," she said. "Plead for our children's lives."

"I won't be pleading for anything, Jae. It's going to be all I can do to keep from tearing the man apart."

"Just stop him," she said. "That's all. Please."

Paul didn't understand the traffic. He knew long lines of cars were escaping the shelter, of course, but they were all to take different routes once they reached the main roads. What was all the other traffic? It was crawling, and a light snow was making the roads treacherous. And here he was with Roscoe Wipers, neither of them wearing coats. Paul cranked the heat and settled into the traffic jam crawling south on 29.

"I don't get it," Wipers said. "What good am I to you? Why didn't you just leave me there to die?"

"Like the NPO did?"

"They think I'm dead already. You accomplished that. They would have got me out before this if they'd known."

"You really believe that."

"I'd like to."

"Dream on, Roscoe. Think about who's behind this."

"Decenti, of course."

"Of course. You know he's my father-in-law."

"Yeah."

"And his daughter and grandchildren are in there."

"Yeah."

"And he's lobbing bombs on the place. You think he cares more about you?"

Wipers shrugged. "But still, if I'm you, I'm leaving me there. I helped bring this on you."

As they crept past the Walter Reed Army Medical Center, Paul got an idea. He could shoot southwest and then west on Military Road to Nebraska Avenue, then head southwest across Connecticut to Massachusetts. The cathedral would then be just southeast of him at Wisconsin Avenue and Woodley Road.

Bad idea. Once he was on Military Road, Paul was committed, but the traffic was, if anything, worse. "What is goin' on?" Roscoe said.

Paul turned on the radio.

• • •

Now Jae *could* hear something through the pile. But what was it? She didn't want to delude herself or imagine her own kids' voices. But neither had she ever been as focused. Every time she heard a creak or groan in the structure, Jae imagined another cave-in, or worse, another shelling.

The others heard what she heard, and she could tell they were digging faster. There had to be an end to this, and once they and the loader got through, there would be a mad dash to get the kids to an exit where cars awaited.

• • •

"So why, Stepola?" Wipers said. "That's all I want to know. I mean, I think I know why you flipped. I studied enough religion to fool them until my so-called son got snuffed in The Incident. You're a believer, okay, fine. But that doesn't explain why you came for me."

"What kind of a person would I be if I hadn't?"

"You'd be like me, that's what."

"And you said yourself, Roscoe, you're not a believer. Believers do the right thing. At least we're supposed to."

"That's what you're doing now? Looking for your father-in-law so you can give him a hug?"

Traffic was too dense for Paul to shoot Roscoe a look. "I might as well be. I'm no less human than the next guy, and a huge part of me would like to take him out."

"I can imagine."

"But I don't plan to shoot him."

"Yeah, right."

"I'm serious."

"Then you're crazy, Doc. Really."

"People know where I'm going and who I'm going to see. Ranold tries anything with me, he'll never get away with it."

"So he gets caught! You get dead. What are you thinking? You want your family left without you if they do survive?"

The news had been droning in the background, Paul listening with one ear for any explanation for the exaggerated rush hour.

Finally it came: "Traffic continues to mount from the north in Washington, D.C., where two explosions have ripped through an abandoned industrial park. The blasts sparked a panic that had many residents fearing a military attack, though there is no evidence to suggest the same. People fleeing the area have joined the normal rush at this hour in the District, causing tie-ups on every major artery."

Paul took a call from Straight.

"You listening to the news?"

"Yep. Where are you?"

"Mr. Davis and I are where you told us to be, no thanks to the traffic. Where are you?"

"Probably still half an hour away. You want to get Davis set up in there? The doors are always open."

"Where?"

"I'll see if I can lure Decenti into the main narthex and close to the altar. The government has covered the statuary and icons with heavy draperies that might give Davis good cover. I have no idea how the lighting will be. Just tell him to keep the camera rolling and pick up all the sound he can too."

•  •  •

Ranold did not even have to sign out an NPO sedan. The carpool guy said he would handle the paperwork. "I don't even have to see your license, huh?" he said, laughing and apparently trying to elicit the same from Decenti.

But the interim chief of the NPO was off without a word, even of thanks, and he wasn't a happy man when he hit traffic. He radioed a SWAT team and told them where he'd be. "And I want no one—repeat, no one—inside without my expressly asking for it."

Ranold was convinced someone was on to him and following him. His eyes darted from the windshield to the rearview mirror, and every chance he got, he drove erratically, getting off the main road and onto side streets. He couldn't tell if anyone followed or stayed with him or was really behind him or not. All he knew was that he was already running late. He checked the nine millimeter on his hip, ground his teeth, and pounded the steering wheel.

His phone rang. "Please hold for Governor Haywood Hale."

When the governor came on, he shouted, "Decenti?"

"I'm here," Ranold said. "You still in Bern?"

"Oh yeah, and we're making headway."

"On what?"

"The world should know within an hour or two."

"Know what?"

"Exciting news, General. We still on for Monday morning?"

"Unless you plan to fire me. You can do that right now, over the phone."

"No need for that, Ranold."

Ranold decided Hale might not think that if he accomplished his mission with Paul Stepola.

# 45

**ROSCOE WIPERS** thrust a hand in Paul's face. "Shake."

Paul shook his hand. "What's that about?"

"I was planning on just walking away when you let me," Roscoe said. "I'm going to have to answer for not trying to bring you in, but you don't have to worry about me. As far as I'm concerned, you're a free man. I owe you. Even if I am sitting here unarmed in the cold with no coat."

"Don't worry; I'll drop you somewhere warm."

"You would."

"Yes, I would. And in the meantime, while I'm doing my thing, you can wait here with the heater running."

• • •

Now Jae was sure she heard something. And not just anything. The voices of children. They couldn't have been three feet away.

Angela must have had them trying to dig through from the other side. Jae signaled the front-end loader to shut down and called out, "Kids! Can you hear us?"

A chorus of yeses came back, and the sound of excavating increased from both sides. Finally, pinholes of light, then tiny tunnels, and finally a hole big enough for a child to climb through.

"Wait!" Jae called. "Angela, line them up and let us make the way bigger!"

Jae was the first through the opening, and she stumbled and fell at the feet of the squealing kids. When she was upright again she could tell by the looks on their faces that she must have been a sight. Brie and Connor jumped on her.

"Everybody ready? We're going to be walking a long way in the dark, but we're going to get out of here." *Thank You, God.*

· · ·

When the three-hundred-foot-tall and five-hundred-foot-long limestone edifice came into view, Paul, as usual, had to stare. "A hundred and forty years old," he said. "Took more than eighty years to build."

"What're you," Roscoe said, "a tour guide?"

Paul shook his head. "Religion major. Wait here."

Paul dialed Straight as he jogged through thick underbrush toward the south entrance. "Our boy Davis in place?"

"Yeah, but no sign of your father-in-law."

"Believe me, he'll be here. Where are you?"

"I'll be around. I've got your back."

"You armed, Straight?"

A chuckle. "You wouldn't want that. I'd shoot my remaining foot. I assume you are."

"Yeah, but I'm trying to talk myself out of putting two between Ranold's eyes."

Inside the dark, airy cathedral, Paul found it hard to move without his shoes echoing throughout the cavernous place. He stopped every few feet to listen. Footsteps? His own, still echoing? No, someone was here.

Paul entered the massive nave and peered at the round, colorful stained-glass window at the west entrance. Streetlights and snow caused it to glow and shimmer. He moved to the arches at one side, moving in and out of the shadows. Finally he stopped and waited.

Heavy, slow footsteps.

He imagined Ranold, could almost see him. Was it possible the man had come alone? Unlikely.

The footsteps stopped.

"You alone, Dad?" Paul called out.

"Of course," came the reply. "And unarmed. You?"

"Better not count on it." For the first time he saw Decenti on the opposite side, moving from behind one pillar to behind another. "How would you feel, Dad, if you knew more of your family was dead because of what you did tonight?"

"Tonight? What did I do tonight? And quit calling me Dad! You're not my son. I didn't choose you."

"That's more important than whether your daughter or grandbabies are dead or alive?"

Did Ranold hesitate? Paul couldn't imagine actually getting to him. Paul moved past two arches toward the main altar.

"Where're we going, Paul?"

"Just staying out of your line of fire, Dad."

"You don't trust me."

Paul snorted. "You must be a trained observer."

"Don't mock."

Paul strode quickly to the last arch before the altar and knelt behind the pillar.

Ranold seemed content to stay where he was, about twenty-five feet from the front on the opposite side of the sanctuary. Because of the acoustics, the men didn't have to even raise their voices.

"I know why you killed Commander Balaam, Dad."

Silence. Then, "I killed her? I did no such thing."

"Had her killed then. She was the one who could connect you with the murder of the chancellor."

Another pause. "*Murder* is such a civilian term, Paul. *Assassination* has a better ring to it, don't you think? We are at war. Something had to be done. Just like now. I'm in the same room with a traitor, and I'm on duty. I aim to take him in."

"You finished trying to wipe out the underground, Dad?"

Ranold hissed as if the moniker pierced him. "I don't know what you're talking about."

"C'mon! I thought you'd be proud of yourself."

"I *am* proud of myself. At least I'm not a turncoat. My career speaks for itself. And if I am the only stalwart left, so be it. We can do without the Denglers and the Hales and the Tamikas."

"The populace seems to be standing against you now, Dad. Deal with it."

That did it. That seemed to push Ranold. He moved up a couple of pillars, and Paul thought he heard another set of footsteps, maybe two sets.

Ranold must have thought so too. He stopped short and dropped to one knee. "I told you men to wait outside!" Ranold said.

The footsteps retreated, but not far.

"Backup, eh, Dad? You're that scared of me?"

Paul heard an explosion, and a blast to his shoulder threw him back against the wall. He dropped, unable to move.

Ranold swore at him from across the way. The pair of footsteps came running again. "I'm all right!" Ranold said. "I said to wait outside! I got him!"

But it sounded to Paul as if Ranold hit the ground.

"Who are you?" Ranold demanded as his weapon clattered away. "Wipers? Get off me or I'll have you—and who are *you*?"

"Call me Straight." Then he called out, "You all right, Paul?"

"'Fraid not."

Straight ran to him and helped Paul onto his back. "Hold on, brother," he said.

"Not feeling so good," Paul said.

"Not looking so good either, pal. Stay with me."

Paul thought it strange that Straight talked that way. Surely the wound was not life threatening. It had not been that close to the heart, had it? His pulse was fast and ragged, but that was to be expected.

Straight was on the phone, calling for an ambulance.

And Paul lost consciousness.

# EPILOGUE

**PAUL AWOKE**—he didn't know how long later—in a room at Bethesda Naval Hospital, surrounded by Straight, Jack, Greenie, Jae, Brie, and Connor. He had never been so relieved to see anyone in his life. He tried to sit up and reach for the kids, but Jae assured him there would be plenty of time for that.

"You've got a lot of damage in there, Paul," she said. "But you'll be all right. Oh, there it is! Let's watch!"

They pulled the curtain back so Paul could see the TV. Scooter Davis's grainy, dark footage rolled with the echoing sound as Ranold appeared on national television. The big man awkwardly knelt in the old cathedral, aiming his weapon and firing.

"Now listen to what preceded this attack," the anchorwoman said. "Recently exposed NPO double agent Dr. Paul Stepola—ironically Ranold B. Decenti's own son-in-law—is the first to speak. He's referring to one of Director Decenti's own top operatives, Commander Bia Balaam, who was found ritualistically murdered in her car at the NPO garage earlier."

*"I know why you killed Commander Balaam, Dad."*

"I killed her? I did no such thing."

"Had her killed then. She was the one who could connect you with the murder of the chancellor."

"Murder is such a civilian term, Paul. Assassination has a better ring to it, don't you think? We are at war. Something had to be done. Just like now. I'm in the same room with a traitor, and I'm on duty. I aim to take him in."

"You finished trying to wipe out the underground, Dad?"

"I don't know what you're talking about."

"C'mon! I thought you'd be proud of yourself."

"I am proud of myself. At least I'm not a turncoat. My career speaks for itself. And if I am the only stalwart left, so be it. We can do without the Denglers and the Hales and the Tamikas."

"The populace seems to be standing against you now, Dad. Deal with it."

The anchorwoman returned. "After the shooting, Decenti was subdued by two unidentified men, then taken into custody by his own backup squadron. Here now is footage of Director Decenti being taken from the cathedral."

A SWAT team member was interviewed by the press as the phalanx edged toward their vehicles with Decenti in tow. "We all heard him. He as much as admitted he assassinated the chancellor and launched those missiles on the underground."

"I did nothing of the sort!" Ranold raged, his face red, spittle flying. "I said what I had to say to take down a fugitive! I—" His own men shoved him into a Hummer.

"And now," the anchorwoman said, "this from Bern, Switzerland, where interim international chancellor Hoshi Tamika is prepared to address the world. She has been in meetings since early this morning with heads of state from all over the globe."

Paul squinted at the screen. What could it mean?

The interim chancellor took her time arranging her notes

while microphones were noisily adjusted to a smattering of applause. Then the soft but anything-but-timid voice of the chancellor:

"Ladies and gentlemen of the world community. This is a historic day. I stand before you with heads of state or their designates from all over the globe. They stand with me here in solidarity and unanimity, having spent the last several hours in spirited debate and discussion.

"Our goal? A midcourse adjustment on an international scale so that all men and women might continue to live in peace. As you know and many of you remember, the world embarked on a bold new initiative thirty-eight years ago in the wake of a devastating war that nearly destroyed us all. As the result of a holy war, we almost lost our planet.

"The criminalizing of religious activity was believed the only recourse in an attempt to ensure that nothing like that would ever again occur. And for most of the time since, we have lived in relative peace. Most of us have.

"We are here today to acknowledge that this has not been true of all our citizens. Peace-loving people of faith have been forced underground and treated like second-class citizens. They have not enjoyed the privileges and rights of the free in this world.

"Ironically, this has resulted in yet another holy war, this time necessitated by oppressed, disenfranchised, devout people who share our commitment to peace. It has become foolhardy to suggest that a Supreme Being does not exist since The Incident, when as many firstborn males died as we had casualties from World War III. I myself lost a loved one, as did countless of you.

"The pendulum has by no means swung all the way back, despite today's vote and the edict I am about to announce. People of this earth remain free to be atheists. I confess I am one no lon-

ger. No one will be forced to acknowledge any form of spiritual-
ity. However, the following was voted into international law just
moments ago:

"'No citizen of the world community shall be penalized or
otherwise discriminated against due to his or her practice of the
religion of their choice. The recommitment to the loyalty oath is
hereby rescinded. Further, all citizens incarcerated, indicted, suspected, or forced to live underground due to violating the same,
are hereby now and henceforth exonerated and awarded full
amnesty.'

"That ends the document. Be assured, there are technicalities
and conditions relating to this edict, some yet to be worked out.
These apply to those who broke other laws in the course of prac-
ticing their religion. But the above-stated edict becomes operative
immediately and shall be disseminated as widely and quickly as
possible by the news media. Thank you and good day."

The small cadre surrounding Paul's bed high-fived and
hugged each other. "There *is* a God!" Jae said.

Paul shook his head. It *was* hard to comprehend.

"Guess I don't have to pray down the flood of justice," Jack
Pass said.

"Thank God for that," Paul said. He opened a hand to Brie
and Connor, and they shyly approached.

"Aren't we the bad guys anymore, Dad?" Connor said.

"Nope," Paul said. "Not anymore." He had to smile at
Connor's frown. He'd have made a good little outlaw.

Paul knew he would still face charges for what he had done
in violation of his oath of office at the NPO. And something told
him the new ruling, glorious as it was, would hardly be the end
of the story.

Less than half an hour later, because of the gleeful jabbering
of those at his bedside, he could no longer hear the television,

but over Jae's shoulder Paul saw footage of demonstrations already breaking out around the world.

Some showed underground believers pouring into the streets, singing, dancing, and raising their hands toward heaven. But others showed angry people of all walks of life, rioting, snarling, and shaking their fists at the sky. He could only imagine the threats and epithets directed at the newly freed people of faith.

Paul shook hands with and gingerly embraced the friends and family celebrating around his bed, careful not to aggravate his wound. He could hardly fathom the difference the news would make in all their lives, including those of believers around the world, and especially his own.

He found himself suddenly overcome with emotion, but despite tears of joy, Paul had to wonder how long the reprieve would last. How long before the world once again fell under the shadow of persecution?

THE END